Seasons Under Heaven

Also by Beverly LaHaye and Terri Blackstock

Showers in Season
Times and Seasons
Season of Blessing

Seasons Under Heaven

Book One

Beverly LaHaye
Terri Blackstock

Grand Rapids, Michigan 49530

ZONDERVAN™

Seasons Under Heaven

Requests for information should be addressed to:

Zondervan, *Grand Rapids, Michigan 49530*

Library of Congress Cataloging-in-Publication Data

LaHaye, Beverly.
Seasons under heaven / Beverly LaHaye and Terri Blackstock.
p. cm.
ISBN: 0-310-23519-7 (Softcover)
I. Blackstock, Terri, 1957– . II. Title.
PS3562.A3144S43 1996
813'.54—dc 21
98-56104
CIP

Published in association with the literary agency of Alive Communications, Inc., 7680 Goddard Street, Suite 200, Colorado Springs, CO 80920.

Interior design by Melissa Elenbaas

Printed in the United States of America

---

02 03 04 05 06 /❖ DC/ 10 9 8 7 6 5 4 3 2

Dedication

This book is dedicated to Annie M., Susan B., and Mary K., plus the many other women who have shared their "seasons of life" with me, wondering if they were alone in their struggles, disappointments, and heartaches. And also to my husband, who has helped me through my own "seasons of life."

Beverly LaHaye

This book is also dedicated to my husband and children, through whom the Lord has taught me some of my greatest lessons. And, as always, to the Nazarene.

Terri Blackstock

Acknowledgments

We would like to thank Dr. Fred Rushton for taking time out of his busy surgical schedule to read our manuscript and check our facts. We couldn't have done it without you. Thanks also to Jim Gleason, whose Internet account of his illness, *A Gift of the Heart*, gave us so much information. And special heartfelt thanks to the family of Susan Hattie Steinsapir, for sharing her poignant transplant story on the Internet. Susan didn't survive, but the story she left behind will help thousands.

We'd also like to thank Greg Johnson, Dave Lambert, Sue Brower, and Lori Walburg for their vision and active interest in this book. You're all a dream to work with!

There is a time for everything,

and a season for every activity under heaven:

a time to be born and a time to die,

a time to plant and a time to uproot,

a time to kill and a time to heal,

a time to tear down and a time to build,

a time to weep and a time to laugh,

a time to mourn and a time to dance,

a time to scatter stones and a time to gather them,

a time to embrace and a time to refrain,

a time to search and a time to give up,

a time to keep and a time to throw away,

a time to tear and a time to mend,

a time to be silent and a time to speak,

a time to love and a time to hate,

a time for war and a time for peace.

ECCLESIASTES 3:1–8

CHAPTER *One*

Joseph Dodd was not one of those kids who feigned illness to get attention. His ten-year-old sister Rachel might have, since she was the one among the four children who leaned toward hypochondria. Leah, her twin, had been known to fake an occasional stomachache in the interest of competition. And Daniel, their twelve-year-old brother, often used a headache excuse to escape pre-algebra.

But not Joseph. Brenda, their mother, knew that the eight-going-on-nine-year-old was the kind of kid who harbored no deceit at all. His feelings and thoughts passed across his face like the Dow prices at the stock exchange, and Brenda could read them clearly.

That's why she knew something was wrong on the day before his ninth birthday. He'd gotten up with dark circles under his eyes, and his skin was as pale as the recycled paper on which they did their schoolwork. His red hair, which he took great pains to keep combed because he had three cowlicks, was disheveled, as if he hadn't given it a thought. On the way into the kitchen, he reached for the counter to steady himself and hung his head while he tried to catch his breath.

Brenda quickly abandoned the eggs she was scrambling and bent down to look into his eyes. "Joseph, what's the matter, honey?"

"I dunno," he said.

"Are you sick?" she asked, feeling his forehead.

"Sorta dizzy."

"It's his blood sugar," Daniel commented, before slurping his cereal. He wiped a drip from his chin. "Remember, I studied about the pancreas last week? The book said you could get dizzy if your pancreas didn't work right."

"What's a pancreas?" Joseph asked, frowning.

"Daniel, don't slurp," David, their father, said. "Brenda, what are you teaching him? Endocrinology?"

Brenda grinned. "More like he's teaching me. We're touching on anatomy in science. I got him some extra books."

"What's a pancreas?" Joseph asked again. He was still breathing hard and beginning to sweat.

David pushed aside his coffee, leaned across the table, and felt Joseph's forehead. "You okay, sport?"

Joseph didn't answer. He was still waiting for an answer to his question.

"The pancreas is a gland," Daniel mumbled around a mouthful of cereal. "It's near your kidney."

"Mom, Daniel's talking with his mouth full," Leah spouted.

"It is not near the kidney," Rachel said. "It's near the heart."

"How would you know? You aren't studying the human body."

"No, but I have one," Rachel said, tossing her nose up in the air as if that won the argument.

"I'm going to get my book," Daniel said. "I'll prove it to you."

"Sit back down, young man." Brenda turned back to the scrambled eggs and took the pan off the stove. She turned to the table—only a step from the stove in the small kitchen—and began scooping eggs onto their plates. Her blonde hair waved across her forehead, but she blew it back with her bottom lip. It was already getting hot in the house, and the sun hadn't even come all the way up. Despite the cost of electricity, she was going to have to lower the thermostat today or she'd never get the kids through their lessons.

She reached Joseph's plate and scooped out some eggs.

"I don't want any," Joseph said.

"Joseph, son, you've gotta eat," David said.

"I will later."

Brenda set the pan back on the stove and put her hands on her hips, gazing down at her son. "Rachel, will you go turn the thermostat down? Maybe if it gets cooler in here Joseph will feel better." As Rachel popped up to do as she was told, Brenda said, "I hope you're not getting sick again, Joseph."

"You can't be sick on your birthday," Leah said. "Mom, if he's sick, can we still have the party tomorrow?"

"Of course not. We'd just postpone it."

"But I don't want to postpone it," Joseph said, sitting straighter. "I'm fine. I changed my mind. I'll eat some eggs."

Brenda grinned and spooned some eggs onto his plate as she heard the air conditioner cut on. "He'll be fine. Probably just needs to eat something. Sometimes I wake up like that, Joseph. If I didn't eat much the night before, I get up and feel downright shaky until I eat."

"Blood sugar," Daniel observed.

"Of course, mostly I eat too much." She patted her slightly overweight hips. "Somehow my body can always convince me I'm starving." She ran her fingers through her hair and studied her youngest. "Joseph doesn't need to be worried about his pancreas, though. I'm sure it's working just fine. But I have to say, Daniel, that I'm bursting with pride over your interest in the pancreas. David, don't you think he's doctor material? I mean, he's practically ready for medical school."

David smiled and patted his oldest son on the back. "I think you're right. I've always said that Daniel had a sharp mind."

"Me, too, Daddy," Rachel said, coming back to the table.

"All of you. There's just no telling what you'll be," Brenda said. "I'm going to be one of those mothers who can't open her mouth without bragging about her important children. People will run when they see me." She fixed herself a plate and pulled out a chair. "Okay, now, before Daddy goes out to the shop, let's talk about this party. Nine years ago tomorrow, the doctor put that precious little bundle into my arms. Nine years, Joseph! Think of it! Bet it seems like a lifetime to you, huh?"

Joseph didn't answer. He propped his chin on his hand and moved the eggs around on his plate.

"It seems like nine long years to me," Daniel said.

David snickered under his breath, and Brenda shot him an amused look.

"I've already called all of our homeschooled friends," she told Joseph. "I told them to be here at two tomorrow. We'll have it outside. We need to start making the cake this afternoon. Joseph, do you want white cake, yellow, or chocolate? You need to consider this very carefully, since you'll be licking the bowl."

He didn't answer.

Brenda's eyes met David's across the table again. "Joseph?" David asked, taking the boy's hand.

He looked up. "Sir?"

"Your mother asked you something. What kind of cake do you want?"

"Um . . . rectangle, I guess."

"What *flavor*?" Daniel prompted. "Mom, he really is sick."

Brenda frowned. "Baby, do you want to go back to bed?"

He nodded and pushed his plate away, got up, and headed back to his bedroom.

"I'm taking him to the doctor," Brenda told David, getting up and heading for the phone. "Something's not right."

"Yeah, you better."

"Tell 'em about his pancreas," Daniel said. "They might not think of it."

David laughed and messed up his son's hair as Brenda dialed the number.

❧

They waited at the doctor's office for an hour, only to have a five-minute examination. David, who was busy in his workshop behind the house when they got home, rushed out and met them in the driveway.

"How's my boy?"

Brenda got out of the car. "The doctor says it's probably a sinus infection. He just needs antibiotics."

"I can still have my party," Joseph piped in. "The doctor said."

"You sure you're up to it?" David asked.

"Yes, sir," Joseph said. "I'm just tired. I'll go to bed early."

"How about right now?" Brenda asked. "Why don't you take a nap while we do school?"

He didn't argue, which spoke volumes about his fatigue. He fell into bed and slept for four hours, while Brenda homeschooled his siblings.

David came in frequently to check on his son. "He's all right," he told his wife. "He's just been staying up too late."

"Yeah, maybe," Brenda said. "I think his color's back, don't you?"

David grinned. "Never had much to start with. The curse of the redhead."

Brenda hugged her red-haired husband and laid her head against his chest. "Poor little thing. He doesn't want to be sick on his birthday."

"He won't be. He's tough, ole Joseph. It'll take more than a sinus infection to get him down."

Brenda tried to push the worry out of her mind, but it had begun to take root. She only hoped the doctor's diagnosis was reliable.

Chapter Two

The next morning, in the house next door to the Dodds on the little cul-de-sac called Cedar Circle, Tory Sullivan struggled between tears and rage at the sight of the strawberry Kool-Aid congealing on her computer keyboard. A plastic cup lay on its side in a crimson puddle. Two soaked tissues in the center of the puddle, and one lying across the keys, testified of a half-hearted attempt to clean up the mess.

"Brittany!" she screamed, succumbing to the rage instead of the tears. "Spencer! Get in here!"

There was no answer, but of course, she had expected none. The children were probably hiding in their toy closet, trying to blend in with their stuffed animals, or hunkering under the bed until the crisis passed.

She ran to the kitchen, grabbed a roll of paper towels, and tried to blot the mess. But it had been there too long, and the quicker-picker-upper failed her.

The tears came, after all, as she looked at the monitor. Its blackness testified that someone had turned the computer off, as if hoping to make it disappear. What had undoubtedly disappeared, instead, was the four pages she had written but not saved to the hard drive because she had meant to come right back to it after her shower. Her heart plunged further, and her freshly applied mascara dripped with the tears down her cheek. Frantically, she sat down on the sticky chair, ignoring the Kool-Aid soaking into her white shorts, and turned the computer back on. An error message accused her of turning it off without properly exiting. She tried to repair the problem and boot it up, but the computer wouldn't respond to the commands she tried to enter using the sticky keyboard. Besides the damage to the keyboard, she knew that her precious four pages had been sucked into the vortex of her personal cyberspace, never to be seen again.

"Brittany! Spencer!" She bellowed the names with less fury and more despair now, and grabbed a paper towel to blot the tears running down her nose. She headed straight for the closet in the first room she came to: Spencer's room, with clouds and alphabet letters and Ninja Turtles painted on the walls. "You can run, but you can't hide!" she bit out. "Who spilled the Kool-Aid?"

There was no answer, and no sign of her children among the stuffed animal faces on the closet floor. She went to the bed and threw up the bed skirt. No children hid underneath.

She tore out of Spencer's room and headed into Brittany's. Her five-year-old daughter sat at her little table with wet eyes, frantically coloring a picture of a flower. "I made you a picture, Mommy," she said quickly. She resembled a Cabbage Patch Doll as she looked up at her mother with those big round eyes. She held out the masterpiece like a sin offering, but her bottom lip began to tremble. "Spencer did it. I don't even like Kool-Aid."

The red mustache at the upper corners of Brittany's mouth would have belied the child's declaration, if Tory hadn't already known better. Tory set her hands on her hips as the anger drained out of her, leaving only the tears. "Britty, my computer. How could you blame your brother?"

"He's always knockin' stuff over," Brittany said as a sob thickened her voice. Her red lips puckered out. "I told him not to touch the computer, but he wouldn't come away, and when I pulled him . . ."

The truth came out on a squeaky, high-pitched wail, and Tory knew it was genuine. She sighed heavily and stooped down in front of her daughter. "Britty, I've told you a million times that we don't take food or drinks into that room. Now the computer won't work . . ." Her voice broke off, and she wiped her wet cheek. "Where's your brother?"

"I don't know," Brittany cried. "I hope he ran away. I hope he never comes back."

"Brittany!" Tory scolded. "That's an awful thing to say. Now where is he hiding?"

"He's not hiding," Brittany said. "He doesn't even care. He went outside while you were doing your hair."

"Outside? Britty, why didn't you tell me?" She sprang to her feet and headed out the back door. "Spencer Sullivan!"

She saw him in the yard next door, hanging on the fence that corralled the Bryans' horses. "Spencer! Get back!" She lit out across the yard toward her child.

The four-year-old looked back at her, saw that he was in trouble, and ducked under the fence, as if that would render him invisible. One of the horses whinnied in disapproval, and the colt backed up, startled.

"Spencer! Get out of there!"

She reached the fence and ducked under it, grabbed her child, and quickly pulled him out. When they were out of harm's way, she set him down and stooped in front of him, holding him firmly by the shoulders. "Spencer Sullivan, if you keep defying me, you may not make it to eighteen years old, and it won't be because of the horses."

"Sorry."

"You're in big trouble," Brittany chanted, just arriving on the scene. "You're not allowed to come see the horses without Mommy or Daddy. Boy, are you gonna get it." Her brown ponytails swayed with her words.

The red Kool-Aid mustache on her daughter reminded Tory of the busted computer and the lost pages of her novel, and her tears returned. "You're both in trouble," she said, getting up and grabbing one hand of each child. "You're both going to get it."

A mockingbird in a chestnut tree between the two homes chided her as she pulled them back toward their house. She would have sworn it said, "Fail-ure, fail-ure, fail-ure." Her cat, hunkering under the back porch steps, took offense and launched across the lawn and up the tree trunk.

The bird flew away, leaving the cat stranded in futility. Spencer stopped and began pulling to get away. "Get him down, Mommy. Get him down!"

"He can get down," she said, trying to grab his hand again before he could make another escape. "Spencer!"

As if in response, the neighbor's dog Buster began to bark, and bounded around the house to the foot of the tree. The cat squalled and climbed higher, the dog barked and stood threateningly on its hind legs, and the kids began to scream. "He's goin' higher, Mommy! Get him down."

If it hadn't been for the fact that the blasted cat had been stuck up in that tree so many times before, and that Barry, Tory's husband, had had to climb the tree to get it down more than once, she could have ignored the crisis and made it to the house. But this one wasn't going to pass.

It was nearing noon, and the sun was straight up in the sky, too hot for late May in eastern Tennessee. The little town of Breezewood was named for its cool temperatures in the summer, but today the sun seemed to have forgotten that and beat down on them with further malice. Already, Tory's dark brown hair, which she'd spent too much time rolling and spraying, was beading with sweat and pasting itself to her forehead. Her kids, who'd been freshly bathed not an hour ago, were beginning to glisten. Spencer already smelled like one of the steel mills in town—that metallic dirt-and-sweat kind of odor that made you want to hose him down. She eyed the little inflatable pool in the yard and thought of stripping him down and dunking him in it. But that would seem too much like fun to him.

The dog's barks turned to howls, and the cat scrabbled higher up, still making that skin-crawling noise like a wounded person with laryngitis. She looked around for something, anything, to stop the commotion. The green hose lay curled like a snake ready to strike, and she let go of Brittany, grabbed the head of it, and turned it on full blast. Adjusting the nozzle to shoot in a hard, steady stream, she blasted the dog.

He danced away from the tree, distracted as he tried to nip at the water stream to get a good gulp. She turned the hose up to the top of the tree, where the cat still clung for dear life. It whopped him without much force, but frightened him enough to make him jump to a lower branch.

The children laughed and jumped up and down as the cat began to parry the water blows with one fighting paw. He leaped to another, lower bough.

The cat was low enough now to jump to the ground, so she tried to center the water right over his torso to make him take the plunge.

In his excitement, Spencer ran to the wet German shepherd and hugged it exuberantly. Tory's heart deflated further as she realized that now her son smelled like sweat, rust, and wet dog. And *she* wasn't smelling much better.

"He's down!" Brittany squealed, and took off across the wet grass to chase the soaked, angry cat.

"Britty, come back here! Now!"

"But I have to dry him off, Mommy! He hates to be wet."

"Brittany, I said *now!*"

Brittany stopped and gave her a hangdog look that would have wilted a weaker mother, but Tory ignored it. Instead, she turned her attention to prying her reeking son's arms from around the wet dog. "Inside, Spencer! Hit the tub. Do not pass go, do not collect two hundred dollars."

"Huh?"

"The tub, Spencer."

"Why? I already took a bath."

"You need another one."

"But I'm still clean."

"*Now*, Spencer. Brittany, *inside*."

"Do I have to take a bath, too?" Brittany asked. "I didn't do nothin' bad. Besides, Joseph's party is outside, so we'll just get stinky again."

"I don't want you going to the party stinky. I want you going clean, and getting stinky while you're there. Head for the tub."

"Can I take a bath in my bathing suit?" Spencer asked. "Britty can take it with me."

"Fine," she said. "Britty, yours is hanging over the washing machine."

"But we didn't have lunch yet. I'm hungry."

She realized the child was right. The telephone rang as Spencer agreed that he, too, was hungry. Rolling her eyes, she shoved them inside and headed for the phone. She didn't see the dirty pair of sneakers strategically placed between her and the phone. She tripped over them and caught herself on the table, then swung around and drop-kicked them as far as she could. "Get your shoes out of here, Spencer!" she shouted, then snatched up the phone. "Hello!"

"Hey, hon." It was Barry, her husband, and she imagined him sitting in his nice quiet office with his organized desk and his functioning computer and all his metalworks accomplishments photographed and displayed like trophies around him. "What's up?"

"Oh, nothing," she said, her chin stiffening. "My computer has drowned in congealed Kool-Aid, I just rescued Spencer from the Bryans' corral, then I got the cat down from the tree, and we're all about to take our second bath of the morning because we're soaked in sweat and Spencer smells like Buster the dog . . .

and we haven't even had lunch yet." She forced a saccharine tone. "And how is your day, honey?"

"What do you mean the computer drowned? I told you to keep the kids out of there."

"I was in the bedroom for maybe five minutes, getting ready for Joseph's party."

"Joseph's party? It's not for hours."

"That's not the point, Barry! It won't type. The keyboard is dead. And all the work I did this morning—four pages during *Sesame Street*—is gone."

"Tory, that computer cost over a thousand dollars."

"Tell it to the kids." She glanced at the pantry, where the kids had gotten too quiet, and saw that they'd gotten into a ziplock bag of gummy worms. "Put those down and head for the tub. I'm not telling you again!"

"Thank goodness," she heard Spencer whisper, and Brittany giggled.

"Barry, tell me what to do about the computer. I have to save it."

"Call the company. Ask them what they advise."

"All right. As soon as things get quiet."

"And Tory, punish them. Don't let them go to Joseph's party today. They've been looking forward to it, so make them stay home. It'll teach them."

She heard the bath water running, and the cat began scratching at the back door to get in. "Barry, if I do that, *I* have to stay home. And I was looking forward to some adult companionship. Even if it is with a dozen kids around." She sighed and realized she sounded like a shrew. "Look, I'll try to save the computer. And I've got to go bathe the kids. Please don't be late this afternoon. I'll have turned gray and lost my sanity by then."

"Uh, well . . . that's kinda why I'm calling. I mean, not about your sanity. About me being late."

"No, Barry!" she whined, collapsing into a chair. "Please, not tonight. This is not turning out to be a good day."

"I can't help it. I have to work late."

"So what are we talking about? Seven o'clock? Eight?"

"Maybe eight-thirty. A big client wants to have dinner with some of us. It's a huge account, for some great stuff we bid on. I can't say no."

"Of course not." She felt a headache coming on. "Look, I've got to go. I wish I had time to chat, but you've probably got to skedaddle off to lunch, anyway. Tip the waiter nice for me, will you?"

"Tory, come on."

"Bye, Barry." She hung up the phone and headed back to the bathroom to see if her kids had drowned each other yet.

They were both in their bathing suits, sitting in four inches of cold water that didn't have a prayer of getting them clean, and playing battleship with some plastic sailboats they kept on the tub. Taking the opportunity, she went to the living room and sank down on the couch. Barry was probably nursing his wounds, she thought miserably. It wasn't his fault that he had a job he liked and got to eat in restaurants and talk to adults all day. He believed her staying at home was a terrific blessing, and she knew it should be.

But as long as she was here, there was no hope of her ever making anything of herself. No hope at all. What had happened to the Miss University of Tennessee who'd edited the literary magazine, wowed her professors with papers they'd claimed were publishable, and been chosen "Outstanding Senior English Major" because her professors believed she was the one most likely to publish? Whatever happened to the girl who'd been "Most Beautiful" *and* "Most Likely to Succeed," all in the same year?

If they could see her now, she thought morbidly. Instead of mopping in the money, she was mopping up spills. Instead of nursing celebrity, she was nursing earaches and skinned knees. Instead of winning awards, she was winning free hamburgers from the scrape-off cards at McDonald's.

It wasn't what she'd had in mind when she'd become a mother.

If only they were older. If only they could entertain themselves and tie their own shoes and fix their own sandwiches and clean up their own messes. If only she had two hours a day—even one hour would do—of uninterrupted time to pursue her own dreams, without someone undoing it all with the flick of a Kool-Aid-stained finger.

She sat there crying for a long time, until finally she knew that she had to feed her kids lunch or surrender the bag of gummy bears—resulting in a sugar high that would be sure to make the afternoon as challenging as the morning.

CHAPTER *Three*

Sylvia teetered atop the ladder in her living room and carefully removed the white bow from its place near the ceiling. She'd hung bows all around the room, one every three feet, and draped lace between them. Even from this height, she could still smell the sweet fragrance of the white roses and orchids that sat in huge pots around the room. It had made for a beautiful wedding reception for her daughter. But the biggest hit of the party hadn't been the lace and ribbons and roses but rather Sarah's childhood pictures that Sylvia had blown up, placed in gold gilded frames, and hung in an arrangement on one wall of her living room. Jeff, her son, was in many of the pictures as well. Across the room was a similar display of photographs Sylvia had gotten from the groom's mother. She had finished taking that display down earlier this morning, but it was more difficult removing the ones of her own children.

Not for the first time that morning, reality hit her, and the vast emptiness of the house after all the madness of the past few weeks caught up with her. The silence seemed to scream mocking cruelties into her ear about her empty nest and her outlived usefulness. Tears came to her eyes, and she sat down on one of the ladder rungs and tried to get hold of herself.

Longingly, her gaze swept over the photograph of Sarah as a little girl, her brother Jeff hovering over her. Had it been in second or third grade that Sarah had played the Statue of Liberty in the school play? That picture had caused a lot of laughter among their family and friends. The costume party—had that been for Jeff's sixth or seventh birthday? Had Jeff gone to college yet when they'd taken the youth group to the Alpine Sled in Chattanooga? Half of those kids had come to the wedding, and the stories they'd told . . .

"Are you taking those down?"

She jumped at the sound of her husband's voice, making the ladder teeter. Harry rushed forward and steadied it. "Harry! I didn't hear you come in." Her voice was cracked and choked with emotion, and when he looked up at her, she knew he saw the tears. Quickly, she wiped them away.

"This is dangerous, Sylvia," he said gently, indicating the ladder. "You shouldn't do this unless I'm home. Wait till later and I'll help you."

She sighed and came down. "I wanted to get it done. The sooner the better."

"Why don't you rest? The wedding took a lot out of you. You deserve to do nothing today. You remember how, don't you? Think way back to before we had kids."

"I can't remember that far back," she whispered, looking up at those pictures again.

He gave her a tender look, then moved behind her and set his hands on her shoulders. Kissing her hair, he said, "You know, you don't have to take them down at all."

"They're not right there," she said. "I'll spread them out around the house. I'll have to patch the holes in the wall, you know, and repaint. There's so much to do." Again, those tears came, constricting her throat.

Harry turned her around and made her look up at him. Though his hair was more gray than black, his face had retained its youthful look, and his eyes still twinkled with mischief. The very sight and feel of him reminded her that she was not completely alone today, that her life's companion was still here, and that he would not forsake her. "Your children haven't fired you, you know," he said. "You're still their mother."

"I don't know how to be a long-distance mother," she said. "Why did we let them move to other states? They're both so far away. Before we know it, they'll have kids of their own, and we'll be long-distance grandparents who see them once or twice a year. The grandkids will have to be reminded who we are."

"Fat chance," Harry said. "Honey, when Sarah gets back from her honeymoon, she'll be calling you every day to find out how to make meat loaf and pumpkin pie, and to cry when she's homesick or mad at Larry, or just to talk because she misses you. Mark my word. You might just be the one who's not available."

Sylvia wiped her face again. "What do you mean?"

He started to say something, then seemed to think better of it. "Listen, I had a cancellation for my first patient after lunch, so that's why I came home. I was hoping to take you to lunch somewhere nice. When's the last time we went out? I thought maybe that little South American restaurant over on Hilliard Street. We could talk—"

"Harry, I don't want to go out. Look at me. I'm a mess. Could I take a rain check?"

"A mess? You're beautiful. Slim and young-looking. I heard at least three people at the wedding asking if you were Sarah's sister."

She couldn't help being amused. "Don't lie."

"Well, okay, just one. But it happened. Scout's honor."

"I'm fifty years old and I feel sixty-five. Forced into mandatory retirement. Totally obsolete."

Harry's grin faded and he frowned down at her. "You really are depressed, aren't you?"

"And you aren't?"

He slid his hands into his pockets and looked down at his feet. He was thinking, trying to answer honestly, she knew. Harry wasn't one to just tell her what she wanted to hear.

"The other night," he said seriously, "after Sarah and Larry drove off, and the guests started going home, I went in the bathroom and cried. It was tough. My baby, Daddy's little girl, riding off into the sunset with some guy who's going to take care of her for the rest of her life." His eyes misted up even now as he recalled those emotions.

Sylvia smiled softly. "I should have known. And there I was flitting around, laughing and smiling for the guests, ignoring you completely."

"I wanted to be ignored when I felt like that," he said. "But it passed. This morning, I started thinking differently. I started thinking of this time of our lives as a beginning instead of an ending. We can do whatever we want now. All these years, when we've wanted to do things, but couldn't because we had the kids to think of—well, now we can go anywhere, do anything, and it's just the two of us. No more excuses. No more reasons to stay in the same old place. I started getting excited, Sylvia."

Sylvia looked up at him, frowning, wondering where he was going with this. "So where is it you want to go? What is it you want to do?"

Again, he looked down at his feet, searching for honest words, and she realized this midday homecoming wasn't just a whim. He had something specific to say. She tried to brace herself. "Harry?"

"You sure you don't want to go eat?" he asked her. "Even just a burger? We could eat in the car, even."

She sighed. "This must be really big if you have to say it over food."

"I'm just hungry. It's really nothing. In fact, we can talk about it another time."

"Let me run a brush through my hair, and we can go," she said.

Harry grinned, and she knew it was what he'd really wanted. She went into the bathroom, brushed her just-permed hair, and applied some lipstick so she wouldn't look so pale. She powdered the redness over her nose and decided her eyes were hopeless. It was just as well that Harry wanted to go out, she decided. She did need a diversion today.

She followed him out to the Explorer and waited while he unlocked it for her. She looked around at the little houses on the cul-de-sac where they'd lived for so long. Near the neck of the little circle, she saw three of Brenda's kids helping their dad drag picnic tables into the empty lot between their house and the Sullivans. Today was Joseph's birthday, she remembered. They had invited her to the party, but she'd almost forgotten.

She remembered when her own were little, before the cul-de-sac called Cedar Circle had been developed around them. Their own house had been built on a huge, twenty-acre plot at the top of Survey Mountain. It had been much smaller then, until Harry's surgical practice had gotten off the ground. Almost yearly, they had added something to their house.

When she and Harry had made the decision to sell some of the land to a builder to develop into a cul-de-sac, they had done it for the kids. The children needed playmates, she'd told Harry, and he agreed. The developer had plotted out Cedar Circle, paved the streets, and three houses had gone up with wisteria and jasmine-covered picket fences, oaks, and elm trees. None of the homes was quite as large as the Bryans', and none had the stretch of land in the back that the Bryans had kept for their horses. But the neighbors had become close friends, and their children had always had playmates.

But all those children had grown up, and their families, one by one, had moved away. Now the cul-de-sac was populated with younger mothers with active children who only reminded her how she longed for the former days.

"Are you planning to get in, or just stand here all day gazing down Memory Lane?" Harry teased.

She looked up at him. "Sorry. I was just remembering the way it looked before those houses . . ." She got in, and he closed the door behind her, then slipped in on the other side. "I'm sorry, Harry," she said. "It's one of those days when you can't seem to keep your thoughts going in the right direction. It's the classic, textbook case of empty-nest syndrome. I read all about it when they went off to college. But they were close by, and I knew they'd be back for meals and laundry . . ."

"Yeah, this is different. This time they're really gone."

"I need a hobby," she said. "A project. Maybe that would get my mind off of it."

"Well," he said, drawing the word out a little too long, and hooking her attention. "Maybe I have the answer. I'll tell you while we eat."

A few minutes later he pulled into a Burger King, and they both went in and ordered food that was a cardiac surgeon's nightmare. When they'd found a table in the corner, Sylvia brought the subject up again. "Okay, Harry. Shoot. What's your project?"

He gazed out the window. "I'm torn. I don't know whether I should tell you while you're depressed because it might make you more depressed, or whether it'll be just the thing you need to shake you out of it."

"Well, you'll never know until you try." She took a bite of her hamburger.

"You know how we've always said that someday when the kids are grown, we'd go to the mission field?"

"Sure. Do you want to take some extra medical mission trips to Nicaragua this year?"

"No, not mission trips. Longer term."

She set her hamburger down and dabbed at her mouth with the napkin, keeping her eyes fixed on him. "You can't be serious."

He looked like a schoolboy trying to convince his mother to buy him a sports car. "Haven't we always said that, Sylvia? Even these last few years, every time we went on those little trips, we've talked about how great it would be if we were unencumbered and could just go and take the miracles of modern medicine to those people who can't afford it?"

She couldn't deny that they'd talked about it many times. She had agreed that it would be wonderful to be an ambassador of grace, to make sacrifices, to give of herself to people who needed what she could bring them. But what was that, exactly? Harry could take them medicine—she was mostly just there for support.

"It's a great ministry, Sylvia. I've felt called to do it most of my life, but I also felt responsible to give the kids a normal life. But now the kids are gone, and it's time for me to stop making excuses."

She looked in his eyes and saw the joy building there like a cresting tide. The emotions in her own heart felt like those same waves crashing against a bleak and rocky shore.

"Sylvia, just think about how much good we could do there."

"*You* could do so much good there," she said, that tightness returning to her voice. "But what could *I* do?"

"What could *you* do? You're the Doña. The one they all respected."

"I'd be useless there, Harry. Even in our own home, I wouldn't have a purpose. Every home there has a maidservant to clean. What would I do all day?"

"You could start a ministry with the mothers and children, Sylvia. Teach parenting skills, Bible studies, evangelism. You'd be such an example to them. A mother figure for them to look up to."

Tears erupted in her eyes again, and she shook her head. "I'm not prepared to be a mother to anybody but my own kids, Harry, and they're gone."

"They're not gone. You talk like they're dead. They're still alive, honey, they're just proving that we succeeded. They're happy and healthy and building lives of their own."

She shook her head and looked down at the burger. She couldn't eat another bite. Her stomach wouldn't accept it. "I'm not ready, Harry," she said through tight lips. "Not yet. Maybe next year, or the year after that. The kids still might need me, and I can't be out of the country."

He reached across the table and took her hand. "Honey, the kids will always need you. But God may want us somewhere else."

She couldn't believe this was so important to him. Had he been biding his time, chomping at the bit throughout the whole wedding process, counting the days until Sarah was gone, so he could fly off to Managua?

"Are ... are you finished? Eating, I mean?"

He looked down at the half-eaten burger. "Yeah, I guess. Honey, this is upsetting you. I'm sorry. I should have waited until a better time, but I thought it might cheer you up. You said you wanted a project."

"Can we go home?" She was making a valiant effort to fight the tears, but she was losing.

"Sure."

She slid out of the booth and threw their wrappers away, then headed through the door. The drive home was quiet.

When they pulled back into the driveway, she got out and dashed inside.

Harry was behind her in an instant. "Honey, listen," he said, wrapping his arms around her, "I can see how upset this has made you. The timing is all wrong. Just forget I ever said anything."

But that wouldn't be right either, she knew. Harry rarely asked for anything for himself. For years, he'd been catering to his family's wants and needs. This once, he had some of his own. But they were just too hard for her to accept.

She looked around her. Over the years, she'd decorated their home exactly as she'd wanted it. It was a showplace—and it bore the sentimental, beloved scars of a family that had grown up here. The growth chart on the pantry wall, the mural they'd painted in Sarah's room, the little stained glass windows the kids had made one summer.

"What would we do with the house?" she asked on a whisper.

He seemed reluctant to answer. "I don't know. Whatever you want. I was thinking we could sell it."

"*Sell* it?" The words flipped out of her mouth with such disgust that he might have suggested setting it on fire. "Harry!"

His expression fell further. She was the archer shooting her arrow straight into his dreams. She hated playing that role. She tried to breathe in some courage and took his hands, strong surgeon's hands that saved lives with such skill . . . but there were many such hands here in the states, and so few overseas. Maybe these hands were meant to be used in Nicaragua.

She dropped them again. "You've got to understand, Harry, that this is a little sudden. Maybe you've been thinking about it for a long time. But I haven't."

"You're right." He found his smile again, and she saw that his twinkle was still there. "It's just that I've been thinking about it a lot over the last few days. I miss the kids just like you do, but I keep seeing it as a new beginning, not an end. I keep thinking that God has a purpose for us, that all the training and skill He's given me here could be used to take the gospel across the world, and take medicine to people who can't get it otherwise. Sylvia, I've never felt as needed as I felt when we were in Masaya last year. Remember all the people we led to Christ? Remember Carlos, the playboy with a string of mistresses? We were able to lead his wife to Christ for a very important reason: she trusted us after I did the appendectomy on their son. And then Carlos came to church with her, and his life changed—"

"There are lost people *here*, Harry. Some right in this cul-de-sac. Why do we have to go across the world?"

"Because someone has to."

With both hands, she wiped the tears forming under her eyes and tried to think logically. "Let me think about it, okay, Harry? Do we have to make a decision right away?"

"Of course not. Take all the time you need."

"Are you sure?" she asked. "I don't want to destroy your dreams."

"God wouldn't give this kind of calling to just one of us. If He's calling me, He'll call you, too."

She looked at him for a long moment, her eyes filling with tears again. "Is it your practice?" she asked. "Are you just bored with it?"

Again, he stared down at his shoes, thinking. "I could use a change," he said, meeting her eyes again. "But that's not all this is about." He opened his arms and pulled her again into a hug, held her there for a long moment as her tears soaked into his shirt. "It's not the end, honey. You'll see."

"I know," she said in a high-pitched voice. "I really do know that. I just don't feel like I have a lot to contribute, either here or there. It seems kind of pointless to me."

"Then I'll pray that God will reveal to you how important you are."

She laid her head against his chest. He was her best friend, her lover, her confidante, her provider and supporter. He'd always been so strong, so masterful. He'd also often been right.

But right or wrong, she was thankful he wasn't asking for a decision now.

After a few moments, he let her go and ate a dessert of petit fours left over from the reception. She sat with him, eating chocolate groom's cake. She supposed a few extra pounds on her hips wouldn't make much difference. Wasn't food always supposed to make you feel better?

But she didn't feel particularly well as she walked him back out to his Explorer. She leaned in and kissed him when he was in the car. She heard a "hello" shouted from the driveway next door, and she waved at Cathy Flaherty, her neighbor on the other side.

"Why don't you go visit with Cathy?" Harry asked. "She always cheers you up."

"I've got those pictures to take down, and all that misery to wallow in," she said with a smirk. "I wouldn't be very good company."

He kissed her and pulled out of the driveway. Sylvia tried to smile until he was out of the cul-de-sac, but it quickly faded. Her gaze drifted up to the hills in the distance. The mist that normally floated like angelic breath above them had been chased away by the bright sun. Everything looked so clear.

She only wished she could see her own future that clearly.

Chapter *Four*

Cathy Flaherty intercepted her German shepherd as he bounded from the Bryans' house. He was damp, she discovered as she bent down to pet him, and he smelled like a stray mutt. She wondered where he'd been. She slammed the door of her pickup truck and looked back at the Bryans again. She saw Harry kiss Sylvia before pulling out of the driveway. What a day it must be for them, she thought, to finally have all the kids married off and find that your marriage was still strong.

She went into the house, fighting jealousy. She wasn't naive enough to think marriage was always bliss. Heaven knew hers hadn't been. But some part of her—the largest part—wanted one more shot. It wasn't easy being a single mother of three kids from eleven to seventeen. She'd spent a lot of the past couple of years looking for a husband for herself in an attempt to start over. She had never expected to be forty and single, nor had she ever intended to raise her kids alone. That had been decided for her.

She went into the house, breathing in the silence as if it were a balm that could heal a troubled soul. Though her veterinary practice kept her busy, she tried to come home for lunch every day while the kids were at school, just to regroup and do the housekeeping chores she hadn't had time to do that morning. Soon the kids would be out of school for the summer, though, and the whole dynamic of her days would change.

She opened a can of soup and poured it into a bowl, stuck it in the microwave, punched out three minutes. While it was cooking, she went into the laundry room and began pulling blue jeans—the most common and indispensable item in the entire family's wardrobe—out of the mountain of laundry to wash. Even Cathy preferred jeans over anything else. She shoved pair after pair into the washing machine, emptying pockets of change and gum wrappers and breath mints. She tossed the garbage and kept the change. That was the deal, she'd told them. If they were careless enough to leave money in their pockets when she washed, she got to keep it. She saved it in a dill pickle jar and took them all out to eat when enough had been saved.

She stuffed six pairs into the machine, decided the load could take one more, and grabbed up a pair of Rick's long, lanky jeans. Two quarters fell out, and by rote, she reached into the pockets and grabbed hold of the rest of the contents. Her fingers came upon a small square. She pulled it out . . .

And her heart crashed.

It was a condom, in the pocket of her seventeen-year-old son.

She dropped it as if it had burned her. Her son hardly even dated. When would he have time enough to get into a relationship that would require a condom? Feeling sick, she backed to the wall, slid down it, and sat on the floor, hugging her knees. It couldn't be. Not her boy.

Slowly, her mind worked past the shock and began to evaluate options. Maybe she should go to the school, snatch him out of class, confront him face-to-face, and demand an explanation. But would that be overreacting? Shouldn't she be happy that her son was interested in safe sex?

No! her heart screamed. She didn't want Rick to be engaging in sex of any kind. Despite her liberal leanings, she hated the idea of her own children becoming sexually active.

The microwave beeped, and she got to her feet. As the shock gave way, rage seeped in to fill the void. Where had he gotten it? With whom was he planning to use it? Did his father know about this? Was it *his* idea?

Yes. Her thoughts seemed to crystallize as it all became clear. He'd been with his father this past weekend. It was just like Jerry to do something stupid like giving his son a condom. The man probably assumed that Rick had the same loose morals he had, and he wanted to protect him from any "mistakes." The microwave beeped again, and as if it had been the one to corrupt her son, she threw it open, grabbed the glass bowl of soup, and pulled it out. It sloshed over the side and burned her hand, so she flung it into the sink, breaking the bowl. That was all right; she didn't want to eat it anyway. She wasn't hungry anymore.

Instead, she jerked up the phone and punched out her ex-husband's work number in Knoxville. "Jerry Flaherty," he said innocently.

"What do you think you're doing?" she demanded.

"Cathy?" He seemed genuinely confused.

"Yeah, it's me. Who else can you get into a frothing rage without even being present?"

"What, pray tell, have I done now?"

"Did you or did you not give our son a condom?"

"A *what?* No, I didn't give him a condom!"

"Then who did? Could it have been Sandra?"

"No! My wife did not give Rick a condom. That's ludicrous. How could you even think that?"

"Oh, well, excuse me," she said sardonically. "But your past moral slipups tend to keep me from being too surprised at anything you do. Did you *talk* to him about condoms?"

"No. It never came up."

"Is there someone there that he's seeing?"

"No. Annie's the one we can't keep home. She's got that friend, Joni, who has a car, and who knows what they do or what boys they meet when they leave here?"

Newer, hotter rage flared up inside her like a Fourth of July display, and she forced herself to sit down on the stool at the breakfast bar. "Has it *ever* occurred to you to tell her she can't go?"

"For what reason? We haven't caught her at anything yet."

"Do you *know* where she goes?"

"Movies, Burger King, Blockbuster, that kind of thing. Come on, Cathy, calm down. It's not like we let her stay out all night. She's home by curfew."

"Then why did you just say she's probably meeting boys?"

"Because she's a girl. That's what they do."

"Have you checked up on her to make sure she's where she says? Do you know anything about this girl Joni? Have you met her parents?"

"No, Cathy. I have these kids every other weekend. I'm not intimately acquainted with the parents of their friends, and I don't see why that would be necessary. I just brought that up to say that Rick is not the one I'd worry about, if I worried about any of them. Now what's this about a condom?"

She let out a deflated breath and stared at the counter for a moment. "I found it in his pocket. If he doesn't have a girlfriend there, and he doesn't have one here, why did he have a condom?"

"Got me. Maybe he's just saving it for a rainy day."

The flippancy of his remark seared her. "You act like this is no big deal, Jerry. This is your son!"

"My son is seventeen, Cathy. Eventually, he is going to get involved with a girl, and frankly, if you want to know my opinion, I don't think a condom is a bad idea. He probably ought to keep one with him."

She ground her teeth together. "Spoken like the Father of the Year. I don't know why you still amaze me, Jerry."

"Cathy, relax. They're growing up. You can't stop them. Even Mark's going through puberty. Twelve years old, and his voice is starting to change."

"I'm not trying to stunt their growth," Cathy bit out. "I'm trying to raise them right."

"Maybe raising them right means getting them to adulthood without pregnancy or disease. Maybe that's the best we can hope for."

The words filtered through her like scorching water, and she dropped the phone from her ear and stared at it as if she could see her ex-husband through the little holes in the mouthpiece. Why was she even talking to him? He had the morals of a canine.

No longer enraged, she dropped the phone back on its hook on her wall, cutting off the connection. It was like the stages of grief. She had moved quickly from shock, to anger, and now into depression. All she could do was wait for the kids to get home, so she could find out where Rick had gotten the condom. She had exactly two hours to come up with a plan of action. Should she yell, lecture, punish? Or was it possible that she would be struck with a burst of wisdom on how to turn this from a crisis into a wonderful learning experience that the kids would always hold dear?

Fat chance.

It occurred to her to call the clinic and tell her receptionist to close the office for the afternoon, but she knew she had two litters of puppies coming in to be dewormed. She could put them off, she supposed, but she couldn't really afford to turn the work away. Knocking off at four every day and refusing to work Saturday afternoons left her few enough office hours as it was. No, she needed to get back.

She went back to the laundry room, started the load of jeans, and slid the condom into her own pocket. Then, trying to ignore the dismal thoughts flitting through her mind, she went back out to the pickup. Across the street, her neighbor Brenda stood in a huddle with her four kids, all with different shades of red hair. They were up to something, but that wasn't unusual. Brenda, who homeschooled her children, had the most creative mind Cathy knew when it came to stimulating them. She was probably doing some sort of nature hunt or demonstrating the food chain by collecting bugs in the yard, imparting some type of life lesson that they'd never forget.

Suddenly, Cathy felt like a terrible mother who didn't deserve the children who'd been entrusted to her.

As she backed out of the driveway, she saw David, Brenda's husband, dragging picnic tables to the lot between the houses. He was always there, an active partner in raising the children, making a living as a cabinetmaker from the workshop in the backyard. With his wavy red hair and his slight paunch, he had never been the catch of Breezewood. But given the chance, Cathy would have traded every material possession she had to have one just like him. She gave him a cursory wave, swallowing her swelling anger at her ex-husband. She deserved better than to be raising three children alone. More importantly, *they* deserved better.

CHAPTER *Five*

"*Come* on, hurry up, let's go. We've got to get the decorations up before the party." Brenda Dodd's tone was more grand marshal than drill sergeant as she looked around at the empty lot between her house and Tory's house next door. David had moved the two picnic tables he'd built to the center of the lot for Joseph's birthday party.

Though Joseph had sprung out of bed that morning and declared that he was well, he still looked weak. "But we don't have any crepe paper," he pointed out. "What are we gonna put up?"

Brenda grinned and lifted her eyebrows. "Did you grab a roll of toilet paper like I told you?"

"Yes, but I don't see why the kids can't just go in the house if they have to go to the bathroom," Daniel said.

Brenda laughed. "The toilet paper's for decoration, Kemo Sabe."

All four children looked down at the rolls of toilet paper in their hands, expressions of complete bewilderment on their faces. "We're decorating with *toilet paper?*" the birthday boy asked, his flaming red hair making him look even paler in the harsh sunlight.

"Isn't there some rule against that in Amy Vanderbilt?" Leah had found a thirty-year-old copy of Amy Vanderbilt's *Book of Etiquette* at a used book sale, and read it like a novel when she wasn't doing schoolwork. "I mean, I never saw it in the book anywhere, but it just seems kind of rude, don't you think?"

"Trust me," Brenda said. "Observe." Like a scientist attempting to demonstrate a life-changing experiment, she unrolled two yards of toilet paper from her own roll. "Follow me, troops. I'm about to show you how to do the most fabulous party decoration known to man, and all for the price of a six-pack of toilet paper."

The children all followed, doubtful.

Brenda laughed at the looks on their faces as she reached the center of the empty lot. "Oh ye of little faith." She looked up at the canopy of huge oaks and elms throughout the yard. Rearing back, she threw her toilet paper roll into the branches overhead. The paper caught on a limb, and the roll fell to the ground, unrolling a stream of paper behind it.

"Cool!" Daniel shouted. "Mom's letting us roll our own yard!"

The confused looks turned to expressions of sheer delight as the children joined in the act, squealing and laughing and flinging their rolls. When Brenda's naked cardboard roll fell to the ground, she stood back, watching her kids send long swoops of white toilet paper draping through the trees like crepe paper purposely placed.

"Brenda! For Pete's sake, what are you doing?" David called, leaning out the window of the workshop behind the house. "What have you taught them?"

"How to decorate on a shoestring, David," she called with glee. "Come help us."

He came out in a moment and stood there with his hands at his sides, a worried grin on his face. "How are we gonna get this stuff down?"

"Don't worry. It'll come down. We'll just pull it all off after the party."

"What if it rains?"

"It wouldn't dare."

The look on his face was so comical that she had to laugh out loud. "You up for blowing up balloons? We couldn't afford the helium kind, so I figured we'd just all blow until we ran out of air."

"Mama, can we have more toilet paper?" Rachel asked. "I ran out of mine."

"That's enough," Brenda said. "Look at it. Isn't it beautiful? Now, come help with the balloons. We're going to blow them up, tie them in bunches, and set them on top of the birdhouses."

Her children's faces testified that they had caught their mother's vision. She could have suggested that they grab some shovels and dig a ditch, and they would have been convinced they were having fun. They worked on the balloons until they'd blown up half of them, but it was getting hot, and she realized that by the time the party began, they would be nearing meltdown. Joseph was looking particularly peaked. He was pale, perspiring, and breathing hard. "David, why don't you hook up the sprinkler in the backyard while we blow up the balloons?" she suggested. "That'll be one of the activities at the party. They can run through the sprinkler when they get hot."

"Good idea," David said. He was sweating himself, and his red hair had separated into wavy wet strands.

"But they'll be soaked," Leah said. "Whoever heard of going to a birthday party soaking wet?"

"Ms. Vanderbilt would have loved it," Brenda assured her as David headed to the backyard. "Come on, now. Get some more balloons and start blowing."

She watched the kids huff and puff. But when she noticed that Joseph, too, was only watching, she tousled his damp hair and said, "Joseph, are you feeling okay?"

"Yes, ma'am," he said. "I'm just hot."

"Wanna go sit in the air-conditioning for a minute? Get a drink?"

"No, ma'am, I'll just stand in the sprinkler to cool off."

"You're the birthday boy. Have at it."

She would have expected him to run at the rare treat, but instead he only walked around to the back of the house. "Joseph," she called after him, "remind Daddy to make sure the water doesn't reach the toilet paper."

"I will."

They finished blowing up balloons, and by the time two o'clock came, the yard looked festive and inviting. Two cars pulled up at the same time, and out spilled eight delighted homeschooled youngsters. Brenda sent the parents on their way for some rare time alone, assuring them that there would be plenty of supervision. She saw the front door of the Sullivan house open, and Tory came out with Spencer and Brittany.

Spencer took one look at the toilet paper draping the trees and sprinted away from his mother. Brittany began to jump into the air like a pogo toy. "Look, Mommy! Look!"

Tory, dressed in a pale blue shorts set that enhanced the color of her eyes, looked like a model about to do a photo shoot. Brenda wondered why she bothered to fix her hair and makeup when she would probably sweat it all off. Tory gave her a what-have-you-done-now grin as she reached the crowd. "Brenda . . ."

"It'll come down, I promise," Brenda said, raising her right hand in a mock vow. "The kids love it." She knew Tory didn't consider that a good enough reason to risk a potential mess in both their yards, but it was the best she could do.

Spencer and Brittany flung their presents to the center of the table, where the other gifts were piled. "Open mine first, okay, Joseph?" Spencer demanded. "Open it now!"

Joseph, who was cooler now that he was soaking wet, shook his head. "I can't, Spence. It's not time yet."

"Aw, man," Spencer said, then immediately switched gears. "How come you're wet?"

"There's a sprinkler going in the back. You can play in it if you want."

Spencer didn't wait to hear more. He leaped down from the picnic table and tore around to the back of the house.

"Spencer, no!" Tory shouted. "I've bathed him twice today, and he's on his third outfit."

"It'll dry," Brenda laughed. "Come on, Tory. It's part of the activities. David's back there supervising."

"Well, we could run back home and put on bathing suits . . ."

"Nooo!" Spencer protested. "It's more fun in clothes!"

Tory sighed and seemed to resign herself to a fourth outfit.

Brittany almost had a conniption fit. "Me, too, Mommy? Can I get wet, too?"

Brenda knew that Tory didn't see the appeal of "getting wet"—to her it represented another mess—but finally, she surrendered her second child to the water. As if to force her own mind off wet children, Tory looked around at the other kids. "These kids are all different ages. Aren't any of them in school?"

"They're all homeschooled," Brenda said. "We go on field trips together and stuff. I thought they'd enjoy a party. I sent their mothers away—they could use a break."

"Mama doesn't make us do school on birthdays," Joseph said, putting a balloon to his mouth to blow up. The balloon inflated slightly, and his face began to redden as he tried harder to blow it up.

"Here, I'll help," Tory said, taking one. She blew it up quickly, tied it in a knot, and handed it to Rachel, who was waiting with ribbon to tie around it.

Joseph was still working on his. Finally, he gave up and let the balloon go. It twirled in the air and collapsed on the table.

Brenda stopped what she was doing and gazed down at him. "You couldn't blow it up, honey?"

"I don't want to," he said.

"You want to run through the sprinkler again?" She pushed his wet hair back from his face and touched his forehead. It wasn't feverish. "Go ahead. It might pep you up a little."

"Yeah, maybe." He got up from the bench as if to do just that, but stopped and steadied himself.

Brenda bent over to meet his eyes. "Joseph?"

He didn't answer right away, just stared blindly into space, wobbled slightly, then went limp and hit the ground.

"Joseph!" Brenda fell to her knees beside her unconscious son. "Tory, go get David!"

But David was there before Tory could move. "What's wrong?"

"He passed out! Get me a cold rag or something."

Daniel, who was soaked from the sprinkler and had run up behind his father, pulled his wet T-shirt off and thrust it at his mother. She was shaking as she began to stroke Joseph's face with it. "Honey, wake up. Joseph?"

His eyes slowly opened and rested blankly on her.

"He's awake," Brenda cried. "David, we've got to get him to the doctor."

"But the party!" Leah cried. "We can't leave all the guests. Their mothers aren't here!"

Tory looked helplessly at David and Brenda. "Look, you two take him on. I'll take care of things here."

"He's okay, aren't you, sweetie?" Brenda asked, trying to calm her voice to keep from frightening Joseph. "I can take him by myself. David, you can stay and have the party. Just save Joseph some cake and all his presents. There's no need for everybody to go home, is there?"

"Okay," he said, and Brenda knew that he too was trying to keep the concern out of his voice. "Joseph'll be fine, and all this loot'll be here when you get back. Leah, go get him a change of clothes so Mama can get him out of the wet ones when they get there."

Already, she had Joseph on his feet and was walking him toward the car. She fumbled with the door, and David came to her aid. "David, I'll call you when we see the doctor, okay? Just have fun. Joseph is fine." How many times had they said that? she wondered. And were they saying it for the sake of the kids—or themselves?

David helped Joseph into the car as the children, some wet from the sprinkler and some from sweat, crowded around. Leah cut through them and handed Brenda her purse and a change of clothes for Joseph. As the car pulled out, Joseph looked sadly out the window.

"Well," Brenda said cheerfully as they left the cul-de-sac. "This will be a party to remember, won't it? For years, we'll say, 'Remember Joseph's ninth birthday when he passed out cold?'"

Joseph was still gazing out the window. "Toilet paper is better than crepe paper, isn't it?" he asked quietly. "Prettier, too. It was fun even before the people got there."

Brenda tried to blink back the tears in her eyes as she sped to the doctor's office.

CHAPTER *Six*

The pediatrician's office was packed to capacity with sick children and babies waiting for their monthly checkups. As they waited to be worked in, Brenda could only imagine the disappointment that Joseph must feel at having to miss the birthday party he'd spent weeks talking about. Her own heart was deflated, and she couldn't put aside the fright she'd experienced watching her child pass out before her eyes.

Maybe it *was* his blood sugar, as Daniel had suggested. Maybe the cinnamon rolls she'd made for breakfast had been a mistake, but she'd wanted to make something special for his birthday. Maybe he still wasn't a hundred percent after his virus a few weeks ago. Maybe it was just too hot for him.

As badly as she wanted to believe these simple and non-threatening explanations, her heart found no comfort in them. Something was wrong with Joseph. Something was terribly wrong.

He laid his head back in the chair, his little body almost limp. His face still lacked color, and his hair was mussed from drying without being combed first.

She racked her brain trying to think of something to help him pass the time. She had promised him no school today, so she didn't want to practice his multiplication tables or drill him on his spelling words. No, she would keep her word. Today would only be for fun. Even if they did have to have it in a doctor's office.

She reached into her big purse that carried all sorts of child-occupying paraphernalia and pulled out a miniature legal pad. She got a green marker from the ziplock bag of markers and crayons in the bottom of her purse. Joseph looked as if he expected her to hand it to him, but instead she dropped the bag back into her purse and began to draw with the green marker.

"Whatcha drawing?" he asked.

"Never you mind. Just wait."

"Is it for me?"

She grinned and covered her paper so he couldn't see. "Just a minute. You'll see."

She finished drawing, then tore out the page and brandished it.

"What is it?" he asked.

She wrote a one and then six zeros in the center of the page. "It's a million dollar bill," she said proudly.

"A million dollar bill?" he asked. "They make those?"

"I wouldn't know," she said. "But I was just thinking a kid like you on his ninth birthday probably deserves nothing less than a million dollar bill. So I wanted you to have it." She handed it to him.

He grinned. "Gee, thanks, Mama."

"And now you have to spend it."

He looked skeptically up at her. "Spend it? How?"

She reached back in her purse for a pen, and handed him the legal pad. "You have to write down everything you'd spend your million dollars to buy, and you have to spend every cent."

His smile turned to a suspicious frown. "Are you tricking me into doing math?"

It would have been a good trick, but she'd had no such intentions. "No, it's just a game."

His eyebrows arched as his grin crept back.

"Let's just see if you can. A million dollars is a lot of money, you know."

He smiled down at the bill, as though he couldn't believe his good fortune. "Okay."

"What's the first thing you would buy?"

He leaned his head back on the chair and closed his eyes for a moment, thinking. When he opened them, she saw the twinkle there. The excitement. Already he was feeling better. "I know," he said. "A truckload of toilet paper so we could roll everybody's yard in our whole neighborhood, and up and down the streets, all the way down the mountain."

She gave him a disgusted look. "You've got a million bucks and you'd use it to buy toilet paper?"

"Well, it was fun."

"Okay, then. Write it down."

"How much is that?"

"Depends on where you get them. At Sam's Club, I guess it'd be about ten, fifteen bucks. What else?"

He thought for a while. "How much does a swimming pool cost?"

"Depends," she said. "One of those little inflatable jobs? Or an Olympic-sized pool with marble sides and lily pads floating on the top?"

"Yeah, one of those."

She shrugged. "I wouldn't know, but thirty thousand dollars ought to be safe. What else?"

He subtracted the thirty thousand. "I've still got a lot left over. How about a convertible?"

"A convertible what?"

"A convertible . . ." She imagined him flipping through his mind's database of minivans and used pickups.

Finally, he surprised her. "A convertible Jaguar!"

Television, she thought. There was a whole database he got from the hour a day she allowed him to watch.

"Okay, what color?"

"Red." He started to write it down, and she began to think about what a car like that might cost.

"Put a hundred thousand dollars. No telling what a car like that costs, but it's probably in the ballpark. How much left?"

"Too much," he said. "I'll never spend it all." He spent some time thinking, then looked up at her with wide eyes. "How about a big nice house for you? Like something that cost forty thousand or something like that."

She didn't want to burst his bubble with the real value of real estate, or break it to him that the house they lived in, which they scraped to pay for, was worth far more than that. "Thank you *very* much. What else?"

"The Bryans' new horse?" Joseph asked. "You know, the baby."

"You'd want to buy that horse?" she asked.

"If I had a million dollars I would."

"Okay, put it down."

She let him make up the price. "What else?"

"Rude lessons for Leah, since she's so worried about it all the time."

"You mean etiquette lessons?"

"Whatever. She's so afraid she'll do something wrong. We need to send her to good manners school so she can learn all the right things to do."

"She'd appreciate that."

"And ... golf lessons for Daddy and Daniel. And clubs. Daddy works too hard."

"Good idea. I agree."

"And for Rachel," he added, "some new dresses. She's obsessed with her looks."

Brenda grinned. *Obsess* had been one of this week's vocabulary words, and she was proud to see him use it. "What else?"

His eyes drifted off as he considered the possibilities. For a moment, he seemed to watch the chattering children in the waiting room running to and fro, playing with the toys in the corner, but she knew he was still thinking. "A video camera," he said more softly. "So I could tape my birthday parties when I'm not there."

The amusement left her eyes, and she gazed down at him. "I know you're disappointed."

"It's okay," he said, grinning. "It was really fun rolling the trees and all. How'd you think of that, anyway?"

"It just came to me." Necessity *was* the mother of invention. Most of her creative ideas came from being broke. "We never have money to throw around. Just toilet paper."

Joseph giggled. "Do you think Daddy'll pull the toilet paper down before we get home?"

She thought that over. It would be just like David to do that, in an effort to spare her the work. "Tell you what," she said. "Before we leave here we'll call him and ask him to leave it up."

"But what if it rains tonight? Then it'll get mushy and fall in the yard."

"Stop worrying. It was a beautiful day today and it's going to be beautiful tomorrow. Tomorrow we'll take it down. But today is your birthday for the whole day, and that toilet paper stays up."

He smiled up at her as his eyes grew distant again. "What about the cake?"

"They're saving you some," she said. "They promised. And the presents will still be there when we get back."

"Okay," he said. He went back to his list and was still trying to think of other ways to spend his million dollars when, finally, a nurse came to the door.

"Joseph Dodd?"

Brenda stood up quickly and nodded to the nurse, and Joseph handed the legal pad back to his mother, then followed the nurse into the examining room.

The doctor put on his stethoscope and listened carefully to Joseph's heart. As he listened, Brenda could see that something troubled him.

At last, he finished and pulled the boy's shirt back down. "Brenda, I think we need to have some tests run on Joseph."

"What kind of tests?"

"Oh, several things," he said evasively. "We just want to take every precaution, make sure we don't overlook anything. Can you take him over to St. Francis Hospital?" Though his voice was calm, the question conveyed urgency.

She frowned. "Right now?"

"Yeah, I'd really like to get the results of these tests. It's not normal for kids as strapping as Joseph to go around fainting on their birthdays. Is it, son?" He patted Joseph gently on the back. "I'll have my nurse call and set up the tests. You may be there a while."

She nodded silently and tried to push out of her mind the thought of the bills that would mount as a result of these tests. She wondered briefly whether they were all necessary, but then she shook off the thought. Joseph's health was at stake, and if the doctor thought Joseph needed the tests, then he would have them.

When Joseph was out in the front room picking through the reward bucket for the perfect scratch-'n'-sniff sticker, she stopped the doctor in the hall. "Doctor, could this be something serious?" she asked softly.

He had trouble looking her in the eye. "I can't say, Brenda. He's probably just fine. Just got a little too hot, a little too excited. But I'd like to be sure." He busied himself jotting on his chart as he tried to walk off.

But Brenda stopped him again. "What are you looking for?"

The doctor still didn't look at her. "Nothing specific. It's just that the tests will go a long way toward helping us diagnose him, if there's a diagnosis to be made."

Anger sparked in her heart, and she wanted to grab him by the throat and force him to look at her. But that wasn't her way. Feeling disheartened, she went to pay the bill, knowing they'd have to stretch their grocery budget a lot further now. But she was willing to give up food entirely if it meant helping her son.

She fought the tears threatening her eyes as she led Joseph back to the car.

Chapter Seven

Cathy turned into Cedar Circle and saw the toilet paper draped on the trees in the lot between the Dodds' and Sullivans' houses. What on earth was that about? She thought only homes of teenagers had stunts like that pulled on them. Twelve-year-old Daniel was probably getting old enough to have prank-playing friends. But in broad daylight?

Too preoccupied to worry about it, she pulled into her driveway just as the school bus drew up to the neck of the cul-de-sac. She got out of the car and waited as her dog, who'd been heading for her, changed his direction and loped toward the bus.

Mark got off of the bus and rubbed the dog's ears before ambling up the driveway. "Hey, Mom. Check out Daniel's yard. Cool. Why are you home so early?"

"I needed to talk to your brother." She kissed him on the forehead, but he recoiled, as if afraid someone might see. She accepted the rebuff without taking offense. "How was your day?"

"Okay." He headed into the house, and she followed.

He dropped his backpack just inside the door, and she grabbed his shirt before he could get away and turned him back around. "Take it to your room, kiddo."

"But I have homework."

"You planning to do it right here on the kitchen floor?"

"Well, no, but—"

"To your room, Mark."

He moaned and jerked the backpack up. She heard a car pulling into the garage and looked out the door. Rick and Annie were obviously embroiled in some kind of argument. She sighed. She had wondered about the wisdom of letting them ride to and from school together when they barely tolerated each other at home. On the other hand, she wasn't willing to let Annie ride home with Mario Andretti wanna-bes with more tickets than miles under their belts.

Rick got out and slammed the car door.

"You're such a jerk!" Annie shrieked as she got out and slammed hers harder.

"Make her get off my case, Mom!" Rick said. "I'm sick of it!"

They both tornadoed into the house. "Okay, what's going on?" Cathy demanded.

"He's just such a jerk," Annie repeated, slapping her long brown hair off of her shoulder. "I asked him to take one of my friends home, and he said no, right to her face. It was so embarrassing."

For two teens who were so at odds, their choreography remained identical. Simultaneously, they dropped their backpacks at the door and headed for the refrigerator. "It's not my job to run your friends all over town," Rick said, shouldering her out of his way.

Annie elbowed him like a Roller Derby queen.

"She doesn't live 'all over town.' Just a mile down the mountain. It was on the way. It wouldn't have hurt you a bit."

"When you get your car, you can drive it anywhere you want. I'm not a taxi service for you and your friends."

"Well, it doesn't look like I'm getting one since you're Mom's golden boy and I'm the middle child. I'm the one who always does without."

"Maybe if your attitude changed she'd get you—"

"Hey!" Cathy shouted. "*Hey!*" On the second yell, they both swung around, as if united in their resentment of her intrusion.

Cathy picked up the two-ton backpacks. "Put them in your rooms," she ordered.

"What are you doing home, anyway?" Rick asked, as if she had no business here.

"I wanted to talk to you," she said. "Now take these backpacks out of here!"

They both grabbed them, and Rick muttered, "Great. Can't get a minute's peace around here, what with Annie screaming in one ear and you yelling in the other. I hate this place!"

Though a more fragile mother might have been hurt, Cathy took it with a grain of salt. Rick did have a flare for the dramatic, and since he spoke with equal affection of school, his job, and his father's house, she didn't take it personally. She simply determined not to let his anger distract her from her course.

All afternoon she had worked herself into a lather thinking about that condom in her pocket. Now she couldn't decide whether to confront Rick in front of the other two, or to follow him into his room. She decided to follow him.

He didn't realize she was behind him until he dropped the backpack on the pile of dirty laundry on his bedroom floor. He turned around and saw her in the doorway. "Are you following me?" he accused.

"Yes, I'm following you." She came into the room and closed the door behind her, vowing not to ask the origin of the rancid smell wafting on the air. "We've got to talk."

He kicked some of his clothes out of the way and dropped onto his bed. "I work hard at school all day, get chewed out all the way home, and now this."

She thought of reassuring him that "this" wouldn't be so bad, but then she felt that foil square in her pocket again, and decided that it would be even worse than he thought. She felt her knees shaking and decided she had to sit down, so she knocked the clothes from a chair into a new pile on the floor, and sat. "Rick, I found something when I was doing the laundry."

"Oh yeah?" he asked, unworried. "Did I leave money in my pockets again?"

She fixed her eyes on him, wondering if he was playing innocent. "No, Rick. It wasn't money."

"What then?" Suddenly, his face changed, as if it hit him what she was talking about, and he caught his breath. "Oh! You found the ..." He let his voice trail off, as if he didn't dare say the word.

"Yeah, it was the condom," she said. She felt her face turning red and knew that she was going to launch into a high-octave sermon that would draw the other kids from their rooms and send Rick into a defensive rage. She didn't want anything so futile and destructive to happen, so she set her elbows on her jean-clad knees and tried to think. "Rick, I want you to tell me why you had it."

He stared at her, frowning as his mouth hung open, and she braced herself for his accusation that she'd invaded his privacy. "You think I got that for *myself?*"

It wasn't the response she'd expected. "Rick, I'm not stupid."

"Neither am I! I don't believe this. I'm in trouble for something I didn't even—"

"Rick, it was in *your* pocket."

"I don't care where it was. Just because I'm carrying around a condom doesn't mean I went out and bought it and planned to use it."

"Then why did you have it?"

"Every guy at school has one."

She closed her eyes, fuming, and ground her molars together. "Rick, I don't *care* if every boy in school takes a dive off the cliff at Bright Mountain. I don't want *my* son—"

"No, you don't get it!" he cut in. "Mom, they gave them to us at school. In a class."

She opened her eyes and gaped at him. She couldn't have heard right. Had he said . . . ? "They *gave* them to you?"

"Yeah. It was 'Condom Awareness Day,' if you can believe that. It's the biggest joke of the school year, every year from seventh grade on up. They get you in the room and start lecturing you about safe sex and stuff."

He said it matter-of-factly, as if she would naturally know and understand. *Oh, yes, of course. Condom Awareness Day.* But she didn't.

Her heart began to rampage, and she stood up, facing him at eye level. "Are you seriously telling me that they gave condoms out at school?"

"Yeah," he said. He was grinning now, enjoying her shock.

"Rick, I know that sometimes I can be naive, but I didn't just ride in on a hay truck."

"Mom, I'm telling you the truth. Call the school and ask them."

It was rare for him to suggest she call the school for any reason. For him to do so now clued her that he was probably telling the truth.

"When did this happen?"

"Last Friday," he said.

"Why didn't you tell me about it?"

He shrugged. "It wasn't that big a deal, Mom. Besides, it's weird talking to my mom about condoms."

"Why didn't you just throw it away?"

"I meant to, but I forgot. Besides, if you'd found it in the trash you would have gone just as ballistic. Mom, get real. Who would I use it with? I don't even have a girlfriend."

She deflated and wilted back in the chair. "I know. That's why I was so confused."

"I mean, it's not like I couldn't get a girlfriend if I wanted one. I could and everything. I've got a date to the prom."

She didn't want to know. "Oh, yeah? Who?" she forced herself to ask.

"Jeanie Bradford."

An image of the girl came to mind. She had been in Annie's dance class for years, and she had a nodding acquaintance with her mother. "Cute girl."

"Yeah, real cute." Pink blotches colored his cheeks, exposing his embarrassment. He turned away. "It's not like I'm in love or anything. This'll probably be our only date. But it is my junior year and I felt like I ought to go."

He was off on the prom, not even interested in the condom anymore, but Cathy couldn't get her mind off of it. "So I'll just throw this away. Because there's no point in your holding onto it."

"Fine. Mom, just because I'm taking some girl to the prom doesn't mean I need *that.* You brought me up right, okay?"

"Right," she said. She thought of telling him that he couldn't go to the prom, couldn't date a girl *ever*, not until he was married. But that seemed a little radical. "I can't believe you got it at school."

"Well, didn't you have sex classes when you were in school?"

She tried to think back twenty-five years. It seemed like three eternities ago. "Seems like we saw a movie called *Splendor in the Grass*, about a girl who got pregnant. But I think that was about the extent of it." She got up and stepped over the clothes on her way out of the room. The telephone rang, and before she could make it to the stairs, Annie cried, "Mom, for you!"

She went to the door of Annie's room. "Who is it, Annie?"

"Some guy," Annie said, holding her hand over the receiver. "I'm like, 'Can I tell her who's calling?' and he's like, 'Her favorite patient,' so I go, 'Oh, the rottweiler?' and he's like, 'Are you calling me a dog?' Real big flirt, whoever he is, Mom."

"Glad you could hold your own with him," Cathy muttered. She made it down the stairs and answered the extension in the living room. "Hello?"

"Cathy, hey, it's me. John. I meant that my cat is your favorite patient, and I am *not* a flirt."

She managed to laugh. "Sorry. I didn't know you could hear that."

"Forgiven. Just wanted to see what time you wanted me to pick you up tonight."

She frowned. Tonight? Had she forgotten? Her hesitation spoke volumes, and he moaned. "You said you'd let me take you out to dinner tonight, finally. Come on, Cathy, you aren't backin' out now, are you? I've been chasin' you for weeks, and it's ruinin' my self-esteem."

"John, it's just that I'm kind of having a bad day."

"Cathy, you promised."

"I know I did, but—"

"Come on, we'll have fun, you'll see. You deserve a break today."

She thought of the McDonald's jingle, and wondered if that's where he planned to take her. John, who brought his Himalayan cat in periodically, was an attractive man. She supposed she should be flattered that he was interested. And if truth be known, she did need some adult companionship. As she held the phone to her ear, she reached up and pulled her hair out of its ponytail. "Well, okay. I guess I can get away."

"Can you work up a little bit more enthusiasm?"

She smiled. "I told you. Bad day."

"Then gimme a chance to turn it around."

There was something charming about his deep cowboy drawl, she thought. She tousled her hair and wondered how long it would take for her to get ready. Too long, but she supposed it would be worth it. "Okay, pick me up at seven."

"Will do. Don't back out, okay? I've heard all the stories. Grandmothers dyin', workin' late, dog havin' puppies . . ."

She grinned and doubted that was true.

After she had cooked supper for the kids, she started to go upstairs and get ready for her date.

"See you later, Mom! I'm outa here," Rick called up.

She went halfway back down the stairs and looked over the rail. "Where are you going?"

"To work," he said. Rick worked weekdays bagging groceries at the local Kroger, when he wasn't helping at the animal clinic.

"You didn't tell me you had to work."

"It wasn't on the schedule. I had to trade with somebody so I'd have prom night off."

"Oh." She came the rest of the way down. "Well, okay, I'm going out, so I guess Annie can stay with Mark."

"No!" From upstairs, she heard her daughter protesting. Annie came bouncing down the stairs. "Mom, I've got a date tonight!"

"A date? On Tuesday night? You're not allowed to date on weeknights."

"But Mom, I'm fifteen, and Dad lets me go."

She didn't want to talk about Jerry. "You're never with him on weeknights. We have rules in this house, Annie."

"Mom, I asked you last week if I could go to the school's baseball game tonight, and you said yes."

"You didn't tell me you were going with a boy."

"I didn't think it was a big deal. Please, Mom. It's Allen Spreway. I've liked him for months and months, and he finally asked me out. I want to go!"

"Well, what am I going to do with Mark?"

"I don't know," she said. "It's not my job to raise Mark. You're the mother."

Mark came in from the kitchen, his hand buried in a bag of potato chips. "I'm not a kid, you know. I can take care of myself."

"I'm not leaving you here by yourself."

"Then cancel your date."

She thought of calling John and canceling, but she hated to put him off again. He might not give her another chance. It occurred to her that she could simply invite him in when he came, feed him here, and they could watch a movie together. But it didn't usually work well to have men around her children. It usually took only one visit for them to decide she wasn't their type.

Funny how single mothers with smart-aleck kids weren't anyone's type.

"Mark, I'd rather not cancel my date, but I don't want to leave you here alone. Is there somebody you could spend the night with?"

"On a school night?"

"No, that won't work." She moaned. "Look, I'll just call John—"

"It's okay, Mom. I can stay by myself. Really. Give me a chance."

"I'm not ready. Maybe you could go to the game with Annie and her date."

"No way!" Annie erupted. "I'll die before I'll take him with me on a date."

"I'll die before I go," Mark threw back.

Frustrated, Cathy headed back for the telephone. She called John's number, but he wasn't in his office. She left him a message to call back. He would know immediately that she was canceling, and he'd give up on her, as he probably should. But she really didn't want him to. He might, after all, be the one.

As she waited for him to call, she went ahead and got in the shower, trying to let the hot water rinse the tension from her body. She should be feeling relief, she thought, that Rick hadn't bought the condom, that he had no plans to use it with a girl, that he hadn't had any objection to her getting rid of it. Still . . .

The fact that the school had doled them out like breath mints riled her. She just didn't know what to do about it.

She was rinsing the conditioner out of her hair when she heard Annie screaming from the hallway. "Mom, telephone!"

She finished rinsing her hair, threw a towel around herself, and ran out to get the phone. "Hello, John?"

"No, Mom, it's me."

It was Mark, and she frowned. "Mark, I thought you were downstairs."

"Nope. Across the street. I came over to see why Daniel's yard got rolled, and found out they did it theirselves. Cool, huh? Mr. Dodd said I could spend the night with Daniel tonight. Since they homeschool, it's no big thing to do it on a weeknight."

"But *you* have to go to school."

"So I'll come home first thing in the morning and get ready. What's the big deal?"

She closed her eyes. "Let me talk to Brenda." He put her on hold, and she could hear him talking to David. Finally, he came back. "She's not here. She took Joseph to the doctor."

"Well, are you sure it's all right with her?"

"Sure," he said. "What's one more? I'll come home and get my stuff."

"Come home and do your homework," she said. "Then you can go back."

She hung up and sat down on the bed, wondering if there was any wisdom in her going out tonight, after all. Didn't she want to be here when Annie got back from her date? Didn't she want to make sure that Rick didn't go out partying after he got off work? Didn't she need to supervise Mark's homework to make sure he did it all?

The door opened and Annie shot in. "Mom, does my hair look all right? Do I have on too much eyeliner?"

Cathy gave her a once-over. Her shirt flaunted too much of the figure that Cathy would have died or killed for when she was fifteen. She tried to think of a good reason why Annie needed to change, but the girl had her on a technicality. The shirt was neither low cut, nor too tight. Cathy tried to shift her thoughts to something positive. "Your hair looks gorgeous," she said. "You look like one of those soap opera stars."

"What about my eyeliner?"

"It looks fine."

"Fine?" Annie asked, stomping a foot. "I *can't* look fine. Not *that* kind of fine, anyway." She ran into Cathy's bathroom and began digging through her makeup drawer.

"Honey, I was about to go in there. I have to get ready for my date."

"But Mom, I need your lipstick. Look at me, I look awful."

"You look beautiful," Cathy said, falling in behind her. "Come on. I need for you to move aside so I can get ready."

"But *Mom!*"

Finally understanding what a crisis this was, Cathy surrendered her makeup table and sat on the side of the tub as her daughter panicked over her date. "So tell me about this boy," she said.

"Oh, he's so cute," she said. "He's got the bluest eyes, and these *luscious* lips."

Cathy didn't want to hear about his lips. She wondered if he'd been given a condom at school. "What time will you be home?"

"As soon as the game's over, unless we go get a burger or something."

"No burgers. Come straight home."

"Mom, what do you care? You won't be here."

The fact that Annie would be coming home to an empty house with no accountability and a boy who'd just seen a film about safe sex riled her. She made a decision to have a quick dinner with John and then beg off. She had to get home before Annie did.

"I'll be here," she assured her. "I want you coming straight home. It *is* a school night."

"Well, I know, but every kid in school's going to be at that game."

"I'm letting you go to the game."

"Well, why can't I go out afterward?"

"Either agree to come home after the game, or stay home and don't go at all."

"And if I stay home, are you staying home with me?"

The smart-aleck tone made Cathy want to throw something, but she refrained. "Annie, why do you talk to me like that?"

"Because you talk to *me* like *that*."

"I'm your mother."

"And I'm your daughter."

It was one of those grueling games they played. Just like when the kids were little and they would repeat every word she said until she was a raging lunatic trying to make them stop.

Sighing loudly, she headed into the closet to find something to wear. She pulled out a simple dress and a sweater, and laid it on her bed.

"You're not wearing that, are you?" Annie asked.

She turned back to her daughter. "What would you prefer that I wore?"

"Something prettier." Annie went into her closet and pulled out something more colorful. "Here, wear this."

Something about her daughter helping her get ready for a date seemed unnatural, and she felt more depressed than ever. "All right, Annie, I'll wear that. Thanks."

"Sure. And if you want me to help you with your makeup, I will. You could use more blush than you usually wear."

"All right." Cathy headed for her makeup, but Annie dashed back to it. "I'm not through, Mom."

Cathy closed her eyes. She was supposed to have been a contented married woman by the time she had teenagers who dated. She was supposed to have been settling into the prime of her life. Not competing with her daughter for the mirror so they could both get ready for dates.

When Annie finally moved aside, Cathy applied the makeup that she rarely wore and slipped on the dress. Maybe it would be nice to get out, after all. She did need a break from responsibility and routine and constant needs and demands. It would be fun to have some adult male companionship for the evening. And who knew? It might turn into something.

As the possibility entered her mind, she began to get a little more hopeful. For the first time, she actually looked forward to the evening.

CHAPTER *Eight*

Brenda and Joseph had been at the hospital for what seemed hours, doing an echocardiogram, a MUGA scan, and other tests she had never heard of before. She wasn't clear on the purpose for any of them, but she tried to stay cheerful and keep Joseph upbeat as the grueling day wore on.

What a terrible thing to have to endure on your ninth birthday, she thought. She would make it up to him, even if she had to have another whole party and decorate the trees again.

No one at the hospital would give her any of the results, so when she finally headed back home with Joseph, she had no more answers than she'd had earlier. They had simply told her to keep him quiet and let him get plenty of rest.

They were eating a late supper of hamburgers David had cooked out on the grill when the doctor called. "I knew you'd want to know—I got the results back on some of the tests already," he told Brenda. "I'd like you to take Joseph to see Dr. Chris Robinson. He's a pediatric cardiac surgeon."

"A what?" She immediately got up from the table and took the cordless phone into the other room where the children couldn't hear. David followed her.

"You think this is his heart?" she asked quietly.

"Some of the tests showed . . . well, it's a little enlarged. It's hard to tell why."

"Enlarged?" The word seemed to scramble the thoughts in her brain, keeping them from any logical order. "What would cause that?"

"A number of things could cause it," he said. "Possibly that virus he had a few weeks ago. Or an illness years ago could have caused damage that's just now showing up. I'd really rather not speculate. I'll be calling Robinson myself first thing in the morning, but you need to make an appointment with him. Try to get in as soon as possible."

"Sure. I'll call first thing."

"I'd really like to keep up with what's going on, so remind him to keep me informed."

"Sure," she said. "What do I do in the meantime? For Joseph, I mean."

"Just keep him quiet."

"Is there medicine?"

"Oh, sure. There are lots of ways to treat problems like this. Dr. Robinson will probably have him back to a hundred percent in no time. Don't panic until you hear what he has to say."

Don't panic. The words seemed so worthless and impossible. Slowly, she hung up the phone.

"His heart?" David asked on a rush of breath.

She met his eyes, saw the terror there. She might have been looking into a mirror.

"Maybe. Maybe not," she managed to answer. "He wants us to take him to a pediatric cardiac surgeon." She covered her mouth with a trembling hand, muffling a sob. "David, he said his heart is enlarged."

"Enlarged? What does that mean?"

"I don't know." She reached for him, and he hugged her fiercely, as though the strength of their embrace could hold back whatever evil had its grip on their son.

They managed to pull themselves together for the sake of the children and didn't speak of it again until the kids were occupied in another room. Cathy's son Mark was over, and had brought a game of Monopoly that they were all engaged in.

When they were alone, David paced across the kitchen, rubbing his face with callused hands. "He needs the best care. The absolute best. Guess I need to take on some extra work," he said. "These bills could get pretty hefty."

"All those tests today," Brenda said. She sat at the kitchen table with her Bible—the source of her strength—but somehow, she couldn't seem to concentrate on the words she had opened to. "What's our deductible again?"

He closed his eyes and leaned back against the counter. "Two thousand dollars. And it doesn't cover but seventy percent after that. The joys of self-employment."

They had decided years ago that this was the best situation for their family, in spite of the tight budget, the self-employment taxes, the poor health insurance, and everything else that came with self-employment. Being a cabinetmaker at home enabled him to help in the homeschooling of their children, to be there when Brenda had to leave, to spend time apprenticing his boys. Already, Daniel helped him in the afternoons. It was a situation that worked, and they didn't want to change it. But at times like this, they both wished they had a company benefit program with health insurance.

"We'll get by, David," she said. "The Lord will provide. He always does."

David averted his eyes, the way he always did when she spoke of spiritual things. He wasn't a believer, and he considered her faith to be nothing more than shallow superstition. She tried not to let it bother her. "David, He *will* provide. You'll see."

She knew he was thinking that *he* was the one who would have to provide. "We'll get by," he finally agreed.

"Besides," she said, reaching deep into herself and finding the optimism she was known for. "I don't really think he's that sick. It's probably some fluke thing. We'll get in to see that doctor, and he'll take a look at Joseph and say there's nothing wrong with him, that I wasted my time bringing him in. And we'll find out that he just fainted because the sun was too hot and he'd had too many sweets. That his heart is enlarged because it's so full of love ..."

David's look told her that this was another one of those times when their faith didn't match. He swallowed hard and got up from the table. "I know it's early. It's not even dark yet, but ... I'm going to bed. It's been a long day."

"Yeah, okay. I'm going to stay up until I get the kids into bed."

She watched as David disappeared down the hall, then turned her eyes back to the Bible again. Her thoughts were in such disarray that she didn't think she could find words to take to God's throne. She wished her husband could share this with her, and that they could pray for each other when one of them had a heavy heart. But David would have none of it.

She sat back in her chair and recalled the night, almost thirteen years ago, when she had gone to a church service with a friend and had come home to tell David that something had happened. She had found Christ that night, and she'd been overcome with joy and excitement and couldn't wait to tell him how the Holy Spirit had touched her.

She had hoped that he would want the same experience, but she'd tried to prepare herself for his indifference. What she had not expected, what had come as a shock to her, was the rage that she had never seen in David before. It was as if she'd joined some evil cult ... as if she had announced her intention to leave him and join her new friends. It was frightening and irrational. He had tried to forbid her to go back to that church, and insisted on her renouncing the faith that he found so distasteful. She had refused.

That night, she had gone to bed in confusion while David stayed up watching late-night television in the other room. She had not been able to sleep, so she had wept and prayed. Those prayers must have reached right into that other room, because sometime after midnight, David had come to bed.

With red eyes and tears on his face, he'd sat down on the side of the bed and asked her forgiveness for losing his temper. "I have reasons for hating church," he'd said.

She sat up in bed. The light coming in from the hall illuminated one side of his face, leaving the other side in darkness. In the half that was visible to her, she saw pain. "But . . . you were raised in church. I thought you, of all people, would understand."

"I understand more than you do," he said. "Those people in that church you went to . . . they're not what you think."

"How do you know?" she asked. "You've never met them."

"I've met people just like them."

Flustered and unable to find a defense, she reached for his hand. "David, it doesn't matter about the people as much as it does about Jesus."

He got up from the bed and lost himself in the shadows. "I thought I'd escaped this. When I left home, I never had to go back. And you never cared about church. Now, all of a sudden, you're all gung ho for this religion stuff, and I'm supposed to just accept it?"

"It'll make me better, David. Not worse."

"I don't think it'll make you better," he said. "I've seen what it does to people."

The conversation had ended, and he'd gone back to the television. She had decided right then and there that she would simply pray for him to change his mind, and make sure he found nothing in her faith to be bitter about. She must have succeeded, for when they began having children, he allowed her to take them to church. But he refused to go himself.

His reasons were locked up somewhere inside him, and he refused to let them out. Over the years, though, she had guessed at some of them, from things his mother said before she died. Things about David's father being a preacher—a fact that shocked her, since David had never mentioned it. Things about that same father running off with the church organist when David was a small boy. Somehow, all of that figured into his bitterness and anger at the church. But she knew there had to be more. And she prayed daily that he would someday open that cage and share its contents with her, and turn to the God who healed past hurts.

That prayer had not been answered yet, thirteen years later, but she hadn't given up.

Her heart was as heavy as it had been in a long time, and she decided to call her prayer partner. She dialed Sylvia's number, hoping she wasn't waking her.

"Hello?"

"Sylvia, it's me. Brenda."

Sylvia had always been able to detect when something was wrong. "What is it, darlin'? Is Joseph okay? I got to the party late, and Tory told me what happened."

"Um . . . I don't really know."

"Are you dressed?"

Brenda looked down at the clothes she'd had on all day, wondering why Sylvia asked. "Yes, why?"

"'Cause I'm coming over. Meet me on the front porch."

Brenda felt better already as she hung up the phone and headed outside.

Chapter *Nine*

John didn't take Cathy directly to the restaurant. Instead, he told her she needed to relax, and he knew just the thing. He drove to the top of Bright Mountain to park at the Point, and as the lights flickered on across Breezewood just before dusk, he tried to skip at least three of the natural dating steps.

She pushed him away and got out of the car.

"Aw, come on. What'sa matter?" he asked as he followed her.

"John, you asked me to dinner, and I said yes, that I'd love to have *dinner* with you. I didn't come out with you tonight to get groped and manhandled."

He looked wounded and misunderstood. "I thought comin' up here would help you relax. I'm tryin' to be romantic."

"I don't want to be romantic with you," she said. "I hardly even know you."

He pretended to pull a knife out of his heart. "And here I thought you liked me. You seemed so free and loose around the clinic."

"Free and loose?" she repeated. "How do you figure that?"

He shrugged. "I just mean that bouncy ponytail and those Keds, and you always have a big smile for me."

"That's free and loose? You must be kidding."

He chuckled as though he *was* kidding. "Come on, get in the car. I'll take you to dinner."

Sighing, she got back into the car, closed the door, and hooked her seat belt. He dropped in on the other side.

"Tell me something," she said, still angry as he pulled the car back onto the road. "I'm just curious. Do other women you go out with really allow you to grope them before your car engine has even warmed up?"

He chuckled under his breath. "Come to think of it, most of 'em don't. Maybe I need to change my technique." He gave her an apologetic glance. "Hey, you can't blame a guy for tryin'. So where do you want to eat?"

She found that she wasn't hungry anymore. "I don't care, John. Frankly, I'd rather just go home."

"But that's scandalous," he said. "I can't take a gal home after less than an hour!"

"Scandalous?" She shook her head in disbelief. "Come on, John, you're not going to get what you came for, so just take me on home. Consider it a dating nightmare."

"Mine or yours?"

"Mine," she shot back. "Only it's usually my nightmare for my daughter. I never dreamed *I'd* be the one to be attacked. I thought the hormones kind of leveled off when you reached middle age."

He was more offended by her assessment of his age than his behavior. "Come on, I'm not that old!"

"Just take me home."

"Man, you can hold a grudge!" he bit out. "I said I was sorry, for Pete's sake! My worst crime was bein' attracted to a good-lookin' woman. Sue me."

When he missed the turn that would have taken them to her house, she shot him a look. "Where are we going?"

"To a restaurant," he said.

"I *told* you to take me home."

"Well, I'm not gonna do it." His tone was softer, more conciliatory. "We're goin' to a restaurant, we're gonna eat, we're gonna enjoy each other's company—and you'll forgive me. I messed up, okay? I shouldn't have got so friendly so soon. It's just that you're such a knockout. I couldn't help it."

She wondered if that was meant to flatter her. "I don't *want* to have dinner with you, John."

He pulled into the restaurant parking lot and let the car idle. "Relax. It's just dinner. I can't do anything to you in front of all these people."

She couldn't believe all the arrangements she'd made, the stupid dress, the makeup. She felt like such a fool. Now she felt like some three-year-old, holding her breath until she got her way, refusing to budge—and it was John who'd put her in this awkward position. She remembered why she hated men.

"Guess I don't blame you for bein' mad," he said in a softer voice. "I really don't behave this way with every woman I go out with. In fact, I don't even date all that much. I'm a real homebody. I was just a little nervous before I picked you up, so I had a glass of wine. It must have just loosened me up a little too much."

She tried to appear disinterested, but finally she sneaked a peak at him. "You were nervous about taking me out?"

"Of course I was. You're a beautiful, classy blonde who has everything goin' for her. I figure you're the town catch. What would you possibly see in a good ole boy like me?"

Something about the vulnerability in his confession softened her attitude toward him. She sat quietly for a moment. He let the quiet pass between them. Finally, she glanced toward the restaurant. It was Alexander's, and she'd been wanting to go there. What harm could it do to let him buy her a steak?

"All right," she said with a sigh. "Let's go."

"Really?" he asked.

"Yes," she said. "But please don't drink anymore. It doesn't become you."

He nodded and they went in, and she tried to forget the first part of the date as the second rolled by.

❧

It wasn't that John was a poor conversationalist; it was just that his choice of topics was limited. After the first half hour of talking about himself, she'd wished they could move on to another topic. But he hadn't exhausted all the possibilities yet. He had just exhausted her.

She had a headache by the time the meal was over. Though he'd had no more to drink, and she hoped the food had dulled his appetite, she found him getting familiar again as they drove home.

"Sure you don't want to go back up to the Point?"

"Positive. Take me home, John. I need to get there before my daughter does."

"How old is she, anyway?"

"Fifteen."

"She doesn't need a baby-sitter. She can take care of herself."

"Take me home, John."

With a huff that reminded her of a frustrated kid, he headed to Cedar Circle.

CHAPTER *Ten*

Barry wasn't home at eight-thirty. With each moment that passed, Tory grew more and more agitated. She got the kids bathed for the third time that day and put them to bed. But instead of going to bed herself or re-creating her four pages in longhand, she decided to ride her stationary bicycle while watching the clock and stewing.

When her odometer registered ten miles, she showered and decided to read for a while. She ignored the novels on her shelf and chose instead a self-help book her mother had bought her for Christmas on fulfilling your own destiny.

By the time she heard Barry pulling into the garage, she had read a whole chapter about setting goals and prioritizing time, something that had only made her angrier about her life. The author of the book obviously didn't have two children, a congealed computer keyboard, and a husband who came home late.

As she listened to the garage door shutting, she tried to decide how to greet him. Should she meet him in anger and lambaste him for being so late, or should she force herself into the submissive role and flutter around him like he was the prodigal son?

By the time he opened the door, she had decided to do none of the above, and instead, had put on her shoes and pushed past him into the garage without a word. He looked surprised and turned around to follow her out. "Where ya goin'?"

"To talk to Brenda," she said curtly. "Joseph got sick today. I want to make sure he's all right. The kids are asleep."

"Bad day?" he asked her back.

She couldn't believe he had the nerve to ask. She turned around and gave him a disgusted look. "*Long* day. Made longer by the fact that my husband and partner in child rearing didn't make it home until after the kids were in bed."

"You could have kept them up."

"I didn't know how long you'd be since you're later than you said."

He rolled his eyes as if contemplating the wisdom of coming home at all. "Well, we got the account."

"Bully for you."

She opened the garage door and headed out. She heard the door slam behind her.

Darkness was just falling over the ridge, a little darker than twilight, but lighter than full-blown night. The sky offered a lunar half-grin much like the birds' "fail-ure" cries of this morning, and she turned her eyes to the ground. It was cool and breezy now, unlike the day that made children smell and mothers perspire and little boys faint. A foggy mist rendered the Smoky Mountains invisible even with all the lights usually dotting their sides.

As she crossed the lot next to her house, she heard voices and saw that Brenda and Sylvia were sitting on the Dodds' front porch swing, talking quietly in the darkness. As she approached, Tory wondered if she was intruding on a private moment. She thought of going back in, but then she would have to tangle with Barry. She decided to take her chances with her neighbors.

"What are you doing out here?" she asked as she approached.

"Tory!" Brenda said. "Come sit down. We were just catching up on the day."

Catching up, Tory thought. Did that ever really happen? "I came to see how Joseph is," she said, stepping onto the porch and pulling two wicker rockers close to the swing. She sat down in one and propped her feet in the other one.

"Well . . . we're not sure," Brenda said. "He may be fine."

Tory fixed her eyes on Brenda. "What do you mean, *may* be?"

Brenda looked as if she was having trouble getting the words out, and Sylvia intervened. "They're going for more tests tomorrow. They're not sure what made him faint yet."

This sounded serious, and Tory dropped her feet and leaned forward, as if that would help her to understand more clearly. "What kind of tests, Brenda?"

Brenda sighed. "His heart . . . it seems to be enlarged a little. We have to take him to a pediatric cardiac surgeon."

"They have those?" Tory asked. It had never occurred to her that there were children with heart problems.

"Yes, apparently," Brenda said. "But he's okay. As soon as the light-headedness passed, he felt fine. We've kept him quiet for the rest of the day, made him take it easy. It's probably just a virus or something. Or they misread the X-rays. That happens, you know. They make mistakes all the time."

Tory felt the pressure on her own chest, and tried to imagine having one of her children pass out at his birthday party, and then being told that it was due to an enlarged heart. "I'd be a basket case," she said quietly. "Brenda, are you okay?"

"Yeah, sure," Brenda said with that smile that seemed a permanent part of her expression. "I mean, it's a little nerve-wracking. But things will be all right."

Headlights lit up the entrance to Cedar Circle, and they all watched a strange car pull into Cathy's driveway. Their neighbor got out and headed for the door. The driver followed a little too quickly.

"Date?" Sylvia asked.

"Guess so," Tory said. She smiled as she gazed across the street. "Cathy's lucky."

"Lucky?" Brenda asked. "Why would you say that?"

"Because. She gets to go out with handsome men who take her to restaurants and shows. Barry hasn't taken me out in two months. He barely comes home."

"Oh, for heaven's sake," Sylvia said. "He's home every night. It's not like he's a traveling salesman."

"He may sleep at home," Tory insisted, "but take tonight. One of the worst days I can remember in a long time, and ten minutes ago he finally strolled in."

"Then why aren't you home with him?"

Tory looked up at Sylvia, almost amused at the point-blank question. But Sylvia wasn't smiling. "No, I'm serious," Sylvia went on. "If you're complaining about him not being home enough, why aren't you there when he is?"

Deflated, Tory started to get to her feet. "You're right. I'll go home." It reminded her of childhood when one of her friends would offend her, and biting her bottom lip she would gather her toys and leave. Hadn't she outgrown that feeling that she didn't belong in any group, and that those who included her were just politely biding their time until she left?

"We're not trying to run you off," Brenda said quickly, ever the peacemaker. "Sylvia wasn't telling you to go home, were you, Sylvia?"

"Of course not," Sylvia said, but her tone suggested that home was exactly where she thought Tory belonged. "I'm just trying to point out that he's there now."

"I know he is," Tory snapped back. "But I'm a little mad at him right now."

"Okay," Sylvia said. "I guess that's fair. Goodness knows there were nights in my younger days when I got mad at Harry for coming in so late. Until I finally grew up and realized that, in his mind, he was doing it as much for me as for his patients. He just thought he was providing, the way he was supposed to."

"Barry isn't out saving lives," Tory said. "It was just a stupid metalworks account, which could have waited, or at least taken less time."

"My point is that you seem to wish you could be like Cathy, dating again. But I don't think you want to be in her shoes. Think how much of your life you've invested in Barry. He's your partner. If all that was gone, you'd have to start over with men you don't know. It doesn't look like much fun."

Tory was skeptical. "Cathy seems to be having fun."

No sooner had those words left her mouth than Cathy's date marched back out to his car, slammed the door, and peeled out of the driveway. They all looked at each other and laughed.

The door opened again and Cathy, suddenly in blue jeans and T-shirt, bounded out. She must have shed her dress the way Spencer shed his Sunday clothes—in five seconds flat. She came across the street, pulling her hair up in a ponytail as she reached them.

"I saw you three out here gawking at me as I drove up," she said, "so I thought I'd come over and tell you every little gory detail before I get Mark to come home."

"So who was he?" Tory asked, undaunted by Cathy's sarcasm.

"Some guy who brings his Himalayan to me every time it throws up. Seemed like a nice guy in the office. Looks can be deceiving, though."

"You didn't have a good time?" Brenda asked.

Cathy took the rocker where Tory's feet had been and plopped into it. "I had a good meal. Let's leave it at that."

"You're home early," Brenda said. "Mark and Daniel are probably still up."

"Yeah, that's the real reason I came over. I figured I'd send Mark back home so I could be the one to scrape him off the sheets in the morning before school." She finished putting her hair in the ponytail and slapped her hands hard on her thighs. "Since we're all here, I might as well make it official. I'm giving up dating. It's not worth it."

"Why?" Tory asked, amazed.

Cathy braced her elbows on her knees, an unfeminine gesture that looked quite feminine when Cathy did it. Her skin looked like that of a porcelain doll, and she was so thin she looked breakable. She had long, tapered fingers that moved like those of an artist or musician, and bright blue eyes that men gravitated to. She was spirited, like the Bryans' mare, but she didn't let feminist convention dictate her behavior. Last weekend at the wedding, Cathy looked almost glamorous.

"I was getting ready tonight, and Annie was getting ready for *her* date, and it just struck me that there's something terribly unnatural about all this. She was giving me tips and telling me what I should wear, and I thought the roles were reversed. I was supposed to be doing that for her, not the other way around."

"But you can't just give it up," Tory said. "You could date on the weekends when the kids are out of town."

"Date who?" Cathy asked. "I've just about had it. This guy tonight was all over me. He seemed like a perfectly nice guy, but he turned out to be an octopus with hands everywhere."

"What a disappointment," Sylvia said.

"You said it. But I don't know where to meet nice men." She shook her head, and that ponytail slapped each side of her head. "I don't go to bars. I'm afraid I'll run into my children there . . ."

There was a moment of stunned silence. No one ever knew for sure when Cathy was serious. But after a moment, she let that deadpan face break into a smile. "Hey, I'm kidding."

They all laughed softly. "Have you tried church?" Brenda asked.

Cathy looked uncomfortable, as she always did when the subject of church came up. "No, but going to church to find a man seems a little wrong, too. On the other hand, it sure wouldn't hurt my kids to get a little spiritual training. You're not going to believe what I found in Rick's pocket today."

"What?" Tory asked.

"A condom. He got it at school. In a sex ed class."

"He didn't," Brenda said.

"Oh, yeah. Imagine the things your kids miss when you homeschool, Brenda."

Brenda didn't seem to find that funny. "So what are you going to do about it?" She had thrown down the gauntlet, and they all knew it. Brenda was big on challenges, but she issued them with such a sweet tone that no one was ever offended.

"What *can* I do? I can't homeschool, like you. I have to make a living. And I can't take them out and put them in private school—some of those are just as bad, and besides, I can't afford it." She looked around at the faces of Tory and Sylvia. "Yeah, I know, I could take on the school board and change all the policies, before they start messing with Mark's hormones. And I'm thinking about how to do that. It's just not easy, and time is not a commodity I have a lot of right now." She looked down at her watch and tried to read it in the light from the street lamp at the entrance to Cedar Circle. "Speaking of time . . . don't you think the baseball game should be over by now?"

Tory was having trouble following the thread of Cathy's rambling. "Baseball game? What's that got to do with condoms?"

"Nothing, except that every boy on the team got one, as well as every boy in the school, including the boy that Annie is out with as we speak." She leaned back hard in the chair and brushed her fingers through her bangs. "I'm sorry. I didn't mean to dominate the conversation like that. It's just been an incredibly bad day."

"We can relate," Tory said. "The kids spilled Kool-Aid on my computer. Oh, and Joseph passed out at his birthday party today." The two events seemed equally tragic to Tory.

Cathy shot Brenda a look. "Is he all right?"

"Yeah, fine, I think." Tory wasn't surprised at Brenda's lie—it wasn't like Brenda to dump her problems out for everyone to examine. Sometimes Tory wished she would. To her, Brenda was some kind of mythical supermom who did all the right things and never had a negative thought. Just once, she'd love to see Brenda fall apart, get angry, lose her cool. It certainly would help Tory relate to her better.

"Sylvia's the only one who's had a peaceful day, I bet," Tory said, smiling at the matriarch of the neighborhood.

"Not really," Sylvia said. The swing stopped, and Sylvia swept her frosted pageboy behind her ears. "See, Harry came home today for lunch and asked me if I would think about going to Nicaragua as a full-time missionary."

"A *what?*" Cathy threw her head back and laughed uproariously, as if she'd never heard anything so funny in her life. Tory found it less amusing, and Brenda wasn't smiling at all. "Has he gone off the deep end? Sylvia, what did you say?"

Sylvia seemed puzzled by Cathy's response. "Well . . . I said I'd think about it. And no, he isn't going off the deep end. It's something he's always wanted to do. We've talked about it before. Now that the kids are gone . . ."

Cathy's smile faded, and she looked at Tory, then at Brenda, and realized that no one but she was laughing. "You're serious. You're really thinking about this."

Sylvia drew in a deep breath and let it out hard. Tory didn't think she had ever heard Sylvia sigh before. "Thinking about it. That's all. I don't know if I could do it. Sell the house, the furniture, leave the country . . ."

"Why would you *do* that?" Cathy asked. "Why would *he?* You have it so good here. You're so happy. He's a prominent cardiac surgeon. He's worked all his life to be where he is. What could possibly be in Nicaragua for you?"

Sylvia thought that over for a moment. "It wouldn't be about us, Cathy." The words were not said in condemnation. They were thoughtful words, meted out carefully. "Harry feels called."

"Wow," Cathy said. "I don't mean to seem so bowled over by this, but it's kind of hard for me to imagine. Most people work all their lives to get where he is. It's just hard to grasp."

"For me, too," Sylvia said. "I understand why he wants to do it. I'm just not sure I'm that selfless."

"Give me a break," Cathy said. "You and Brenda are the most selfless people I know."

Tory couldn't help noticing that Cathy didn't mention her. But she wouldn't have expected her to. She looked down at the boards beneath her feet.

"The first year we went," Sylvia explained, "we worked in León, about an hour and a half from Managua. I lost ten pounds in two weeks. Hardly ate a thing, because it was so disgusting to go to the marketplaces to buy meat that was hanging in the open, covered with flies."

"Gross," Tory whispered.

"The second year, we went to Masaya. I thought it would be better, because it was right on the lake. I pictured a resort area, you know? Imagine my surprise when we got there and all we saw were run-down buildings badly in need of repair. No telling where we'd live if we went there indefinitely."

"Where did you stay then?" Brenda asked.

"In the home of a missionary who was already there. And in spite of my disappointment at the location, it turned out to be a fruitful trip. Harry operated on hundreds of people and treated hundreds of others. He did all types of surgery—not just heart cases. Because of Harry, the little church the missionary started has doubled. Some of those converts are starting churches of their own. There's no doubt, it's God's work."

"For two weeks, maybe," Cathy said. "But forever?"

A strong wind whipped up, dancing in their hair, as Sylvia seemed to think that over. "I'm not sure God's calling us to do this. I'm praying about it. I want to do God's will, but frankly, I'm not sure I'm up to this. I don't have a lot to contribute, you know? Harry practices medicine there, and they flock to him by the hundreds. He helps them. But I just don't think I have that much to offer."

"You have a *lot* to offer," Brenda said. "If you put everything you have experience doing on a resumé, it would never fit into an envelope."

Tory's eyes settled on Brenda for a moment as she tried to let that sink in. Brenda made being a housewife seem noble, yet

Tory couldn't think of it that way. To her, it was a detour on the way to her career goals, something that had gotten in her way.

"So what are you going to do?" Tory asked finally.

"I don't know," Sylvia said. "Harry told me he would wait until I made the decision."

"Oh, great," Tory said. "So he dumps it in your lap?"

"I already know what he wants to do. He's leaving it up to me."

"It's better than having him come home and telling her to pack her bags, that they're on their way out of the country," Brenda said. "I think it's sweet."

"He believes that if God really is calling him, He'll call me, too."

"If I were you I wouldn't answer the phone," Cathy said. Everyone laughed.

Tory looked over at her house and saw that the light in the laundry room was on. She knew Barry wasn't doing laundry. Was he working on the computer they kept there? Cursing her for being so stupid as to leave the children alone long enough to destroy the equipment he'd worked overtime to pay for?

Wearily, she got up. "I guess I'd better go home."

"Might be a good idea," Sylvia said.

She paused a moment, crossing her arms. "Sylvia, did you ever have days when Harry was working long hours, and you just really wanted him to come home?"

"I sure did. And when he finally did, I was happy to see him."

Tory nodded, wishing on one hand that she could be more like Sylvia, and on the other stubbornly holding on to her anger at Barry. "It's just so unfair, these long hours."

"He's doing his job."

"Yeah, I know." She didn't want to talk about it anymore. Sometimes Sylvia's wisdom drove her right up the wall. "Well, I'll see you all later. Brenda, let me know if you need anything."

"Thanks."

Tory tramped back across the yard and into her garage. She took a moment to collect herself before opening the door and going in. Was he stewing now as she had stewed earlier? Was he waiting at the kitchen table, poised to attack?

She made a point of closing the door loudly enough for him to hear, then went in and looked around the kitchen. He wasn't there, so she went to the laundry room. He heard her coming and glanced over his shoulder at her. He was sitting in front of the computer with a bottle of some kind of cleaner he must have brought from the office. He had taken the keyboard apart.

"I don't know if I can fix it," he mumbled.

"Yeah, that's what I figured."

He turned around in the swivel desk chair she'd gotten for Mother's Day. "Look, I'm sorry I wasn't home sooner. This account will mean a million dollars for the company, and a sure raise for me."

It was hard to be mad at him when he put it that way. "It's okay. You just wouldn't believe all that's happened today." She wanted to make a checklist of today's tragedies, so he would understand. She wanted him to be amazed at the things she put up with; she wanted him to submit her name for "Mother of the Year." "You just don't know what it's like," she said. "Staying home all day with two preschoolers. I don't have much adult companionship. And I have no time to write. I look forward to you coming home and relieving me, and then when you don't . . ."

"Tory, we agreed," he said. "When you got pregnant with Brittany, we agreed that you would raise our children, instead of letting them go to day care. Writing a book was way down on the priority list."

She bristled. "So what's wrong with my writing a book, as long as I'm getting everything else done? The house is spotless, Barry. It always is. The kids are clean, they're fed, they're loved. What's wrong with me wanting to write a book?"

"Nothing, unless it makes you miserable when you have to spend time with the kids."

She turned away from the door and went back into the kitchen. He'd left his briefcase and his car keys on the table. She picked them up and put them where they belonged.

He got up and leaned in the doorway, right where she'd been standing. "I'm just saying, Tory, that when I work overtime, it's because I have to do that to make it possible for us to live in a nice house in a nice neighborhood, and still let you stay home with the children."

She didn't want to talk about it anymore. Though the counter was clean, as it always was, she got her sponge from the sink and began wiping it again.

"Tory, do you want to go back to work? Is that it? Do you want to get a job and let me stay home with the kids?"

She knew there was about as much chance of that as there was of her running for congress. "I want to be a writer." She slammed the sponge down and spun around to face him. "I'm smarter than this, Barry. I'm smarter than getting cats out of trees and rescuing Spencer from horse corrals and reading Dr. Seuss. People used to look up to me and admire me when I was in college. I want to make an impact. That was the plan."

"You *are* making an impact. You're raising two children who are secure and happy. You're doing a great job. But if it's instant gratification you want, you're not going to get it in child rearing."

"I'm not going to get it in writing, either," she said, "so that's a low blow. You know it's not instant *anything* I'm after."

"Then what are you after?"

"I just want to write four pages in a day without losing it to a Kool-Aid spill," she said. "I just want to be able to sit by myself and think sometimes. I just want to be able to reach a goal or two."

"Well, if you didn't spend all your time cleaning this house and reading self-help books, maybe you'd get something done."

"Oh, so now you're upset because the house is clean?"

"No, I'm upset because you have to have everything perfect. That's how you are with your writing. Other people do it for a hobby. They work it in. But if you can't have everything exactly like you want it before you start writing, then forget it."

"Barry, don't you understand that I *did* write today? I wrote four pages and it's gone."

"Did it ever occur to you to try to re-create those four pages?"

"How? The computer was broken."

"You could let the kids play in the little pool and sit out there with a legal pad and a pen. You remember those, don't you?"

He was right, she thought. It could be done that way. Lots of people did it that way. It just wasn't the way she wanted to do it.

He went to the table and sat down. "Come here," he said. "Sit down and tell me everything you can remember about what you wrote. It'll come back to you, then you can take a pen and paper and write it again."

She just stood there with her arms crossed. "Barry, it doesn't work that way."

He tapped the chair. "Come on, Tory. Just try. Is this still the story you wanted to do about the nurse in France in World War II?"

"Yes."

"And she falls for a wounded soldier, but he dies . . ."

"I had him get wounded today. He was brought into triage, and she met him. It was really good."

"Great. What else?"

She kept standing where she was. "Nothing else. That's as far as I got."

"Good. Then you don't have so much to re-create. What happens next? He's going to die, right? And while she's grieving, Dr. Right comes along and rescues her from herself?"

"Yeah."

"Then start writing. It's a guaranteed best-seller."

She shook her head. "I can't turn it on just like that. I'm not in the mood."

He stared up at her, his face hardening. "Tory, I'm trying to help you. Look, if you're so miserable, then let's try something else. Plan A was to stay home and raise our kids. But if Plan A isn't working, then let's think of Plan B. Just come up with one, Tory. You could hire a baby-sitter for a few hours a day so you could write. Whatever it takes."

She felt horrible and thought of Sylvia and Brenda telling her how she should be happy to stay home with her husband when he finally came in. She rarely heard them complain. The first time she'd *ever* heard Sylvia complain was tonight when she'd spoken about Nicaragua. Tory wondered if there was something wrong with her that rendered her incapable of appreciating things that other mothers longed for. The truth was, she didn't want to go out and get a job, and she didn't want to put her kids in day care. She *did* want to stay home with them. "It's just that . . . no one puts much value in child rearing," she said, then wished she hadn't said it aloud.

He got up and leaned on the counter, forcing her to look at him. "Just tell me one thing, Tory," he said. "Who is it that you're trying to impress?"

She couldn't believe he'd asked that. "What are you talking about? I'm not trying to impress anybody."

"You said that no one puts value in child rearing. That sounds to me like you're trying to prove something or impress somebody."

She felt her face growing hot. "You'll never understand," she said, "because you can go to work and do your job and meet people and be good at what you do and get awards and recognition and pay raises. You can stand back and look at the work you've done and be proud of it and tell everyone that you did it. I can't do any of that, Barry."

"I think you're wrong," he said. "I think Brittany and Spencer are better awards than any pay raise and any job recognition."

"Great, now you're acting like I don't value them!"

"It sounds like it, Tory. Sometimes it really does."

"That's it." She squeezed out the sponge and went to throw it into the washing machine, then dropped the top loudly.

Then she went to bed angry and cold to the sound of David Letterman in the living room.

Chapter Eleven

Cathy paced the front room of her house, the room they called the formal dining room, though there was nothing formal about it. Jerry had gotten their antique dining-room suite in the divorce, since it had come from his family, and now he and his new wife used it at Thanksgiving and Christmas. Cathy had never had the inclination to replace it—in addition to never having the money. Shopping for furniture was something that took time, and she never had a block large enough to do it. So she had moved a garage-sale table in here, covered it with a tablecloth, and set up her computer and printer on it.

Tonight, what drew her to the room was the fact that it had a window overlooking the front yard. From here, she could see the entrance to Cedar Circle, and each time she passed the window she peered out to see whether any headlights had lit up the street. Annie was three hours later than she'd said she would be.

When she had come home from Brenda's with Mark and realized that Annie should have been home by then, she headed over to the high school's baseball field. The parking lot was empty. The game had long been over. Getting angry, she had gone by the grocery store where Rick worked, and asked if he knew where she could be.

"She doesn't tell me anything," Rick said. "The brat's probably gone to a movie or something."

"She wouldn't dare. Not after I barely let her go to the game on a school night."

"Sure, she would," he said. "Annie does whatever she wants. Usually, you just don't know about it."

Cathy's mouth had fallen open. "Rick, I hope you intend to explain that!"

"Can't, Mom. Gotta go. I'm on the clock."

Frustrated, she had gone back to the car. She'd left Mark in it with the motor running, and he had moved to the driver's seat so people would think he was old enough to drive. The radio was on a heavy metal station and turned to full volume. She was embarrassed when she opened the door and the music came blaring out. "Move over, Mark," she yelled. "And turn that thing down. Good grief!"

He moved over but didn't turn the radio down, so she got in and turned it off.

"Hey, I was listening to that!"

"And so was half the town. There are laws about disturbing the peace, Mark. And I don't want you going deaf. You already do a pretty good job of not hearing me whenever I tell you to do something."

"So did you find her?"

Cathy didn't put the car in reverse just yet. Instead, she sat there, staring out the window, trying to think. "No, Rick didn't know anything. Mark, he said something that really bothered me. He said that Annie does whatever she wants. That I just usually don't find out about it."

"He's got *that* right," Mark said, reaching for the radio again.

She slapped his hand away. "I'm talking to you. What did he mean by that? What has she done that I don't know about?"

He looked at her then, as if trying to decide whether to talk. "I can't tell you that, Mom. It's classified. If I tell on her, she'll tell on me."

Cathy's heart deflated. Was there a conspiracy among her children to dupe her into servitude without asking questions? Were there things going on after she went to bed at night? Did they have whole identities she knew nothing about?

She popped the car into reverse and pulled too abruptly out of the parking space. The tires squealed as she came to a stop and switched to "drive."

"Way to go, Mom!" Mark said. "Burning rubber. All right!"

She felt her face reddening and forced her foot to go easier on the pedal. "Mark, I'm going to make a suggestion to you right now, and I want you to pay close attention. It would be very wise of you if you didn't utter another word until we got home ... unless you plan to tell me what your sister has done that I don't know about."

"Sorry."

"That was a word."

"Ex-*cuse* me."

"That was two words," she said through her teeth. "Why don't you stop by the bathrooms on the way to bed and clean the toilets? Burn off some of that energy."

"Mom! You're mad at Annie and taking it out on me. No fair!"

"No, Mark, right now I'm most definitely mad at you. But it's a good thing, because I'll get clean toilets out of it, and you'll learn to respect your mother. See how these things have mutual benefits? Now, if you'd like to keep talking, there are some dishes in the sink that need washing."

Mark hadn't said another word. And now she had clean toilets, and he was sound asleep in bed. Rick had even come home from work, but Annie was still nowhere to be found.

"Mom?" She turned back from the window and saw Rick in the doorway. "I called Allen Spreway's house. His mom said he still wasn't home either, so she's obviously with him. I asked her if she knew when he had to be home, and she said he didn't have a curfew."

"Terrific. My daughter is out with some condom-carrying kid with no curfew."

He grinned. "Cool. Alliteration."

"What?"

"Never mind. Mom, I could go out looking for her, if you want."

"Where would you look?" she asked, turning back to the window.

"There are places where kids go . . . You know . . . to park and stuff."

She felt nauseous. "So you think that's where your sister is?"

"She could be. Or she could be at Pizza Hut. Lots of people go there after the game. Most of them would be gone after three hours, though."

She turned back to the window. "Why is she doing this to me?"

Rick came closer and peered out over her shoulder. He'd long ago surpassed her in height, and was filling out. He wasn't the lanky, loping kid he used to be. "Mom, don't think of it as her doing anything *to* you. She probably hasn't given you a single thought."

"Maybe we're just assuming the worst," Cathy said, as if she hadn't heard him. "What if she's hurt somewhere? What if they had a wreck? Or what if this guy, this Allen Spreway, is a jerk and won't bring her home?"

"Well, don't get mad at me for saying this, Mom, but Annie's not the victim type. Wherever she is, it's exactly where she wants to be."

Headlights lit up the street, and she caught her breath as the car turned into the driveway. "There she is!" Cathy said.

"I'm outa here," Rick said, heading for the stairs. "I don't want to hear the yelling."

Cathy didn't respond, because she knew there probably would be plenty. She went into the kitchen and waited with her arms crossed as the garage door came up. She stood poised to attack the moment her daughter came in, but she didn't right away. It took several more moments before the door finally opened.

Annie stepped into the kitchen and looked surprised to see her. "Mom? You didn't have to wait up."

Cathy's mouth fell open. "Are you kidding me? You're three hours late and that's all you have to say?"

"The game went into extra innings. I can't help it if—"

"Don't you even try it," Cathy bit out. "I went to the ballpark and the game was over hours ago. Where have you been?"

"Just riding around."

Cathy glared at her, her mind desperately seeking a response. "Just riding around? Annie, how wise do you think it was to stay out three hours late when I almost didn't let you go out on a school night in the first place? How soon do you think I'll allow you to go out again?"

"Oh, Mom. Give me a break. I'm not some little kid. I'm fifteen."

"Well, you're about to be treated like 'some little kid.' You're not going anywhere for two weeks, and right now, you can march up to your room and unplug your telephone. Bring it to me. You won't get it back until I think you deserve it."

"That's ridiculous!" Annie yelled. "I didn't do anything wrong! And I *am* going out this weekend because Allen asked me out and I said yes. There's no way I'm going to tell him that my mommy won't let me go."

"Fine. Then I'll tell him when he comes to get you," Cathy said.

"I can't believe this." Annie threw her purse down on the counter. "What is it with you? Did your date turn out to be a dud again? You *always* take it out on me when you don't have fun, but I am *not* responsible for your love life, Mom."

Cathy tried to follow that thread of logic but realized her daughter was just trying to change the subject. "Go to bed, Annie. I'll deal with you tomorrow."

"Fine. But I *am* going out with Allen this weekend. I've been waiting for him to like me all year, and now that he does, I'm not going to let you blow it for me."

A thousand reactions played through Cathy's mind—from having Annie's mouth sewn shut to chaining her to her bedroom doorknob. The child needed discipline, she thought. She needed to be taught a lesson. She needed to learn respect. She needed . . .

. . . a father in the home.

Suddenly, Cathy was incredibly tired, and she looked at the clock and saw that it was after one. "Go get the telephone, Annie, and give it to me. Then go to bed. And when I try to wake you up in the morning, I'd better not have to tell you twice, because I'm going to be in a worse mood than you are, and I could be dangerous."

Annie jerked her purse off of the counter and huffed up to her room.

Cathy sat in the den for several moments, waiting for the phone, but Annie never brought it down. Finally fed up, she stormed up the stairs and burst into Annie's room. She was in her bed with the light off, talking on the telephone.

Cathy turned the light on, and Annie cried out, "Mom!"

She stormed to the phone jack and jerked the cord out, then grabbed the phone from Annie's hands and flung it across the room. It hit the wall with a crash, then thudded to the floor. She turned back to Annie and saw that her daughter was finally taking her seriously. "I'm not a violent woman," Cathy bit out, her hands shaking with rage and her eyes blazing. "But you're pushing me too hard, young lady. If you have one shred of judgment, you know that I've reached my threshold of maternal tolerance. From here on out it gets ugly."

"Sorry," Annie said.

It was the closest Cathy was going to get to resolving this tonight, she thought. At least Annie wasn't talking back anymore. It was a small victory, but hard won.

Without another word, she picked up the pieces of Annie's phone and stormed to her bedroom. She didn't sleep a wink for the rest of the night.

Chapter *Twelve*

It was all Brenda could do to wait until after eight o'clock the next morning to call in for Joseph's appointment. When she was told that the next available appointment was a week away, she took it gratefully, then hung up and wondered if she should have fought for an earlier one.

Joseph was sitting at the breakfast table with the rest of the children, eating cornflakes. She'd felt guilty for waking him this morning when he looked so tired and pale. But today was a school day, and she didn't like letting the children sleep late just because they didn't have a tardy bell. He had his face propped on his hand and was picking at his cereal. He seemed slightly out of breath, but she wondered if that was just her imagination.

David came into the kitchen and caught her watching Joseph. "Did you call?" he whispered.

"Yes." She busied herself cutting up wedges of cantaloupe and putting the pieces into bowls. "It's just . . ."

"Just what?"

"Just that they couldn't get him in for a week."

David's jaw dropped. "Did you tell them it was a referral? Did you tell them about his X-ray?"

"I did," Brenda said. "But I guess all of their patients are like that."

David turned back to Joseph and stared at him for a moment. Finally, he sat down at the table. Daniel, Rachel, and Leah were just finishing up, waiting for the fruit their mom was working on, but Joseph had hardly touched his cereal.

"You feeling okay this morning, buddy?" David asked Joseph.

"Yes, sir."

David raked his hand through the child's red hair, finger-combing it into place. "You sure? You don't look like you feel that well."

Joseph met his father's eyes. "Is something the matter with my heart?"

Brenda stopped what she was doing and turned back from the counter. The other three children looked up.

"Why would you ask that?" Brenda asked.

"Because ... Daniel said a cardac surgeon—"

"Card-*i*-ac," Daniel corrected.

"—is a guy who works on hearts, like Dr. Harry."

David looked up at her, and Brenda abandoned the cantaloupe and sat down in her own place. "Daniel's right," David said. "Your heart might need a little tune-up, like we did to that old truck of mine."

"A tune-up?" Joseph asked. "How do they do that?"

Brenda didn't trust David's analogies to help the matter, so she touched her husband's hand, silencing him. "Joseph, there may not be anything wrong at all. You probably just have some kind of virus. We just want to check to make sure."

He kept dipping his spoon in his cereal, scooping up cornflakes and letting them fall back into the milk. "I dreamed I died."

Brenda caught her breath and covered her mouth, and tears came to her eyes. "Oh, honey ..."

"That's it," David said, getting up. He picked up the telephone book and began flipping through.

She touched the tears at the corners of her eyes, as if she could hold them back. "Who are you calling?"

"I'm calling Harry. He's a heart surgeon."

"But he's not a *children's* cardiac surgeon. That's what Dr. Gunn said we needed."

"I know, but Harry knows what to look for. If he thinks Joseph needs to be seen right away, he'll find a way to get us an earlier appointment. Doctors listen to doctors."

"But Dr. Gunn said he would call, and it didn't help. Besides, isn't that rude, to ask a neighbor to make a house call like that?" Brenda felt like Leah now, worried that she'd make some kind of social faux pas.

"Hey, if he wants me to, I'll take Joseph over to his house. He's not like that, Brenda. He won't mind."

"Well, you may not catch him. Doesn't he do surgery early in the mornings?"

He got the number, dialed, and waited. "Sylvia? This is David Dodd. Has Harry left yet?" He paused. "No, that's okay. I was just hoping . . . Well, it's just that . . . Brenda called to get Joseph's appointment and they can't get him in for a week. Yeah. That's what I thought. Sylvia, we hate to take advantage of a neighbor . . . If you're sure . . . All right. We'd really appreciate it."

He hung up the phone and turned back to the table. All four children were frozen in silence.

"What did she say?" Brenda asked.

"She said that she would call Harry right now and see if he could come check on Joseph on his lunch break."

"Thank goodness." She leaned across the table and patted Joseph's hand. "Dr. Harry will fix you up." She looked at the other kids. "You can all have some of this cantaloupe if you want it. Rachel, will you give some to Joseph? Then all three of you clean up. Joseph, you don't have to help. You just try to eat."

He nodded as his sister gave him a bowl of cantaloupe.

Brenda took David's hand and headed back to the bedroom. She burst into tears before she reached the room. She turned around, and David pulled her into his arms. "Don't be scared," he said. "It's probably something very minor. Nothing at all."

"He dreamed he died." She let the tears out all at once, as if to relieve some of the pressure on her glands, then quickly dried up. "You're right. Harry will probably just tell us it's okay to wait a week, that there's nothing wrong . . ."

They clung together for a long time, neither wanting to let go. Finally, David loosened his hold on her. "I'll be out back working," he said. "Call me when Harry comes, or if you need me."

Brenda let him go and went back into the kitchen. Already, the table was cleared, and Daniel and Rachel were rinsing the bowls and loading them into the dishwasher. Leah had found a book to put on her head and was prancing around with perfect posture as she wiped the table. Joseph was laughing at her as he carried his bowl to the sink.

Brenda found herself studying his little chest, wondering what was going on inside it. Silently, she prayed that they had caught it in time, whatever it was, or that it was all a mistake and they'd find out today that the anxiety and worry had all been for nothing. She could live with that—even without anger toward those who'd made the mistaken diagnosis. She tried to believe it—that nothing was wrong with Joseph, that he would bounce back within days and be racing around the house with his sisters and brother, playing David and Goliath. But she could not shake the fear that it wasn't going to turn out that way.

Brenda saw the concern on Harry Bryan's face as he finished his examination of Joseph. Harry's face had many lines—lines of joy that webbed out from his eyes and his mouth, lines of concern that pleated his forehead. But the lines she saw now looked like fear. Would she, too, have those kinds of lines before this was over? She glanced up at David, and saw Harry's fear reflected there.

"I'm going to call Dr. Robinson," he said softly, "and I'll make sure he sees Joseph today."

Brenda didn't know whether to be relieved or startled. "What's wrong with him, Harry?"

"I can't say, Brenda. All I know is his heartbeat is slow and weak, and in my opinion, he needs to see a specialist pretty quick."

Joseph looked up at her, his big eyes searching her face for her response, so he would know how he should feel. She wouldn't let herself show the fear she felt. She smiled. "Well, then, we can get this over with today, can't we, Joseph?"

He nodded solemnly.

"I'm going home to call," he said. "I'll call you before I go back to the office and let you know what time your appointment is."

He didn't want them to hear the conversation, she realized. What would he tell Dr. Robinson that he didn't want them to hear? "Thank you, Harry," she said, and gave him a hug.

When he'd gone, Brenda looked up at David. He looked even more shaken now, and she wanted to take him into the other room and ask him to try to smile so that he wouldn't worry Joseph.

"Good grief, Joseph," she said brightly. "You'll do anything to get out of schoolwork."

He smiled. "I think I'd rather do math than go to another doctor."

"That's what you think," she said. "We were about to work on fractions today."

He wasn't amused.

Brenda finished feeding lunch to her kids, then assigned them to separate stations around the house where they worked on different levels of schoolwork. Her heart wasn't in it today. There were ways to stimulate her kids, to challenge them to go farther than they had to go to pass the state tests. Normally, she would find life lessons in everything she taught them. They would go places and experience things. The tests were just a formality. Her kids had always scored very high.

Today, however, she was tempted to tell them that school was letting out early, that they could play and watch videos and find something to occupy themselves so she could worry. She might have to do that anyway, if the appointment came early enough.

True to his word, Harry called back within twenty minutes and told her that Dr. Robinson would see Joseph at one-thirty. She would just barely have time to get him to St. Francis Medical Center. She gave the kids their assignments and put Daniel in charge. Then, acting as if they were heading out on a field trip, she plastered a joyful smile on her face, nudged David into doing the same, and they loaded Joseph into the car.

Chapter Thirteen

Cathy had decided not to wear her usual jeans and tennis shoes today, or the blue lab coat that she wore over her clothes at the clinic. Instead, she had dressed in a blazer and khakis that made her look like any other middle-class mom showing up at the high school to talk about her kids.

She waited nervously outside the principal's office, pacing back and forth, back and forth, her speech playing over and over in her mind, as if one misplaced word would send her whole case tumbling down.

A side door opened and the principal stuck his head out. "Mrs. Flaherty?"

"*Ms.* Flaherty," she corrected. "I'm divorced." She didn't know why that bit of information was relevant, except as part of her argument that, as a single mom raising her kids on her own, she needed the school to be her ally, not her enemy.

"Come into my office, Ms. Flaherty," he said. She followed him in and took the seat across from his desk.

"Aren't you the vet?"

"That's right," she said.

"My wife brings our dog to you. Gussy. Big German shepherd?"

"Of course," she lied. She treated hundreds of German shepherds each year and had no recollection of one named Gussy. There were pictures of older teenagers on his desk—his own children, apparently. She wondered if anyone in school had handed *his* son a condom when he was in high school.

He sat back in his chair and pressed his fingertips together, making a steeple. She crossed her legs, trying to look relaxed, but her right foot began to vibrate, as it often did when she was nervous or upset. She willed it to stop.

"Mr. Miller, I came here to talk to you about the sex education class that my son was involved in last week. I believe you called it 'Condom Awareness Day'?"

"Yes," he said. "It's actually about human reproduction, but naming it like that kind of gives it a sense of importance. I know that some parents have a problem with it, Ms. Flaherty, but the truth is that the teen pregnancy rate in this state is sky-high. Our children are getting pregnant left and right, and the incidence of AIDS and other sexually transmitted diseases are at an all-time high. It's very important that we teach them about safe sex."

Her eyes locked into his. "I prefer that my children have no sex. Not until they're married."

He smiled and leaned back hard. "Don't we all? That's the ideal, of course. But these kids *are* having sex."

"Then wouldn't it be better for you to teach them not to, instead of instructing them on how to do it right?"

He didn't seem to like the way she put that. She hadn't meant to antagonize him, not when he was the one she needed on her side. She picked up the framed portrait of his son on his desk. "Mr. Miller, is this your son?"

"Yes." His face softened into a smile. "He's going to the University of Tennessee right now, playing on the baseball team. He's a junior."

"And your daughter?" She pointed to the portrait of the young woman.

"My daughter is still here," he said. "She's a senior."

"She's pretty," Cathy said, forcing a smile. "I'll bet she doesn't sit home much on Saturday nights."

He laughed, flattered. "No, she sure doesn't."

"And it doesn't bother you that she dates boys carrying condoms?"

Again, his face changed and he shifted uncomfortably in his chair, bracing his elbows on his desk. "I don't think that's the case. Just because they know how to use one doesn't mean they're going to."

"Why not?" she asked. "When you were a teenager, if some authority figure had handed you something like that, saving you the shame and embarrassment of having to go into a drugstore and buy it, wouldn't you have thought it was okay to use it?"

He leaned forward now and laced his fingers together, more of an igloo now than a steeple. "Actually, no."

"Well, that's where we disagree." She shifted in her seat. "Mr. Miller, if I want my son to be instructed in condom use, that's my prerogative, but I don't think you have the right to decide that for me." She sat straighter in her chair and leveled her eyes on his. "I was wondering if I could watch the video you showed them. I realize it's after the fact—the truth is, you should have given parents the right to do that before you ever showed it to the kids. But I'd still like to see it."

"We don't have it," he said. "It floats between the district high schools and middle schools, and the superintendent's office holds it until we need it." He slid his chair back and crossed an ankle over his knee. "Look, Ms. Flaherty, I didn't write this policy. The school board thought it was a good idea. If you don't agree, and if you're set on seeing the video, I suggest you take it up with them."

She pulled a pad and pen out of her purse and poised to write. "So who do I talk to?"

"Well, you could start with Mary, the superintendent's secretary. She could let you view the video, I suppose. And if you want to challenge the policy, you could try to get this put on the agenda of the next school board meeting. Or you could go straight to Dr. Jacobs, the superintendent, and take it up with him."

"And would he listen?"

"Probably not," he admitted. "You see, you're coming from the perspective of a parent with . . . how many children?"

"Three."

"And Dr. Jacobs is coming at this from the perspective of someone who oversees thousands. He's intimately acquainted with the statistics. The problem is so big that they're considering opening a day-care center here for our kids who have kids. Personally, I'm dreading it. As if I didn't have enough to take care of. A few years ago, that wouldn't have been a problem."

"A few years ago they weren't handing out condoms in schools." She slapped her forehead dramatically. "Could there be a connection, ya think?"

"Talk to the superintendent," he said, obviously annoyed at her sarcastic tone. He got up, dismissing her. "Thanks for coming by. It's good to finally meet you, especially since I've never seen you at a PTA meeting."

The observation stung, and she realized that he was accusing her of not being involved in her children's education. Even if it was true, did that mean she didn't have the right to question their policies? "Mr. Miller, I am a single mother with a full-time job trying to raise three kids alone. It's not easy to find the time to make all of the meetings."

"I understand," he said smugly. She knew he really didn't. His home was probably perfectly intact; she doubted that he knew what it was like to have a spouse rip the heart out of the family by deciding they'd rather start fresh with someone younger and more exciting.

"Thanks for your time," she said, and left his office as hurt as if he'd insulted her outright.

Next, she went to the superintendent's office. Mary, the superintendent's secretary, claimed they had misplaced the video, but that she was sure it was at one of the schools and would "turn up" before the next school year. "Perhaps you'd like to meet with Dr. Jacobs," the secretary said.

"Of course," Cathy said.

Dr. Jacobs rose to greet her when she entered his office. But the bald, overweight superintendent shifted in his chair impatiently as she explained her position.

"You could submit a written request to be put on the agenda at the next school board meeting," he suggested. His tone implied that he didn't think she'd bother.

"When is that?" Cathy asked.

"Well, the last meeting of the school year was just last week, and there won't be another one until September."

She decided that wasn't too bad. She would have time to gather resources and allies before she actually went before the school board. And there was still time to get some policies changed before they handed out condoms again next year.

"Can I get a list of all the parents in the district?" she asked.

"What for?"

"So I can communicate with them. See if I can get any support from other concerned parents."

Dr. Jacobs stared at her as if she'd just asked him if she could use all the fifth graders to clean up toxic waste. "I'm sorry, Ms. Flaherty, but we're not authorized to give out the addresses of our students. I'm sure you understand."

"Then how am I supposed to contact the other parents?"

"Maybe you're not supposed to," he said. "If and when the policy is changed, it will show up in the new policy booklet."

"But isn't the new policy booklet given out at registration? Won't it be printed *before* school starts next year?"

"Yes."

"Then wouldn't it stand to reason that we should take care of this before that comes out?"

"There's nothing in the policy booklet regarding human reproduction classes."

"Which is exactly the problem. Parents would appreciate knowing what the administration intends to do with their children. They need to know their sons are carrying school-distributed condoms around in their pockets."

"Ms. Flaherty, if you're so disenchanted with the public school system, perhaps you should send your children to private school."

She couldn't believe the anger that mushroomed inside her. "I happen to believe in the *ideal* of public school," she said. "I pay a huge tax bill every year for these schools. They're *my* schools, as much as anyone's. I'm not going to pull my kids out just because things aren't going my way. Instead, I'm going to fight things and make sure that my tax money isn't going to waste. I want to make sure that what goes on there is not detrimental and not morally corrupting. A wholesome, solid education should not only be available to kids whose parents can afford private schools."

"It isn't morally corrupting to explain sexual safety to our children. People are dying because they're not having safe sex."

"For kids, the *only* safe sex is abstinence. Passing condoms out to children doesn't come close."

"Frankly, Ms. Flaherty, we're not sure what works, so we hedge our bets."

"Sounds like nothing's working, which is why you're considering day-care centers in the high schools." She could see the fatigue lines on the man's hard face, and she realized he had the weight of the whole school district on his shoulders. She didn't imagine that was an enviable job. "Look," she said, trying to sound less confrontational. "I think we're both out for the best interests of these children. I just happen to disagree with you on what is best."

"That's allowed."

"I'm going to fight you."

"I expect you will."

"And somehow I'll get a list, and I *will* contact all the parents."

He smiled. "Somehow, I believe that you'll manage to do just that, but I'm not going to help you."

"Fine," she said. "I'll see you in September."

His smile was weary but without hostility. And as she left the office, a seed of hope began to take root in her heart.

CHAPTER *Fourteen*

Dilated congestive cardiomyopathy.

The words exploded in Brenda's head with the power of dynamite. She was glad Joseph was not in the room to see the effect this diagnosis was having on his parents; he'd have been frightened to death.

"It's a condition probably caused by a viral infection," the doctor was saying in a slow, deliberate voice. "It causes the muscle of the heart to weaken, making the chambers dilate." He held up a diagram of the heart, trying to demonstrate what he was explaining. But the alarm bells wouldn't stop ringing in Brenda's mind. "As the virus damages the heart muscle, the chambers of the heart dilate and the contractions become ineffective. Right now, Joseph's heart is not able to pump enough blood to adequately maintain his circulation."

"What virus?" David asked the doctor in a voice that sounded far away. "When?"

"There's a remote chance that he's had cardiomyopathy since birth and it's just now presenting. Or somewhere along the way, another illness may have done some damage. But my guess is that it was the virus he had a few weeks ago."

"So what do we do?" Brenda choked out, fighting tears. She couldn't go out of here with a red, runny nose. Joseph would sense her despair immediately. Nine-year-old boys shouldn't have to worry about the condition of their heart.

"Well, we have three options. There's a very good possibility that, with the proper medication, the heart muscle will make a full recovery."

"Medication?" Brenda asked as the first balloon of hope inflated in her heart. "Really?"

"It's a possibility," he repeated. "The second option is that, if it doesn't heal itself with medication, we'll have to medicate Joseph for the rest of his life to keep his heart functioning."

Her hope deflated. Medication for the rest of his life?

"And the third option?" David asked.

"Well, surgery. But it all depends on the biopsy," he said. "I'd like to put Joseph in the hospital today and perform a biopsy first thing in the morning. We need to find out the full extent of the damage to his heart before we can take any action."

"And . . ." she swallowed, trying to steady her voice. "What will that entail?"

"I won't lie to you," Dr. Robinson said, leaning on his desk. "It's a pretty tedious process for a little boy, so we'll need your help. What I'll do is cut into the artery and insert a catheter. This isn't painful. He'll be semi-awake for everything, and you'll be able to watch on the monitor as the catheter goes through the arteries and into the heart's chambers. We insert dye to help us see what we need to see, and this sometimes causes discomfort. It's a warm sensation, and passes pretty quickly. If we tell Joseph what to expect, he should take it just fine."

"Is that all there is to it?" David asked.

"Well, no. He'll have to lie flat and be immobilized for several hours afterward while we keep pressure on the incision.

That's where we'll really need you. This is difficult for adults, so you can imagine how hard it'll be with a little boy."

"Joseph will do fine," Brenda said.

"What will all this tell us?" David asked.

"It'll tell us how bad things are," Dr. Robinson answered. "And what we need to do to save his life."

❧

They found Joseph sitting up and playing a game of Memory with the nurse, who seemed used to entertaining children while the doctor fulfilled their parents' worst nightmares. Joseph looked up at Brenda, and she knew that she hadn't done a very good job of hiding the evidence of her tears.

"How you feeling, honey?" she asked, hugging him so tight that she feared she might break him.

"Okay, Mama," he said.

David stooped down next to him, meeting his eyes. "Doctor tells us you're sick, buddy. He wants to put you in the hospital and do some more tests."

Joseph's hazel eyes grew round. "Now?"

"That's right."

"Don't worry, honey," Brenda said. "I'll stay with you. And you won't be in long. Just a night or two."

"Will I get to eat ice cream?"

Brenda smiled. Daniel had had his tonsils out two years ago, and the other three kids had felt deprived because of all the attention and ice cream lavished upon him. "Probably. We'll see."

As they headed for the car, Brenda wished with all her heart that ice cream was all that Joseph needed.

❧

The catheterization went well the next morning, and Joseph took it all as if it was another of their field trips. Brenda patiently tried to explain everything that was happening, taking advantage of the opportunity to teach him a little anatomy.

It was late that afternoon when the doctor came with the results. David and Brenda stepped out into the hall while the nurse fussed over Joseph.

"How is he, Doctor?" David asked anxiously.

"Well, I'm really very pleased with what we found. His heart valves and his veins and arteries look pretty good. That's good news. His left ventricle is still not pumping like it should, and it's enlarged. But it's possible that he'll make a full recovery with medication."

Brenda caught her breath. Had he really said that medication was all Joseph needed?

"Medication?" David asked as if voicing her thoughts. "Not surgery?"

"Not yet," Dr. Robinson said. "We're going to start with a couple of drugs that will lower his blood pressure and reduce the force of the contraction of the heart. We'll want to keep him another day or so. I'd like to transfer him to the telemetry unit. We'll hook him up to a transmitter and monitor his heart. He'll be able to walk around the halls and get some exercise, but the nurse's station will have the heart monitor so we can watch him. After we release him, we'll give him a portable heart monitor to wear all day, and then you can bring it back in so we can analyze his cardiac activity and see how he's doing."

Brenda didn't like the sound of any of this, but she did appreciate that they were planning to watch things so closely.

"What if things don't go like you hope?" David asked.

"They may not," the doctor admitted. "Then we'll have to look at surgery. But if he's lucky, he'll be back to normal in just a few months. And he looks like a lucky kid to me."

After Joseph fell asleep that night, Brenda and David sat quietly in the darkened hospital room, watching him, saying nothing. Sylvia, who was staying with their other three children, had encouraged David to stay as long as he wanted to, and Brenda knew that if there had been enough room, he would have spent the night there, too.

She touched Joseph's forehead. He was cold, clammy. She straightened his covers, trying not to move the cords and wires attached to his chest. The *tick*, *tick*, *tick* of the heart monitor beside his bed was getting on her nerves—especially the occasional blips that broke the rhythm, startling her. But she had been impressed by the diligence with which the nurses watched him. They had ten heart monitors over their station, monitoring ten patients, and whenever Joseph's heart stumbled, they ran to check on him.

David's hand touched her shoulder and she turned around. He pulled her into a reassuring hug. She began to weep, and afraid of waking Joseph, she pulled out of his arms and walked out of the room.

David followed her into the corridor. Not knowing where else to go, she went into the stairwell next to their door, sat on the top step, and buried her face in her hands. He sat down next to her and stroked her back helplessly as she wept.

After a while, she looked up at him. "David, if Joseph is out of here by then, I want you to go to church with us Sunday."

He looked away. "Brenda, we've talked about this a million times. I don't do church."

"I know, but this is different. We've never had a child with a heart problem before."

"And how does that make things different?"

"Because we both need to believe, David." Her words were uttered urgently, tearfully.

"Honey, I know how much you want me to believe. But wanting me to won't make it happen. I just don't. I can't."

She wiped her face and tried to look stronger. "I'm going to ask them to lay hands on him Sunday," she said. "I'd like for you to be there. It's very important."

"No way." He got up and his face began to redden. "They'll lay hands on Joseph over my dead body."

His outburst stunned her, and she got to her feet. "David, why?"

"I have my reasons." He pointed a trembling finger at her. "So help me, Brenda, they're not gonna touch my son."

Her face twisted as she tried to understand. "David, this is ridiculous. I know you're bitter about church, but for heaven's sake, the Bible tells us in the book of James that we can go to the elders of the church and they can pray—"

"I've kept my mouth shut all these years, Brenda," he cut in. The rims of his eyes were beginning to redden, and the anguish on his face astonished her. "I've let you drag all four children to church with you. It didn't seem to do any harm, so I've allowed it. But I draw the line when it comes to laying hands on my boy."

"David, if you don't believe in God, then what difference would it make to you?"

"It'll make a difference to Joseph!" he bit out. "You don't know what it's like to be a little kid and have a bunch of hateful, Scripture-chanting hypocrites surrounding you with their hands all over you. It stays with you for life, Brenda. It changes the way you think! They're not going to do it to my son!"

Brenda gaped at him, desperately trying to put this new information into the context of David's background. "Stays with you for life? Changes the way you think? David, did someone lay hands on you?"

He swung around and reached for the door handle. "I'm going home. I'll be back in the morning."

"No, David. Please! We need to talk about this. How can I understand you when you won't talk to me?"

He stopped before opening the door, and turned slowly back around. He was trying to calm himself, taking deep, deliberate breaths. His voice was low when he finally spoke. "All right. Let's talk. You want rational reasons, I'll give you some. It doesn't work, for one. If it did, everybody would be doing it, and we wouldn't need hospitals. They have funerals for Christians every day, just like everybody else."

She tried to think. Somehow, this was a conversation vital to David's life. She had to answer wisely. "Because God doesn't choose to heal everyone."

"That's convenient," he said. "You're told that He'll heal you, and then if He doesn't you can say He just didn't choose to. So how does anybody ever know what to believe?"

Her tears assaulted her again as this disappointment she had grown accustomed to hurt her as if it was new. "Faith, David. It's just faith."

"What about Joseph's faith, when he expects to be healed but walks out of there still sick? And what happens when nothing changes, and your church friends start saying it must be because there's sin in your life, or in Joseph's life—or better yet, in *my* life, since I'm the one who doesn't buy into all this? What they'll be saying is that God is cursing our little boy, because otherwise their prayers would have healed him. And then they'll say it's a demon, not a heart problem, that's keeping him from getting well. How's he going to feel about having a demon in him, Brenda? What do you think that'll do to a little kid's mind?"

She wasn't angry anymore, for suddenly she understood. These weren't hypotheticals, thrown out to win an argument. This was a scene right out of David's childhood. It had happened. New tears trickled down her cheeks as she looked at him. "They told you you had a demon?" she asked.

"I was one angry kid," David whispered, as if saying it too loudly might shatter him completely. "I had reason to be. And not because of any demon. It was disappointment."

"About your father," she whispered.

He shot her a look, as if surprised she knew.

"Your mother told me before she died," she said. "You had never told me you were a preacher's kid."

He breathed a laugh and rolled his eyes, as if he couldn't believe she would call him that. "Why didn't you ever tell me you knew?"

"I wanted you to tell me yourself," she admitted. "It seemed like such a painful thing."

"Then she told you about the organist he left town with?"

"Yes."

He nodded and stood there for a moment. Was he thinking that his mother had betrayed him? Brenda hoped not. He was angry enough at his mother already.

"So I suppose she told you about the parsonage, too—how the dear church gave us a week to get out because they had to make room for their new preacher. How we had to live in a garage apartment . . ."

No, his mother hadn't told Brenda that. She listened to him carefully, gratefully. She'd been so desperate to understand. "No wonder you were angry," she whispered.

He laughed bitterly as tears misted in his eyes. "They were sure I had a demon. Tried to cast it out."

"David, those people didn't know God. They couldn't have, or they would have loved you and cared for you. They would have seen what you needed."

He shook his head. "I know you think your church is different, Brenda. On the surface, maybe it seems that way. But it's not."

"Come and see," she pleaded. "You can stand right there as they pray for him. It won't be a bunch of people yelling and pushing on him, David. Just a few of the elders, gently touching him, talking to God and asking Him for healing. Nothing angry or evil. Just people of faith taking their needs to God. Look at me."

He raised his eyes, and she saw the trepidation, the pain there.

"David, you know how much I love our children. Would I ever put them in jeopardy? Would I let anyone frighten them or hurt them in any way?"

"Not on purpose."

"It's not going to hurt Joseph to have a group of people praying for him. It'll just remind him that God is there, with him, that He won't let him down."

Anger flashed across David's face again, and she knew what he was thinking: That there was, as Brenda had admitted, no guarantee that God would heal Joseph—and if He didn't, then in David's opinion God would indeed have let Joseph down. She knew David couldn't understand. Nor was it something she could explain to him. It was something only the Holy Spirit could convince him of.

"David, you've let me take the kids to church. You've even said it was good for them. Don't start putting limits on that freedom now."

He looked down at his feet. "Brenda, this is serious, what Joseph has. I don't want anyone playing head games with him."

"What do you want me to do, David?" she asked. "Prepare him to die?"

"No," he bit out, his face reddening. "He's *not* going to die. He's going to be all right with this medication. You'll see. With or without those people praying."

She wept at the arrogance of that statement. Softening, David held her as she cried into his shirt, her eyes so raw and heavy that she knew sleep was nearby.

When David finally left, she made up the cot next to the bed and tried to sleep, but the sound of Joseph's heart beating and stumbling, beating and stumbling, kept her awake. So she passed the time praying again for her little boy's heart . . . and her beloved husband's soul.

CHAPTER *Fifteen*

Cathy didn't really know why she decided to take Sylvia up on her invitation to go to church Sunday morning. She supposed part of it had to do with the fact that her kids were going down the tubes. They needed some spiritual instruction. She had never been much for church herself. It wasn't that she didn't believe in God. It was just that she couldn't imagine why it was necessary to get up early on her only day off, don a dress and panty hose, and force her children to put on decent clothes and come to church with her.

That part had certainly been a challenge this morning. Annie had come out of her room looking like a runaway. Cathy had sent her back twice before she'd come out wearing anything remotely presentable—which had reminded Cathy that she hadn't made it a priority to shop for dresses for Annie, except on the rare occasions when she had to wear them for a dance. And none of those dresses was appropriate for church. They'd finally settled on a skirt that was too short, and a hot pink blouse that gave Cathy a headache. But it was the least offensive outfit Annie had come up with.

Mark and Rick had fought her tooth and nail about having to wear anything other than blue jeans, but she'd finally gotten them into khakis and dress shirts. When Mark came downstairs in filthy Nikes, she told him to go back up and change his shoes.

"I can't, Mom. I don't have any other shoes."

"You have a pair of dress shoes, Mark. Now put them on."

"You bought those last year! They don't fit me anymore. What's wrong with these?"

She looked helplessly down at Mark's feet. "They're dirty, and just not right for church. Are you sure the others don't fit?"

"Positive, Mom. This is it."

"All right," she said, giving up. "Get in the car."

They had argued all the way there that they didn't know why she had to visit church on their weekend home, when she could just as easily have done it when they were with their dad.

"I want you to come," she said. "I'm doing this as much for you as I am for myself."

"Oh, so all of a sudden you think we're heathens," Annie said.

"Mom!" Mark shouted. "*I'm* not a heathen."

"I don't think any of you are heathens," she returned. "It's just that nice people go to church, and I want you to be nice people."

"We can be nice people at home," Rick complained. "Aren't we nice people?"

His sister and brother agreed. Cathy couldn't help laughing. "It's not like I'm asking you to shave your heads. I just want you to go to Sunday school."

"Sunday school? Come on, Mom!" Rick said. "We're too old for Sunday school!"

"Is that so?" she asked, giving him a sideways glance. "I didn't know there was an age limit in Sunday school."

"So what are we supposed to do? Sit at a little desk and paste Bible verses on construction paper? Sing 'Jesus Loves Me'?"

Had it been *that* long since she'd had her children in church? "I doubt very much that they still do that in your age-group."

"Then what do they do?"

"They talk about God," she said. "Believe it or not, it's an important subject. You do believe in God, don't you?"

He shrugged. "Yeah, I guess."

"You guess." That made her feel even more like a failure. "Look, Rick, I know I haven't made church a priority in this family, but that doesn't mean I can't set things right now. I think it's important that we all go to church."

"Give me a break," Annie said from the backseat.

She looked in her rearview mirror at her daughter's scowl. "And what is that supposed to mean?"

"It means the only reason you wanted to go to church today is that there's a huge singles department at the Bryans' church. You're looking for a husband."

"*What?*" Cathy gasped, appalled at how close to the truth Annie's guess was. "Where do you get this stuff?"

"I hear things," she said. "I happen to know that the Bryans' church has one of the biggest, most active singles departments in the state, and they have it for all ages, even for older divorced people like you. And I've heard Miss Sylvia talk to you about it, so I know that's why you want to go."

"This may come as a huge surprise to you, my dear," Cathy said sarcastically, "but it is not my aim in life to get tangled up with another man."

Annie looked out the window. "I'm just saying that it's a lot to put us through just for a date."

Cathy had to hand it to her. Annie knew how to give her a one-two punch. "Look, we all need to go to church." Her voice rose with each word. "So if you don't mind, I'd appreciate it if you'd stop complaining. Who knows? You may really like it."

"Yeah, right," Mark muttered.

As she drove, Cathy realized that there was a lot about the way she had raised her children she wished she could change. First and foremost, she wished she had started out making them treat her with respect. Who would have dreamed when they were adoring toddlers that they'd ever turn on her this way? It was her own fault, she thought miserably. Now it was almost too late.

They pulled into the massive parking lot at the Bryans' church, and she sat for a moment, looking at the crowded walkway that would take them across the street and into the huge building. "Look, kids, let's just do our best not to embarrass each other, okay? I promise not to act like a floozy with the single men I encounter, if you promise you won't act like little brats."

None of the children said a word.

She got out of the car, and one by one they followed her, grudgingly, none of them walking together. They were a group of people who didn't want to be seen with each other.

When they reached the visitors' booth, she glanced back at her children to make sure they were put together properly.

"I hate being the new kid," Mark said.

Personally, she didn't mind being the new person, because she liked meeting new people. She just wondered if everyone in the Sunday school department would know instantly that she had come in hopes of meeting a decent man. If they did, was that punishable by death or eternal embarrassment? Would they all turn and look, point at her and hiss, like something out of *Invasion of the Body Snatchers?*

She swallowed her anxiety and stepped up to the booth. As she did, she glanced at her watch. A little over two hours, and she could go home with her humiliated children and a clear conscience.

❧

After a pleasant hour with other divorced men and women her age, Cathy rounded up her kids, and they sat with Sylvia and Harry during the worship service. The Bryans seemed proud that her family had agreed to join them for worship, though Cathy couldn't imagine why. Mark scribbled a note on the church bulletin and tore it off, making a loud ripping noise that caused the people in front of them to look over their shoulders. Cathy clamped Mark's leg, warning him to be quiet. Mark passed the note to Rick, who passed it on to Annie. Cathy opened her own bulletin, found a blank space, and scribbled out, "Stop writing notes!" She started to tear it off, then stopped herself. Instead, she passed the whole bulletin down. By the time it got down to Rick and Annie, they were giggling quietly at the absurdity of her writing a note to tell them to stop writing notes.

She glanced at Sylvia and saw that she'd seen. Sylvia smiled, and Cathy wished she hadn't come.

When the sermon was over and the choir director asked them to stand and sing hymn number 132, Mark muttered, "Stand up, sit down, fight-fight-fight." Cathy had to admit that the constant standing baffled her. Why did they have to keep popping up like jack-in-the-boxes, just to sing a song? Couldn't they sing it as well sitting down?

When the service was mercifully over, Cathy braced herself. She had made the mistake of raising her hand as a visitor, but she'd really had no choice, because Sylvia had been nudging her. Would she be greeted by a dozen well-meaning strangers before she could get to the door? Would they send someone to her home to talk to her about heaven and her responsibility to her children? If they did, she hoped they would call first so she could get the front room picked up.

She was on the way across the parking lot when she spotted one of the better-looking men in her Sunday school class heading toward her. She tried to look approachable.

"Hi, Cathy," he said, reaching out to shake her hand. He was tall, blonde, and had intriguing brown eyes. "I'm Bill Blackburn. I didn't get to meet you in Sunday school, but I'm glad you came. You from around here?"

"We live up on Survey Mountain," she said.

"Nice area."

"We like it. My next-door neighbor invited us to visit. Sylvia Bryan?"

He didn't show any sign that he recognized the name. "Good, good. I'm outreach chairman of the Sunday school class you visited today," he said. "Did you like it?"

"Sure, it was nice." Behind Bill, Annie leaned against the car with her arms crossed and a smug I-told-you-so smile on her face. Cathy began digging into her purse for her keys.

"I heard you were a vet," he said.

"That's right." She glanced at Mark and Rick over his shoulder, hovering behind him like judges, mentally recording the tangible proof that she had come here to meet men.

"Would you mind if I called you sometime?" he asked. "Maybe you'd like to go to the social with me this Saturday. We try to have one every weekend. I could introduce you around."

She thought of telling him no just to shoot down her kids' theories about her intentions, but she did want a life, and the kids needed to get used to it. "Maybe," she said. She jotted her phone number on the bulletin, tore off a corner, and gave it to him. "Just call sometime this week and tell me more. It sounds fun."

"Good," he said. "It was nice meeting you."

"You, too."

He turned back to the children, eyed them one by one. "Great-looking kids you got there," he said, as if they couldn't hear.

"Thank you," she said.

When he'd gone, they got into the car one by one, and she cranked the engine. "So what do you think?" she asked.

"I think you dragged us here so you could meet men," Annie said again.

Cathy pulled out of the parking lot. "I mean about your Sunday school class. Did you like it or not?"

"Not," Annie said.

"How about you, Rick?" Cathy looked across at her big, lanky son. He had already put his Walkman headphones on and was listening, no doubt, to Jimi Hendrix. She gave up on him and glanced at Mark in the rearview mirror. "So Mark, how was yours?"

"Okay," he said. "I knew a couple of people."

She took that as a ringing endorsement. "Did you really?"

"Yeah," he said.

"Who?"

"Brad Lovell. He's pretty cool."

"And he goes to church," she said. "Imagine that. So you'll want to come back?"

"No," he said. "Not unless I have to."

She looked over her shoulder at Annie. "Did you know anybody?"

"Yes." She looked out the window, uninterested in this conversation.

"Who?"

"Sharon Greer. I can't stand her."

"Why not?"

"Because she's after Allen Spreway. She used to date him, and she thinks he's still hers. And she's not a nice girl, Mom, but she sits up there in Sunday school answering all the questions with those hypocritical church answers that the teachers are looking for, and they're like, so out of it, that they don't know she's a fraud."

Cathy's hopes wilted. "Anyone else?" she asked weakly.

"No, that was plenty."

Cathy sighed and thought that maybe they were right. Maybe she needed to attend church on weekends when they were with their dad. She wasn't sure all this pain was worth it.

Chapter Sixteen

Monday morning story hour at the local library was a blessing for Tory, and she never missed a session. Brittany and Spencer loved sitting at the feet of the grandma-like librarian in the children's section and hearing picture books. Tory loved it because it allowed her time to linger alone in her favorite sections. For months, she had spent this time researching her book, reading countless articles on France, World War II, and the nurses and doctors who served in the war. Her head was a smorgasbord of little-known facts, enough to fill a dozen-novel saga.

Deciding that it was not research but motivation she needed today, she floated through the self-help section, searching for the perfect book to inspire greater progress toward her goals. She lingered over a book on personal organization—then realized that if someone could return to her all the hours she'd spent reading books on organizing, she would have written three novels by now.

She moved to the self-esteem section, with books running the gamut from knowing thyself to discovering past lives.

When nothing there appealed to her, she moved to the fiction section and scanned the spines for the names of her favorite authors. Someday, her name would be up here, she promised herself. Someday she would have a book that people would ask for in libraries and go into stores intending to buy. She pulled out a book, scanned the blurb on the back, decided against it, then pulled another one. When she had put that one back too, she looked up and noticed a display of brand-new novels. The name of one of her favorite authors caught her eye, so she crossed the room.

On the cover was a woman in a nurse's uniform, and behind her were flames as if something had just been bombed. Frowning, Tory grabbed the book off the shelf and turned it over to read the blurb. "World War II . . . Annabelle Hopkins serving as a nurse. France . . ."

Tory heard a chuckle and looked up—a woman down the aisle was grinning at her. With a touch of embarrassment, Tory realized she'd been reading aloud. She looked at the woman with annoyance, then turned back to the book, whispering the words with a rush of dread. "Will Annabelle's heart be forever buried with the soldier she loves—"

Her stomach plunged and her heart began to race. Her hands trembled as she bit out the rest: "—or will she find love again in the arms of Dr. Frank James?"

She thrust the book back onto the shelf and backed away as if it had burned her.

How could it be? How could this novel have the same plot she was trying to write—only this one was finished and published, and already a best-seller?

Her chest constricted into a tight fist, and a scream of rage rose up in her, though she knew she would never let it out. She grabbed the book again and began flipping through the pages. Yes, the story was similar to hers—but so much better. She turned page after page, searching for something to reassure her that she wasn't wasting her time, that no one would even suspect the similarities between the two stories. Instead, as she skimmed the pages, she became more and more convinced that this book would make hers seem like a rip-off.

Returning the book to the shelf, she backed against the bookshelf opposite it, closed her eyes, and began to cry. It wasn't fair. She hadn't had *time* to write her book, and now someone else had done it, someone with a famous name and a following of millions of devoted readers.

The door to the children's room swung open and a dozen kids burst out, chattering with excitement. Her kids' homing devices zeroed in on her immediately. Brittany looked up at her tears. "Whatsa matter, Mommy?" she asked loudly, and three mothers turned around to look.

"Nothing, honey," Tory said, still shaking. "Come on, let's go."

"But can I get a book? Please?" Spencer was holding two huge hardback books that he'd grabbed off a table. One was a coffee-table book on antique cars. The other was a picture book about merry-go-rounds.

"No, honey, put them back."

"But you said—"

"I didn't say."

"But we always—"

"Please, I've got to get out of here!" She wiped her eyes, and Brittany kept staring at her. She hated to cry in front of them. It wasn't fair.

She put the books back, then escorted them to the car. They marched like little soldiers beside her, wondering what they had done to upset their mother now. There were no computers or horses close by, no Kool-Aid disasters, no cats in the tree . . .

She got them into the car, hooked their seat belts, slid behind the wheel, and peeled out of the parking lot.

"What is it, Mommy?" Brittany asked again in a small voice.

"Just something stupid," she said.

"I like stupid things," Spencer spouted, leaning up on her seat back.

"Spencer, hook your seat belt!"

"It is hooked. See?"

"Spencer, if you can sit on the edge of your seat, it's not tight enough. And if you keep this up, I'm going to make you use the car seat again."

Spencer moaned and sat back, and she heard him pulling it tighter.

"Mommy's okay," she said finally. "I just had a little surprise. See, the book I'm trying to write? Somebody's already written it."

In the rearview mirror, she saw that both children stared at her as if trying to figure that one out. What were they picturing? A balloon floating around in the air with a book's worth of words in it, and the first one to let the air out got to publish it? She wished that was the case.

"It just makes me feel like my work is a waste of time," she told them. "All the research I've done, and all the ways I've developed the characters. Finally, I've got three whole chapters, and what do you know? Somebody else has done it! So I guess I should just give up and get real. What do you think of that?"

The children seemed to consider it for a moment. Finally, Brittany spoke. "Can we go to McDonald's?"

Tory shoved her sunglasses on, hoping to hide the tears. She thought about Brittany's innocent, selfish request. Did she really want to go home, fix them tuna sandwiches, and look at that mocking computer screen with her three pathetic little chapters? "Yes," she said. "We'll go to McDonald's."

The children cheered.

They went to the McDonald's with the playground in the front. And as the children bounced around on the balls and in the tunnels, Tory sat on a bench wondering why she'd ever thought she could be a writer in the first place.

CHAPTER *Seventeen*

Because Joseph wasn't feeling up to it, Brenda didn't take him to church Sunday. They celebrated the Lord's Day at home, singing hymns and reading Scripture, while David worked out in his shop. That afternoon, as the children scattered around the house, engaged in their own activities, Brenda closed herself in her bedroom and began to read the book of James again. She found the passage she was looking for, and read it again. "Is any one of you sick? He should call the elders of the church to pray over him and anoint him with oil in the name of the Lord. And the prayer offered in faith will make the sick person well."

She closed her eyes and recalled her argument with David. Was it better to submit to her husband on this, or follow the instructions in Scripture? She began to pray, deeply, earnestly, that the Lord would show her direction.

Finally, she told herself that David didn't have to know. She could take Joseph to the elders, and they could pray over him.

She had never defied David before, and she wouldn't do it now if her son's life wasn't at stake.

But as she saw it, she really had no choice.

The next day, she convinced David not to go with her to Joseph's doctor's appointment. It might be a long wait, she told him, and he had too much work to do. Then she called her pastor and asked him to get the elders of the church together on their lunch hour.

She was torn and tearful as she pulled into the church parking lot, and Joseph frowned and looked up at her. "Why are we at church?"

"I just wanted to stop by for a minute before we go to the doctor. Pastor Mike and some of the men want to pray for you." Her eyes misted over as she reached for her son's hand. "Is that okay with you, Joseph?"

He nodded. "Sure."

She just sat there in the car for a moment, staring across at him. "The thing is, your dad can't know."

"Why not?"

She swallowed. "He had some bad experiences with church people praying over him when he was a little boy."

"Daddy went to church?"

"Yes. But it wasn't like our church, and he doesn't understand." She gazed at him for a long moment. "I've never asked you to lie to Daddy, Joseph. And I'm not asking you now. If it comes up, you can tell him. But if it doesn't, then just don't bring it up, okay?"

His eyes were wide as he considered that. "Okay."

"Okay." She got out of the car and went around to help Joseph out. The doors to the church opened, and the pastor rushed out to help her. Several of the elders came out behind him, fussing over Joseph like doting grandfathers.

Brenda knew that she had done the right thing . . . even if it meant defying David.

Chapter Eighteen

Cathy waited three weeks before agreeing to go to a church social with Bill, the man she'd met in the parking lot at Sylvia's church. He had called a couple times a week since she'd met him, and had piqued her interest with talk of the fellowship they had as a singles group. He had offered to take her to Thursday night volleyball, but to avoid having Annie remind her of her reason for taking them to church, she decided to wait for a weekend when the children would be at their father's.

She agreed to go to a Saturday night ice-cream social sponsored by the singles department, and she looked forward to making some new friends.

Bill's Porsche had only two seats, and she felt as if she was crawling into Spencer Sullivan's Flintstone-mobile as she folded into it. He drove like a Nascar driver with a death wish, and she wondered if her fingernails were cutting holes into his armrest whenever he slammed on the brakes. She checked to see if he had air bags. Thankfully, he did. But she worried that if they hit anything she would shoot through the bag like a torpedo.

"So . . . where do you stand on the perseverance of the saints issue?" he asked as they curved down Survey Mountain.

"The what?"

"You know. Once saved, always saved, or predestination, or foreknowledge. I'd like to hear your take on free will versus God's sovereignty."

Was this his idea of an icebreaker? "I don't think I have a take on it," she said. "Uh . . . could you slow down just a little?"

"Sure." He glanced over at her, grinning. "I attended seminary for two years. Was going to be a preacher."

She wondered if churches looked at people's driving records before hiring pastors. If so, it was clear why he wasn't preaching now. "I didn't know that," she said, trying to appear interested.

"That's right. But they were so narrow-minded there. I was obviously at the wrong school, so I dropped out and got a job in computers. But I still study. And I consider myself in ministry—priesthood of believers and all that. I help with the soup kitchen every Thanksgiving, before I have my family over. I invite a few friends, too. An occasional vagrant."

She wondered if he wanted applause. "That's very nice of you."

"You ever do anything like that? 'Cause it's real rewarding. They always need extra hands. And if you can cook, it's even better . . ."

He seemed like a nice guy, she told herself. If it wasn't for his driving, maybe she could even like him. Wasn't a man of faith, a man of principle, what she needed? Someone strong who could be a helpmeet to her? Annie would hate him instantly, but Mark and Rick would be impressed with the car.

"So have you ever been married, Bill?" she asked, half expecting him to say that he had been widowed when his wife was thrown through the windshield.

"Yes."

Suddenly, a short answer? Suspicious, she tried again.

"Divorced?"

"Yes."

"Any kids?"

"Nope."

She couldn't decide if that was a plus or minus. If he had no children, then she didn't have to worry about them liking her. On the other hand, his tolerance level for teenagers was bound to be low.

"How about you?" he asked. "Divorced or widowed?"

"Divorced," she said.

"How many times?"

The question insulted her, and she looked over at him, frowning. "Just once."

"Oh."

She hadn't thought of it before, but now she was curious. "How about you?"

He shrugged, suddenly shy.

"Bill?"

"Three," he said. "I was married and divorced three times. Three mistakes. I have bad taste in women, I guess."

"I see." He picked up his speed again, and she clung, white-knuckled, to the armrest. "I got the impression you'd been in the singles department a long time. How long since your last divorce?"

"Six months."

She gaped at him. "Months? Then how—"

"I met all three women in the singles department," he said proudly. "We have a real high success rate there."

"Success?" she asked. "You call three divorces success?"

He shot her a look. "What are you saying?"

"Just that ... well, it sounds like the marriage ceremony is the standard by which you judge success or failure. I mean, if you get married, you've succeeded. Never mind whether it works out or not."

"Look, those divorces were not my fault. Everybody knows that."

"Well, of course. I didn't mean ..." She didn't know what she did mean, but suddenly she wished she'd never met Bill Blackburn.

"I had biblical divorces, you know. That makes a difference."

She didn't know much about the Bible, but she thought she understood what he meant. "Oh, so they cheated on you?"

"No. They were unbelievers and they left. I thought they were believers, but obviously they weren't, or they would have been better wives. Paul said that we aren't accountable if unbelieving spouses leave us, so that lets me off the hook. It's almost like the marriages didn't exist."

As unschooled as she was in theology, she felt sure that was a misinterpretation. Maybe he could make that explanation work once, but three times?

"What about yours?" he asked. "Was yours a biblical divorce?"

She looked at him, wondering how to politely tell him it was none of his business. As if he read her mind, he said, "It's pertinent, you know. I don't want to date anyone with unconfessed sin."

She almost laughed, but with great effort managed to keep a straight face. "Rest easy. I'm off the hook, too."

He seemed happy with that. So happy, that he picked his speed up from eighty to ninety.

She was worn out by the time they reached the farm where the social was to be held. "You sure are quiet," he said as they screeched into the driveway. She considered telling him it was difficult to talk when your jaw was clenched in terror.

"I hope my driving didn't scare you," he said as if reading the fear on her face.

"'Scared' isn't the word I would use," she said.

He chuckled. "I bought this car after my last divorce, and I go a little crazy when I drive it. It just handles so well."

She tried to look impressed. "Boy, it sure does."

He opened the door and got out, and she found herself struggling with her own door. Her hands were still shaking. He came around and opened it, and she unfolded from the car.

As they approached the crowd, Cathy saw the heads of all the women turn. Were they asking themselves if she knew about his marital history? Or were they his ex-wives?

Bill wasted no time greeting everyone like a politician the morning of an election, ignoring her completely.

Not one to play the shrinking violet, and desperately glad to be safely on her own again, she introduced herself to those on the fringes of the group who looked as if they were as new as she was. Before long, she had joined a circle of men and women basking in the shade of a huge tree, exchanging homemade ice-cream recipes.

As it grew dark and the party died down and the bug zappers began to pop with their prey, Bill made his way toward her. "Ready to hit the road?"

The relaxation that had fallen over her suddenly fled as she realized she'd have to get back in the car with him. She racked her brain for a way out. Another ride home, perhaps, or a taxi . . .

Then it came to her.

"Bill, let me drive. I've always wanted to drive a Porsche."

He frowned. "I don't know. I don't usually let other people drive her. She's delicate . . ."

"But you were telling me how well it—she—handles, and I'm dying to see for myself."

Finally, he grinned, and tossed her the keys. "All right, but be careful."

She almost laughed at the admonition when he'd been so close to liftoff just hours before. She hurried to the driver's seat before he could change his mind.

He seemed bored as she drove the speed limit home, and kept pointing out features of the car she might have missed. He urged her to go faster, but she declined.

By the time they reached Cedar Circle, she was quite proud of her own ingenuity. "Well, Bill, I really had a nice time. Guess I'll see you in church tomorrow."

"That's it?" he asked. "You're not inviting me in?"

"No, it's a little too late. I'm tired."

He looked disappointed. "So how about lunch after church tomorrow?"

She started to ask him why he would want to take her to lunch, when their time together had been so underwhelming. Instead, she chose to lie her way out of it. "I can't. I've already accepted an invitation from my neighbors."

"Tomorrow night, then?"

"No, my kids will be coming home."

"Next weekend?"

She was getting flustered at his refusal to take no for an answer. "Call me. I'm usually pretty busy, but . . ."

"Okay. I'll call. I think we're a good match, Cathy. I can see myself with you."

"Oh, can you?" She tried to hide her amusement. "And why is that?"

"You're my type. Classy. Professional."

Female, she thought. "Well, I appreciate that."

"No, really. People expect me to be with classy women. I like the fact that you're a vet. That's interesting. Pays well, too."

Again, she wanted to laugh. So that was it. He thought she was wealthy.

"So I can call you?"

"Sure." She realized what a blessing caller ID was. "Thanks for taking me, Bill. It was fun."

He started to get out, but she stopped him, desperately trying to avoid a kiss goodnight. "No need to walk me to the door," she said. "Really. Goodnight."

"Goodnight," he said. He leaned toward her to kiss her, but she turned her head and his lips landed on her ear.

Quickly, she got out of the car and waved through the window.

She was giving up dating, she vowed as she got inside. There wasn't a man alive worth wasting time with. Besides, she needed to put all her energy into praying for her daughter to find one decent man on this earth amidst all the losers—and making her sons into decent men instead of the psychos she had been running into lately.

She left the television off and allowed silence—which had never been her favorite sound—to minister to her like a welcome companion.

Chapter *Nineteen*

While Cathy was giving up men, Tory was giving up writing. She had dumped her entire manuscript into her computer's recycling bin, then defiantly pushed the button to erase it all. Systematically, she went about her house collecting all the paraphernalia relating to her writing. Her legal pads, her special pens, her books on technique, her tapes of writers' conferences and seminars she hadn't been able to attend. Then she gathered all the self-help books she had bought over the years, and as she did, she realized that none of them had really done her much good. She might be organized, she might know how to manage her time, she might know how to set priorities, but she had never reached her goals, and she wasn't going to.

So she decided to choose new goals—first among them to have a house so clean it squeaked.

Barry watched her from the kitchen table where he was making a Play-Doh dinosaur with the kids. "Come sit down," he told her, pulling out a chair. "Good grief, the house is clean enough."

"It can never be clean enough," she said. "I'm about to clean out the junk drawer. I'm going to be brutal, so if there's anything in there you want to save, you might want to tell me now."

"Honey, why are you doing this?"

"Because it's Saturday," she said. "And you're home to help with the kids and I can get something done."

"But you could be writing."

"I told you, I'm never writing again."

He shook his head. "Look, why don't you just *read* that book and see what it's like? Maybe you can learn something from it. Maybe God has a reason for this."

"God does have a reason for it," she said matter-of-factly. "It's to tell me that I'm not supposed to be a writer. That's not my destiny."

"Then why have you wanted it so badly?"

"Just because you want something doesn't mean it's God's will."

"But what if it *is* God's will—but it's just something you're going to have to work harder for?"

"How can I work harder?" she asked, looking back up at him. "I can't put any more time into it than I have, so that makes me really slow. When I started it, it was because I heard an editor on one of those writers' conference tapes say they're looking for World War II stories. Now that book is out, it's a best-seller, and they'll probably move on to something else—maybe the Civil War or the Medieval age. By the time I get anything written, it'll be too late."

"Then don't write to the trends," he said. "Write what's in your heart."

She breathed a laugh. "I don't *know* what's in my heart. I make things up, Barry. Besides, I don't have the layers and layers of life experience that that author has. She's probably been to France. She probably remembers the war. She's probably had tragic affairs with passionate men. I'm just me."

"But there are things you love, things you care about. Write about them. Write about things in the neighborhood. Heaven knows, there's enough going on around here."

"I don't want to write about real stuff. I just want to make it up. Fiction, not fact."

"But there is a lot of fact in fiction. Some of the greatest truths I've ever read were in fiction. Think of Jesus' parables."

She looked at Barry for a moment, surprised that he'd made such a profound point. Maybe *he* should be the writer, she thought bitterly. "It doesn't matter. I'm still finished with it."

"Then what about the computer? What are we going to do with that? Sell it?"

"Nope. I'm going to start keeping recipes on it. And I'm cataloguing all my books so I can be as organized as a librarian. And the kids'll use it when they start school. Don't worry, I'll come up with a new goal. I was thinking of building a greenhouse onto the back of the house, so I could start growing things. And I could dig up the yard and plant some tomato plants and lady peas. Okra."

"You hate okra. And growing things is not your gift." He pointed out the fake plants decorating every table and shelf. She had never been able to keep anything alive. As hard as she worked to perfect things, she couldn't perfect nature. It had a mind of its own.

"Okay," she conceded, "but maybe if I devoted myself to it, I could learn to grow things. If I had a greenhouse I could do it."

"Tory, you don't need a greenhouse, and you don't need to plow the backyard. You have enough to do."

"All right, fine. Then I won't grow things. I'll find something else."

He looked at her as if he didn't know what more to say to her, then ambled helplessly out of the room.

Tory dropped into a chair and covered her face with both hands. This was madness, she thought. Obsessive-compulsive madness. And she should know—she'd just finished reading a book on the subject.

Barry was right. She did have plenty to do without dragging out new hobbies. Her children needed her. Her husband needed her.

She took a deep breath, got up, and straightened the chairs. Standing in the doorway between the kitchen and the den, she saw the children lying on the floor watching a movie. Barry was sitting in his recliner, staring into space at thoughts she could only imagine.

"Hey, guys," she said. "What do you say we go out tonight? It's Saturday and we haven't done anything in a while. We could go get ice cream and maybe head down to the river, stand on the footbridge, and watch the barges come through."

"Yeah!" Spencer and Brittany said, jumping to their feet and bouncing like little windup toys.

Barry gave her a puzzled look. "Who are you?"

She grinned. "Don't press your luck."

He got up tentatively. "There must be some drawers you haven't cleaned out. Some closets that need dusting."

She got a pillow from the couch and threw it at him. He flinched. "Okay, so I was being obsessive," she said. "I've been feeling sorry for myself, and I've been making everybody miserable. But look at the bright side. The house is amazingly clean."

"Passes the white glove test," he agreed.

"Come on," she said, trying to work some fun into her voice. "Let's just get out of here."

"You sure you have time for fun?"

"You're about to lose your window of opportunity."

"Come on, kids," Barry yelled. "Let's go while Mom's in the mood!"

She picked up the pillow and placed it perfectly on the couch before she followed her family out the door.

Chapter Twenty

The Smoky Mountain fog had lifted early today, and the mountain range on the other side of the valley of Breezewood was green and majestic. Sylvia felt energized after riding her mare, Sunstreak, through the undeveloped back acres of their property. She trotted back to the stables, her hair mussed from the wind and her cheeks pink from the heat.

Gently, she removed the saddle, blanket, and bridle, and brushed down the horse before returning her to her colt in the corral. Then, dusting her hands off, she headed around the house to check her mail. Again, the sight of the hills took her breath away. She had been born and raised in Breezewood, and when she left for any length of time, her eyes yearned for the sight of those hills. She wondered if Sarah missed their mountains yet, or if Jeff ever thought of coming back. If they did, they hadn't mentioned it to her.

She opened the mailbox, hoping one of them had written, even though she'd talked to each of them on the phone just yesterday. She pulled out the bundle of bills and letters and advertisements, and fought disappointment when she saw that there was nothing from them.

"Sylvia!"

She looked up and saw Brenda coming. She waved and waited for her neighbor to cross the cul-de-sac.

"Time to visit?" Brenda asked.

"On a gorgeous day like this? I've been riding all morning. Just look at those mountains. Let's sit on my porch where we can see them."

Brenda followed her onto the porch and sat down on the swing. Sylvia took the rocker next to a pot of azaleas.

"So how's Joseph?" Sylvia asked her as she flipped through her mail.

"Okay, I guess."

Sylvia looked up. "You guess?"

Brenda's smile was uncharacteristically weak. "Well, Dr. Robinson isn't that sure. We've been seeing him twice a week for four weeks, and he keeps changing doses of medication. I thought Joseph would be better by now, but he always seems so tired and out of breath."

"He'll get better," Sylvia said. "Just give it time. Be patient."

"I'm trying."

She flipped through the rest of her mail. The return address from Masaya, Nicaragua, startled her. "Carlos!" she said, picturing the man they had met last year.

"Who's Carlos?" Brenda asked.

"A man in Nicaragua. Didn't I tell you about Carlos?"

"I don't think so."

Sylvia looked off toward the mountains and smiled, remembering. "Well, last year, when we were there, Carlos's wife Maria brought their son to Harry. He was having serious abdominal pain, and Harry diagnosed it as a ruptured appendix and operated on him."

"Harry saved his life, then," Brenda said.

"He sure did. And Maria was so grateful. After it was all over, Harry led her to Christ. Then she started weeping and telling us about her husband Carlos."

"She wanted Harry to witness to him?" Brenda asked.

"Well, yes, but frankly she didn't see any hope of Carlos's conversion. He's a baker, owns his own shop, and at the time, he was a real womanizer. Very handsome. Of course, Maria is very beautiful, too. But that didn't matter. Carlos kept mistresses and spent a lot of time with them."

"Poor woman."

"Yeah. Only we started praying for him with her, and I shared with her all the Scripture I could find about being a godly wife. I helped her memorize the passage in First Peter about keeping her behavior excellent so the unbelieving husband could be won without a word. She was determined to have a gentle, quiet spirit, and to be a model wife instead of the victim he used to come home to."

Brenda's eyes misted over, and Sylvia suddenly realized that Brenda could relate to Maria, even though David had never been unfaithful.

"I hope you told her it takes a long time," Brenda said. "The Holy Spirit has to do it."

"That's the thing," Sylvia told her, leaning forward with enthusiasm. "The Holy Spirit *did* do it. About ten days later, Maria convinced Carlos to come to church with her so he could thank Harry for healing their son. The missionary who preached that day delivered a sermon that shot right into Carlos's heart. He *ran* down to the altar and fell to his knees, sobbing."

Sylvia saw the emotion in Brenda's eyes as she pictured the scene, probably imagining David in Carlos's place, and she remembered why she hadn't told Brenda this story before. She had feared it would frustrate her spirit and make her question God's silence to her own prayers.

"What a beautiful story," Brenda whispered. "Did it change his life?"

"You bet it did. He's very active in the church there, and Maria has kept in touch with me to let me know what a wonderful husband he's become." She looked down at the envelope and tore it open. "Carlos has never written to us himself. Harry will be so thrilled to hear from him."

Her eyes scanned the first few lines. "Oh, Brenda! He's committed his life to full-time Christian service. His church is raising money for him to come to the States to study in a seminary, so that he can go back to Nicaragua and start his own church." She read further. "He wants to know how much money we think they'll need to raise altogether for housing and food and tuition, and anything else that might come up that he hasn't thought of. And he needs help deciding on a seminary."

Brenda grinned. "What a miracle. It gives me hope."

Sylvia dropped the letter on her lap and stared off into the breeze. "Yeah. That's the joy of mission work. That's why Harry wants to go back there."

"Think of all the fruit Carlos is going to bear," Brenda said. "All because Harry was there to save their son's life, and you were there to teach Maria how to be a godly wife."

Sylvia gazed down at the letter again.

"So have you made up your mind about the mission field?" Brenda asked.

Sylvia shook her head. "I've prayed about it. I've told the Lord that I don't want to go. But I've asked Him to change my heart if He wants me to."

"That's fair," Brenda said. "I'll pray that for you, too."

That afternoon when Harry got home, Sylvia gave him the letter. He shed a few tears of his own and started praying immediately for Carlos and Maria and the plans they were making. Then he got out his calculator and began figuring what it would cost them to come to America to study. He would be on the phone for days, Sylvia knew, trying to line up scholarships and grants and donations from people who could help put Carlos through school. They both knew that the little Nicaraguan church Carlos attended would not be able to raise the kind of money Carlos would need.

Sylvia found her own mind racing with possibilities—and she knew that God had put those thoughts into her mind. He was showing her things she needed to consider, things she needed to offer, priorities she needed to acknowledge—but she knew she wasn't ready yet. Sweetly, generously, Harry continued to give her the time she needed, and nothing more was said.

Chapter Twenty-One

It had been five weeks since Joseph's birthday party, and the medicine had not helped Joseph's condition. They'd had twice-a-week visits to Dr. Robinson, and at every visit Brenda saw the strain and tension on the doctor's face as he changed the medication or juggled doses, hoping to help things along. She'd kept Joseph as quiet as possible for the past few weeks. Even though she normally didn't homeschool during the summer, she'd continued it with Joseph just to keep him still and focused on anything other than his failing heart. He slept much of the time, and during those quiet moments, she would sit on the bed and pray for him. She could see in the pallid color of his skin and the deep circles under his eyes, in his shortness of breath after any exertion at all, in the dizziness that came more often than it went, and in the swelling of his ankles, that he was only getting worse.

All this week he'd been moody and depressed, and she knew that he needed to get out, so yesterday she had made the announcement that they would be taking a field trip today to the Adventure Museum—one of her children's favorite places. Joseph's tired eyes had danced with excitement, though that seemed to be the extent of his celebration.

She had invited Tory, Brittany, and Spencer to come with them, hoping Tory could help by dropping them off at the door so that Joseph wouldn't have far to walk. She planned to borrow a wheelchair when they got there, and she would push Joseph around so he wouldn't have to exert himself as they went from one hands-on experiment to another.

But when she went into his room to see if he was ready, he was sitting on the bed with tears on his face and his sneakers in his lap.

"Joseph, what's wrong, honey?"

He rubbed the tears on his face. "I can't get my shoes on."

"Well, I'll help you, sweetie. You don't have to cry." She took the shoes and stooped down in front of him. When she lifted his foot to slide it into the shoe, she saw how swollen it was. No wonder the shoe wouldn't go on.

"Joseph, do your feet hurt?"

"No, ma'am," he said. "They're just swollen. I can't get them on. But I want to go, Mama. I can't go without shoes ..."

"Wear your flip-flops," she said, going to his closet. "That'll be more comfortable, anyway." She got out the flip-flops and turned back to her son. He was wiping new tears as they ran down his face. "Honey, it's okay. This is nothing new; your feet have been a little swollen every day. The doctor knows about it."

"I know."

"Then why are you crying?"

He shrugged again, and hiccuped a sob. "I don't know."

But she knew. This constant sickness, all the medication, the doctor visits—they were taking their toll on her son. He needed this outing. He needed to get his mind off his problems and have a little fun.

When they arrived at the museum and Tory let them out at the door, Joseph argued weakly that he didn't want to be pushed around in a wheelchair because it was too much like a stroller and he wasn't a baby. But by the time they'd gotten through the ticket line, he'd given in without a fight.

When Tory came in from parking the car, she let go of Brittany and Spencer and they hurried to their favorite exhibits in the art section as fast as they could, as if they feared someone would reach them before they did and suck all the fun out of them. Rachel pushed Joseph's wheelchair into the art room, and Brenda and Tory followed behind.

Tory was dressed in a matching shorts outfit that complemented her trim figure, and her hair and makeup were impeccably done. Brenda had only had time to run a brush through her hair and pull on a pair of jeans and a T-shirt. She felt frumpy in comparison.

"So how's Joseph doing on his medication?" Tory asked softly.

Brenda struggled to maintain her smile for the sake of the kids. "Not well," she admitted.

"I didn't think so," Tory said. "He doesn't look like he feels well at all. So what are they going to do now?"

"I don't know," Brenda whispered. "The doctor seems to think that as long as his heart is functioning at fifty percent, that's good enough. I just keep thinking that sooner or later this has got to get better. But I'm really worried."

"You worried?" Tory asked. "I never thought that was possible."

Brenda knew Tory meant that as a compliment, but she almost resented it. Sometimes, she was just weak, and she hated for people to be shocked by it. She went to a bench against the wall and sat down. Tory followed, still searching Brenda's face.

"You know, it *is* human to worry," Tory offered.

"But what's the point?" Brenda asked. "God knows what's going to happen tomorrow, ten years from now—He knows the very day that we're going to die. What's the point of worrying when He's got it all under control?" She felt Tory's eyes still upon her as she watched Joseph in his wheelchair, having fun for the first time since they'd rolled their yard with toilet paper.

"I know you're right," Tory said, "but worrying is one of my worst faults. I'm trying to give it up, though. That, and writing."

Glad to be off the subject of her worry, Brenda shot Tory a grin. "You're not giving up writing."

"Yes, I am. Already have." She raised her right hand as if making a vow. "I've written my last word."

"Well, you can't do that," she said. "You're called."

Tory laughed sarcastically. "Yeah? Called to do *what?*"

"You have a gift. The stuff you've let me read, it was wonderful. I don't know if you have a right to give it up."

Tory's smile died, and she frowned thoughtfully at Brenda for a moment. "I'm not sure," Tory said finally, "but that might be one of the nicest things anybody's ever said to me."

Brenda laughed. "Oh, come on."

"Really," Tory said, still serious. "I hadn't thought of it that way. As an obligation, I mean."

"Well, you should. Just because it didn't work out that one time doesn't mean it's not meant to be. For heaven's sake, how is God ever going to teach you if things go perfectly well all the time?"

"Oh, I don't know. He could send books. I could read the lessons He wants to teach me." She winked, and Brenda laughed. Brittany flopped by with ponytails wagging and both shoes untied. Tory stopped her and tied them, then with a pat on her bottom, sent her on her way.

Brenda's eyes followed the comical child. "So is Brittany getting excited about starting school?"

"Oh yeah," Tory said. "We've been shopping for school clothes and supplies. I never dreamed I'd have a baby in school this soon. Seems like it's flown by. But I have to tell you, I'm looking forward to it a little. Maybe I'll have more time to think."

"And write?" Brenda asked with a smirk.

"No, not write," Tory said stubbornly. "I told you. I'm through with that."

"Yeah, well, we'll see," Brenda said. "So you're going to send them to public school?"

Tory nodded. "I feel pretty good about our school district. And by the time they get into junior high and high school, I'm counting on Cathy having worked out all the sex ed problems."

"Maybe," Brenda said, forcing herself to keep her mouth shut about the virtues of homeschooling over public education. It was something she felt passionately about, but she didn't want to sound condemning or heap guilt on Tory. They'd had this conversation before, and Brenda knew that Tory thought she was a little paranoid.

Though Brenda chose not to say anything, her silence spoke volumes, and Tory responded. "I know, I know. Homeschooling is the best way. But you have to have a certain temperament for that, and I just don't have it."

"Don't kid yourself," Brenda said. "It's not that hard. I get to stay home and do something important for the four people I love most in the entire world. I don't have to let anybody else's crazy ideas and influences get pounded into their heads. I'm guarding their hearts and teaching them what's important, and I get to learn all over again. What greater calling could there be?"

"I see your point, and I admire it," Tory said. "I really do. But if everybody took their kids out of public schools . . ."

"I know the argument," Brenda said. "Then the schools would really go to pot. And you're right. I'm not suggesting that everybody take their kids out."

Tory smiled. "Just the Christians?"

"No, not even them."

"Because a few minutes ago you told me that I'm called to be a writer, something I can't do as long as I have two kids at home all the time. Plus, there are millions of women who work because they *have* to, who don't have the option to pull their kids out of school and teach them at home. Besides, I loved the school experience. I loved all the friends I had and all the functions and events . . . I don't want Britty and Spencer to miss that."

"I'm just saying that if they go, you need to stay on top of things. Watch carefully what they're taught, what they're learning. Get involved. And then when they get home, spend a lot of time teaching them the important stuff."

"Like the Bible?"

"Yes, like the Bible."

Tory gave her a contemplative look, then asked, "Does that bother David? That you spend so much time teaching the kids Scripture?"

"Not really. He feels like the lessons there are good moral lessons. Of course he doesn't believe there's anything more there."

"Do the kids get confused? I mean, since they know their dad doesn't believe, do they ever question it?"

"Sometimes," she said. "It's a problem, but I'm praying for him." She paused and considered whether to confide in Tory. "David was taught the Bible as a child—but in a real distorted way. The Christians who influenced him growing up probably meant well, but they sent him running the other way. That's just a reminder to me that what my kids are taught, and who teaches them, is critical. You can be taught the right things by the wrong people, or the right things in the wrong way, and have it turn out worse than if you'd never heard it."

Tory seemed to process that as she kept her eyes on Brenda. "Do you ever regret marrying a non-Christian?"

The question almost startled her. "I wasn't a Christian, either, when we married," she said. "David's a wonderful husband and father. I just wish . . ." Her words trailed off, and she averted her eyes.

"That he had your faith," Tory prompted.

"It would be really great to have that in common," Brenda said, meeting Tory's eyes again. "But it's okay. I'm praying hard, and I know the Lord will answer. After all, it is to His glory."

"If a man could love God just by being around you," Tory said, "I'm sure he would."

Tears misted in Brenda's eyes, and she hugged her neighbor. "That's sweet, Tory. Wish it was so."

"No, I mean it," Tory insisted. "You're an exemplary wife, a wonderful mother, a model Christian. If you could twirl a baton I'd have to hate you."

Brenda laughed. "Well, thank goodness I can't."

"Really," Tory went on, leaning her head back against the wall. "I wish I were more like you. If I were one of the Israelites, I'd be grumbling about the manna and quail. I'd keep complaining that the pillar of fire just kept leading us in circles. I'd probably even be one of the people to melt down my jewelry and contribute to the golden calf."

Brenda sighed. "I think there's some of that in all of us."

Spencer came running. "Mommy, they're about to start the art class. Can I go? Please, can I go?"

"Yeah, but I have to come with you." He grabbed her hand and pulled. She winked at Brenda and followed her skipping son to the art room.

Brenda went into the room where Joseph was and stood at his wheelchair. She wondered if the other kids ever resented the fact that she spent so much time with him. It was just maternal instinct to hover over the one who needed her the most. Daniel, Rachel, and Leah were so self-sufficient, and they seemed to understand that their brother was in trouble.

Joseph got out of his wheelchair and took a few steps into the photographic booth where he could make faces, freeze-frame them, and print them out. It was his favorite thing in the museum, and it produced something he could take home and put on his bedroom wall. She glanced back at the other kids. Leah and Rachel were playing with the ink and stamps, and Daniel was creating some elaborate masterpiece they would hang on the refrigerator door. Smiling, she looked back in the booth at Joseph.

He had stopped making faces at himself and was leaning against the wall in the booth.

She ducked in. "Honey, you ready to come out?"

"Just a minute," he said, breathless.

She could see that something was passing over him—dizziness, light-headedness, perhaps. She waited for it to pass, but it didn't.

"Honey, come get back in the wheelchair and we'll go get you something to drink."

He continued to sit, limply leaning against the wall, so she reached in, took his arm, and tried to coax him out. His right hand came up to cover his chest.

And her own heart seemed to stop.

"Honey, does your chest hurt?" The tremulous words came out on a rush. He nodded slightly, got up, took a step toward the wheelchair. "Come on," she said. "Just sit down. You're going to be all right."

But before he could reach the wheelchair he fell and hit the floor like a rock.

Chapter Twenty-Two

As Brenda and David waited for the doctor to come, Brenda found the silence in the hospital consultation room to be smothering—but appropriate. There were no words that could adequately describe the fear she'd felt waiting for the ambulance to come get Joseph. She had wept hysterically as the paramedics barked out Joseph's vital signs and conversed with hushed, panicky concern about the need to stabilize him en route to St. Francis. Although no one had said so, she was certain that his heart had failed. Like a sixty-year-old man, her baby had lain on the floor of the Adventure Museum in full cardiac arrest.

Brenda had ridden in the ambulance with him, and Tory had called David, then taken the other kids home. The emergency room personnel had treated Joseph like a Code Blue, which had frightened her to the point of dysfunction. David had arrived just in time to hold her together, and someone had shuffled them both into this room to wait for the verdict. In her wildest dreams, she had never anticipated sitting in a room waiting to be told if her son was dead or alive.

She'd been thankful when Harry had appeared from his office, after Tory alerted him that Joseph had collapsed. He had gone to check with the doctors and promised to give them news as soon as he knew something. But so far, no one had come to tell them anything.

David got up and walked around the room, staring vacantly at the cheap oil paintings on the wall. Brenda closed her eyes and tried to pray. She wished the words she had given to Tory at the museum could filter into her heart right now. What was it she'd said about there being no point in worrying because God was in control? He knew everything that was going to happen. Why couldn't she rest in that peace now?

Panic rose in her heart, along with the overwhelming sense that there was something *she* needed to do to keep Joseph alive. She could make her heart beat for his, make her lungs expand in and out to give him oxygen—she could keep him alive, if they would just let her go to him . . .

The door opened, and they both jumped. Harry and Dr. Robinson came in, looking like weary soldiers after a crucial battle. It took every ounce of restraint she possessed to keep from attacking them with her questions. Solemnly, Dr. Robinson and Harry shook David's hand, then Brenda's. Desperately, she watched their eyes for a clue.

"I've asked Harry to come in with me to talk to you," Dr. Robinson said, taking a seat across from them at the table.

"Is he dead?" Brenda choked out.

"No, no." Harry sat down next to her and touched her shoulder. "We would have told you."

She felt a rush of gratitude followed immediately by renewed grief, and a fresh onslaught of tears ambushed her. She wilted against David.

"The news . . . it isn't good, is it?" David asked as he held her. Brenda pulled herself together and sat up, unwilling to miss a single word.

Harry and Dr. Robinson exchanged looks. Finally, Harry spoke. "The medicine isn't working. Joseph's heart is functioning at fifteen percent capacity, and what happened today was a very close call."

"*Fifteen percent?*" David threw the words back as if they were dynamite. "Why didn't we know this before?"

"He wasn't this bad at his last checkup," Dr. Robinson said. "His decline has been pretty rapid."

"What's going to happen?" David asked, getting out of his chair, red-faced, and facing off with the two men as if they were threatening him. "'Cause you can't just keep on putting a Band-Aid on it, pouring drugs down him . . ."

"No, we can't." Again, the two doctors exchanged looks, as if silently deciding which one would go on.

"There's really only one option at this point," Dr. Robinson said quietly.

"Surgery, right?" David prodded.

It was not so much what they were saying as what they were not saying that alerted Brenda. She got slowly to her feet, her tears falling freely. "Harry, what is it that we can do to save Joseph?"

"He needs a heart transplant," Harry said.

Brenda's mouth fell open, and she sank back down.

"A heart transplant?" David's words were hoarse, just above a whisper. "But he's just a little boy."

"It's the only thing that'll save him. He's in very bad shape."

"But isn't there some other less risky kind of surgery?"

Dr. Robinson shook his head. "The damage is too great. He's going to have to have a transplant, or he'll die."

Brenda and David stared at each other, horror stricken, as if they each silently urged the other to do something to stop this madness.

"Where . . . where do we have to go . . . for a transplant?" she asked.

"Until a year ago, the only place in the state was Knoxville. But since St. Francis is a teaching hospital, we started doing them here. Our transplant team is excellent. One of the best in the South. They do a wonderful job, and the survival rate is very high."

"Survival rate?" Brenda muttered. It wasn't a question really, just words she never thought would have anything to do with her children.

"So when—when do we do this?" David choked out.

"We have to wait for a heart to become available."

"And how long will that be?"

"There's no telling," Dr. Robinson said. "The wait is usually a couple of months. It could be longer, it could be less. It just depends on when a match is available. The transplant team will meet with you tomorrow, and we have a family support team that will help you tremendously. We'll have to start testing Joseph immediately to make sure he's a good candidate for transplant, but I feel sure he will be."

"But he doesn't *have* two months if his heart is only functioning at fifteen percent," David said. "And what about next week—it could be ten percent, or five. It could stop altogether."

"We're going to put him on a Left Ventricular Assist Device, otherwise known as a Heart Mate. It's a portable heart that will keep him stable until the transplant. We'll have to keep him here in the hospital," Dr. Robinson said. "But that will keep him alive until the heart is found."

"Keep him alive," Brenda repeated mechanically.

"What is this . . . this Heart Mate?"

"It's about the size of a hockey puck, and it weighs about two and a half pounds. We implant it just under the diaphragm, and then we use an air compressor outside the body to power it. It has a battery that lasts up to thirty minutes, so he'll be able to detach from the machine and walk up and down the halls a little, to get some exercise. We'll also have him doing some supervised exercise and physical therapy to build him up for the surgery."

Brenda was speechless. She couldn't find rational thoughts, much less words.

"So he's going to have to stay in the hospital for weeks? Maybe months?" David asked in a shaky voice.

"That's right," Harry said. "It's the only option."

"I don't believe this." Brenda got up and walked across the room. "How could this happen? Just a few weeks ago, he was so healthy. How could one little virus do this?"

Neither of the doctors had any answers.

"Are you prepared to stay with him while he's here?" Dr. Robinson asked gently.

Brenda shook her brain out of its reverie. "Uh . . . yes, of course."

"What about your other children?" Harry asked.

"They'll be fine. I have to stay here with him."

David nodded. "One of us will be with him at all times."

"Doctor, are you sure he'll make it?" Brenda asked. "I mean, until a heart becomes available? Could he die before it happens?"

"Eighty percent of our critical patients on Heart Mate survive the wait for the transplant."

"*Eighty* percent?" she asked, astounded. "That means *twenty* percent don't?"

Harry hesitated, then replied simply, "He's in very good hands, Brenda."

She leaned back hard in her chair, unable to drag her mind away from the odds.

"We'll need to put him in the cardiac unit, rather than the children's hospital," Dr. Robinson went on, "so it could be a challenge to keep him occupied."

"Why there?" David asked. "Wouldn't he be better off with other children?"

"Emotionally and mentally, maybe. But they're not equipped to handle this kind of thing over there. Our transplant teams are located near the cardiac unit, and we really need to have him there so he can get the best of care."

"He's just a little boy," Brenda whispered again.

"A very sick little boy," Dr. Robinson said.

Brenda went into David's arms and buried her face against his chest. He held her tightly and looked over her head to the doctors. "What now?" David asked.

"Well, now we need to admit him and get him on the Heart Mate. Then we start the series of tests that will tell us what we need to know."

"But right now, before we do anything else," Harry said, "there's something I'd like to do. If you don't mind, I'd like to pray with you."

David shot him a surprised look. Brenda knew he'd never met a doctor who prayed with his patients. He didn't argue, probably figuring that anything they tried was better than nothing. He held Brenda tightly as Harry quietly, simply, asked God to see them through this crisis.

As soon as they'd finished praying, David let her go. He got up, slid his hands into his pockets, and faced off with the doctors again. "I have to ask you a question that'll probably seem pretty callous," he said. "But it has to be considered."

"What?"

"How much is all this going to cost?"

Dr. Robinson exchanged looks with Harry again.

"Because I don't have very good health insurance," David said. "We still haven't paid what we owe from the last time Joseph was here. And I don't want somebody in the hospital credit department finding that out and cutting off Joseph's care halfway through this. I'm a self-employed cabinetmaker. We have all the insurance I can afford, but it won't pay everything."

"Most policies cover heart transplants now," Harry said.

"*If* ours does, it'll still only pay seventy percent," David said. "We've got to pay thirty, plus a two-thousand-dollar deductible. How much are we talking?" He looked from one doctor to the other, his eyes glistening with tears. "Look, I'm just saying that I need to know ahead of time so I can work my tail off to earn it. I'm going to provide what my boy needs. I'm not going to let him die because of money."

"It can cost between fifty-seven thousand and a hundred ten thousand," Harry said. "It all depends on how long he has to be here before the heart is available, what has to be done in the interim, and how well his recovery goes."

David did the math in his head. "So, including the deductible, we're talking anywhere from nineteen thousand to thirty-five thousand, out of pocket. Possibly more." He looked at his feet. "Well, we can't get a second mortgage, because we already have one. But maybe if we sold the house . . ."

"Before you consider that, you need to talk to social services. There are programs that can help," Harry said.

David shook his head. "I want any decisions about Joseph's care to be made on the basis of his medical needs—not on the basis of cost. If social services was involved, I'd be afraid of that."

"You don't need to worry about that," Harry said. "It doesn't work that way."

David wasn't convinced. "I'm willing to pay whatever it takes. I just need to be able to plan on it."

"Well, a lot depends on how long the wait is," Harry said. "Look, if I have to pay the bills myself, David, Joseph is going to get his transplant. We'll raise the money. Don't worry about that. You have enough to think about."

Brenda wiped her eyes, praying silently that Harry's open, unashamed prayer—and his willingness to act on those prayers—would affect David. That faith-in-action was something David had rarely, if ever, seen in Christendom; it was just the opposite of the abuses that had soured him to the whole institution.

She was grateful to Harry for another reason, too: His promise to see this through gave her strength, reminding her that God was working.

But she wasn't sure that her faith was much stronger than David's. Not when her child's life hung in the balance.

Chapter Twenty-Three

As David watched over Joseph, who slept soundly in his hospital room, Brenda went to the chapel to have a word with God. Kneeling at the altar at the front of the room, she gave in to the heartbreak and despair closing over her. But as earnestly as she prayed, those prayers didn't feel as if they connected.

What is it, God? she asked fervently. *Is there some sin in my life that's keeping You from hearing me?* She had confessed everything she could think of—even the despair that, she feared, demonstrated a lack of faith. But she did have faith. She knew that God would do His will in her family. She just didn't think that will was going to coincide with hers. Desperately, angrily, she pleaded for mercy, for healing, for God to align His will more closely with hers.

Then she chastised herself for such a selfish prayer. Would it make God turn away and quit listening altogether?

When the door opened, Brenda turned and saw Sylvia coming toward her. She got up to give the older woman a hug, unable to hide the despair on her face.

"David said you'd be here," Sylvia said.

They sat down on the front pew, and Sylvia gave Brenda a handkerchief. Thankfully, Brenda blew her nose and wiped her face.

"Brenda, I know how hard this must be for you," Sylvia said. "You must just be a wreck."

"I am," Brenda admitted.

"Is there anything I can do?"

Brenda shrugged. "You can explain some things to me, maybe." She could see on Sylvia's face that she knew some of the questions she had. That she had struggled with the answers herself.

"The elders prayed over him at church," Brenda said, her eyes glistening with tears. "We prayed for healing, and it didn't come."

"I know," Sylvia said. She touched her shoulder, squeezed it, and wiped her own eyes with her other hand.

"I did that against David's will. He has this . . . this thing . . . against church. It goes back to his childhood. He warned me not to do it, because he thought it would traumatize Joseph. But I did it anyway, without telling him. I thought it was the right thing to do, and what David didn't know wouldn't hurt him. I think that's what messed things all up, my doing it against David's will. God didn't honor it."

"Oh, honey." Sylvia made her look up at her. "God wouldn't punish you for following his own instructions. That's not what's wrong. Brenda, God's not a genie in a bottle. He doesn't answer prayers on demand. If God chooses not to heal Joseph, it must be for some other reason than that. I'm sure you prayed about it before you asked for the elders to pray for Joseph. I'm sure you thought it was one of those times when you have to serve God before your husband."

"I did. I thought that, Sylvia."

"Our prayers aren't buttons we push to get the results we want, Brenda. It's all tied into God's will. We don't see the whole picture, but He does."

Brenda looked up at Sylvia, her eyes pleading. "Sylvia, why does the Bible say that the prayer offered in faith will make the sick person well? Why does it say that?"

"Brenda, have you ever known God's Word not to be truth?"

She didn't even have to think about that. "No, never."

"So that passage must be truth."

"Then why didn't it happen?" Brenda asked. "Why wasn't he healed?"

"Because God's timing isn't our timing, Brenda. Maybe He plans to heal him through this heart transplant. Maybe He just needs for you to trust in Him a little longer."

"I have to," she said. "He's the only one with any power to change things."

"That's true," Sylvia said. "And it would bring real glory to Him if He cured Joseph."

"But see, that's just it." Brenda got to her feet and went to the altar, then turned back to Sylvia. "What keeps going through my mind is that sometimes *death* brings glory to God. Sometimes people are won to Christ through someone else's death, and I'm so afraid that's how He's going to use Joseph." Her voice squeaked with the words, and she broke down and covered her face with both hands.

Sylvia pulled Brenda into her arms. She dropped her forehead against Brenda's neck and held her for a long time. Through her grief, Brenda gradually realized that she was breaking Sylvia's heart, too. That was the last thing she wanted to do. She stepped back and tried to pull herself together. She looked up at the stained glass window with the dove representing the Holy Spirit, flying down from heaven.

"My mother died of breast cancer years ago," Sylvia said. "What God taught me through that death is that God gives wonderful blessings to us, sometimes in the form of people we love. And we have to hold those blessings in open hands, willing to let Him take them back if He chooses. We can't hold them in clenched fists, Brenda, because they're not ours. None of what we have is ours."

Brenda tore her eyes from the window. "I know that's true," she choked out. "I have to be willing to give my blessings back, whenever He comes to take them. But I'm just not there yet."

Sylvia wiped her own tears and shook her head dolefully. "Neither am I. I've been praying that He'll teach me, with my own kids, and they're not even sick. They're happy and healthy—just not with me. I feel so ashamed."

"Don't feel ashamed. We both love our children. For me, you can pray that I'll know for sure that God is watching over Joseph. And that everything that happens, happens because God is guiding it, that there's a reason, and that it'll work for good. I know those things in my head, Sylvia, but please pray that I'll embrace them in my heart. And pray for David."

Sylvia nodded, promising that she would.

"You know, there have been days—before Joseph got sick—when I've prayed so earnestly for David that I've told God if He had to take my life to save David's soul, I was willing. But I never volunteered Joseph's life. And I didn't expect Him to take it."

"What if that is what He has to do to bring David to Christ? What if that is God's way?"

Brenda sank back down. "I know how Jesus felt in Gethsemane. 'Let this cup pass from me.'" She covered her face and sobbed quietly for a moment, then took a deep breath and looked at her friend again. "Oh, Sylvia, pray that this is not the cup I have to drink."

Sylvia hugged her fiercely again. "Can I pray for you now?"

"Yes, please," she whispered.

Sylvia began to pray.

CHAPTER *Twenty-Four*

Tory fed Rachel, Leah, and Daniel at her house that night, an event Brittany and Spencer considered the highlight of their week. They thought it was a party, but the Dodd children knew better. They had seen their little brother lose consciousness on the floor of the Adventure Museum, and it hadn't been the first time. Watching the ambulance carry him away had been traumatic for all of them. Now Tory hoped she could keep their minds off his condition until they heard from their parents.

But when Sylvia came over and asked her to step out on the front porch, she knew that the news was not good. "Brenda's been really busy and preoccupied with Joseph, so she hasn't had the chance to call," Sylvia said, keeping her voice low. "But she asked me to come tell you what they found out."

Tory waited.

"They told Brenda and David that Joseph needs a heart transplant or he'll die."

Tory felt the blood draining from her face. Slowly she reached for the chain on the swing and felt her way down. "Heart transplant?"

"I'm afraid so."

"Poor Brenda." The words came on a rush of breath.

"You said it." Sylvia sat down next to her, and the swing began to creak with their forward and backward motion. "They've admitted Joseph to the hospital. He'll have to stay there until a heart's available."

"How long will that be?"

"We don't know. It could be days, weeks, months . . ."

"And Joseph will have to be there all that time?"

"That's right. His heart's only functioning at fifteen percent. They have to keep him stabilized."

"So what's she going to do? I mean, with the other kids?"

"I'll help as much as I can. But that's not the most pressing problem right now. The biggest problem, according to Harry, is the money."

"What do you mean?"

"Well, they're self-employed, so their health insurance isn't very good. They're going to have to come up with at least thirty percent. A heart transplant is very expensive."

"What will they do?"

"I'm not sure. David told Harry a second mortgage is out—they already have one. He's thinking about selling the house."

"*What?*" Tory exclaimed. "They can't! Don't they have social services or something to help people who can't pay?"

Sylvia hesitated before answering. "David refused to contact social services. He had some stubborn idea that Joseph's care would be inferior if the hospital knew of his financial condition. He's determined to raise the money himself. But I don't think he can, and I'm like you—if he has to sell the house to do it, I don't want him to. But their share of the expenses could easily be more than David makes in a year." Sylvia met Tory's eyes. "So I'm going to do my best to help raise the money, before he has to sell the house. But I'll need help."

"Of course. Barry and I will do what we can. We don't have much extra, but—"

"I'm not asking for money from you," Sylvia said, "but I need some ideas. Ways to get the community involved. People would help if they knew. My church, your church, her church . . ."

"Of course. Surely people will help."

Spencer burst through the front door. "Mommy, Britty got out the gummy bears and she won't give me some. And there ain't enough for all of us."

"Aren't enough," Tory corrected. "Spencer, go back in there and tell her I don't want her to have any sugar before bedtime."

"But it ain't sugar. It's just gummy bears!"

"Tell her not to give them out till I come back in." She got up, and Sylvia followed her to the door.

"I should take the Dodd kids home," Sylvia said. "They need to sleep in their own beds."

"Are you sure?" Tory asked. "I'd be happy to watch them."

"No, it would really make me feel better to do something." Sylvia sighed. "And heaven knows I don't have anything better to do. Harry'll come over and help out when he gets home. Besides, they're good kids. They won't be a problem."

"All right. Are you going to tell them about Joseph?"

"No," Sylvia told her. "I'll let David do that when he gets home."

Tory's pale eyes settled on the Dodds' house. "How are Brenda and David taking it?"

Sylvia struggled for words. "It's hard. Really hard. They're taking it like we would, if Joseph was ours."

"This will be tough on the whole family."

Sylvia nodded. "We'll just have to help." She glanced at the house directly across from the Dodds'. "Look, before I take the kids home, I think I'll run over to Cathy's and tell her what happened. I know she'll want to know, and maybe she'll have some ideas."

Tory nodded mutely and watched Sylvia cross the cul-de-sac.

Chapter Twenty-Five

Cathy sat at her computer in the dining room, typing in addresses for every home she'd been able to find in the school district. Since the school board had refused to give her names and addresses of all the families in the district, she had spent the previous two weekends driving down every street in the area and recording the addresses. She would do a blitz mailing—send a letter to every taxpayer in the district, addressed to "Parents of School Children." It wouldn't apply to every resident, but at least she would know she was reaching nearly all the parents that way.

"So what's this for again?" Mark asked as he faced the stack of letters she wanted him to stuff into envelopes.

"For your education and your moral health," Cathy explained matter-of-factly.

Annie, who had also been enlisted, made a derisive noise of disgust.

"What?" Mark asked.

"It's about sex ed at our schools, meathead," Annie told her brother. "And the fact that Mom is trying to ruin our lives."

"How am I ruining your life?" Cathy flung back.

"Get real, Mom," Rick said, coming in from the other room. "Our friends are already calling you 'the condom lady.' They think it's a big joke that you're fighting the school on this. I may never show my face in that place again. I'll probably run away before school starts in the fall."

"He's right, Mom," Annie said, and Cathy would have marked this rare moment of sibling agreement on the calendar if she hadn't been so appalled at their attitudes. "You wouldn't believe what a hard time we're getting. Today at the Y pool, Selena Hartfield started telling everybody that our mom didn't want them talking to her kids about sex at school 'cause we don't know the facts of life yet. It embarrassed me to death. If you wind up making any more of a deal about this than you already have, I'm going to live with Dad, 'cause I don't need this."

"I'm doing this for your own good," Cathy said. "The school doesn't have the right to pour junk into your heads, and if they can't even let a mother view the video they showed you, something's wrong. If I didn't care about you, I wouldn't go to all this trouble. You think I like spending every minute of my spare time on this?"

"Yes," Annie said. "I think you do. It's given you a life, even if it means that we can't show our faces out of the house for the rest of the summer."

"Isn't that just a little dramatic?" Cathy asked her. "So far, you haven't spent two straight hours in the house, unless you're sleeping. I think your social life is fine. Too good, in fact."

Annie shrugged. "Well, maybe for now. But when you start making speeches at the school board meeting ... Besides, look at poor Rick. His social life was already bad enough, and now he's practically an outcast."

"I am not!" Rick said. "Why don't you shut up?"

"*You* shut up. Mom and I are having a conversation." She turned back to her mother and crossed her arms belligerently.

"Mom, I'm sorry, but I have to take a stand. I refuse to be a part of this. Rick and Mark can stuff envelopes if they want, but I'm standing up for my principles."

"Principles? What principles? You're standing up for the right to have condoms passed out in the school?"

Annie looked flustered, then quickly rallied. "Mom, you just don't understand. Some people need them."

Cathy couldn't believe her ears. "Annie, tell me you don't mean that."

"I *do.* Not me, Mom, but other people. They're going to do things anyway, so you might as well arm them so they don't get diseases and stuff."

"She's brainwashed," Cathy said to no one in particular. "I'm too late. They've already brainwashed her." She covered her face with her hands, then realized she couldn't just play dead. She looked up, breathing in enough energy for the fight. "Annie, it's wrong to have sex before marriage, no matter what your friends or your teachers or your boyfriends say."

"Why?" Annie demanded. "If two people really love each other, and they're not, like, sleeping around, then why shouldn't they?"

"Because!" Cathy racked her brain for a ready reason, but they all seemed to escape her. "It's not the decent thing to do. It's . . . it's bad for you. For a lot of reasons."

"Okay, it's bad because of, like, pregnancy and AIDS. But if they're protected so those things don't happen—"

"It says not to do it in the Bible!" Cathy said, suddenly relieved that the thought had come to her. "It says it clearly."

"Where?" Annie asked. "Show me. Sarah Beth says that it tells you not to have adultery, but that's because someone's getting hurt in adultery. If it's between two consenting people who aren't hurting anybody—"

"Sarah Beth is fifteen years old!" Cathy shouted. "You're going to listen to her word over mine?"

"At least she has documentation."

Cathy wanted to throw something. "Look, I don't know where it says that in the Bible, but I *know* it talks about fornication. I'll find it." She felt flustered and frustrated, and furious at herself for not knowing Scripture.

"Well, even if you do, I'm not sure I buy into the Bible, anyway. It's outdated, Mom. Those rules may have worked in the Stone Age, but things have changed."

"Yeah, things have changed," Mark agreed.

"Things have *not* changed! The Bible is still true." Her voice broke off with the last words, and a lump rose in her throat. How could she have let this happen? How could she have raised her kids without the one value system they needed? How could she explain morals to them if they didn't have anything to base them on?

"I believe it's wrong to have sex before marriage," Rick said quietly, as if he could see his mother needed help.

Cathy fought to hold back her tears. "Thank you, Rick. That gives me some comfort."

"That's just because you're afraid of girls," Annie told her brother.

"I am not!"

"He's shy, Mom. Look at him. How often does he even go on dates?"

"I'm going to homecoming, doofus. I can get a date anytime I want!"

"That's enough!" Cathy belted out. Red-faced, she stood up and grabbed a stack of envelopes. "Sit down, Annie, and don't say another word."

"What? I told you I'm not helping with this! It's propaganda, and I don't want any part of it!"

"Sit!" Cathy shouted. "Now!"

Annie didn't sit, but she jerked the envelopes out of her mother's hand. "Rick, you too," Cathy ordered. "Start stuffing. Mark, you take these."

Annie shook her head with disbelief. "Guess I'll have to run away and live with Dad."

"I'm the one who's about to run away!" Cathy shouted. She forced herself to rein her temper in, and sat back down. "Oh, and Annie?" she said in a quieter voice that simmered with fury. "Don't threaten me with your I'm-going-to-live-with-my-daddy routine anymore, because it sends me into a rage, and I've been known to take away privileges for entire months for that, haven't I, Rick?"

"Yes, ma'am," Rick muttered.

"And you want a good reason not to have sex before marriage? Try this one. Because if I think you're even *thinking* about it, I'll ground you for life. How's that?"

The doorbell rang. Angrily, Cathy shouted, "Come in!"

Sylvia pushed the front door open and came tentatively into the living room.

"Oh, hey, Sylvia," Cathy said, wilting. "Sorry I didn't get up. I figured it was one of the kids' friends. I was ready to lambaste them, too." She noticed Sylvia's somber look. "Everything okay?" she asked. "Harry isn't making you pack for Nicaragua, is he?"

"No," Sylvia said with a faint smile. "I thought you'd want to know that little Joseph's back in the hospital."

"Oh, no. Is it his heart again?"

The kids stopped stuffing and looked up at Sylvia.

"I'm afraid so."

"What's wrong with him, Sylvia? What did they say?"

"He needs a heart transplant."

Silence. Even the three children were stunned. Cathy stood slowly. "A heart transplant? Sylvia, isn't there something *else* they can do before that? I thought that was the last resort."

"This *is* the last resort," Sylvia said. "He collapsed again today, and his heart almost stopped for good. They revived him, but apparently, without a transplant, he'll die."

Stricken, Cathy turned back to her children. Shock and amazement were evident on their faces. Even Annie was speechless. Little boys weren't supposed to experience failure in major organs. They weren't supposed to have to fight for their lives.

She forced her thoughts into a logical sequence. "Sylvia, is there anything I can do?"

"Well, maybe," she said. "We need to raise money. The Dodds don't have adequate health insurance, and David just doesn't make that kind of money."

"Sure," Cathy said. "We'll think of something. Won't we, kids?"

The children all nodded. It was the quietest she'd ever seen them. Crisis always quieted them, she realized. When their father had announced his intentions to divorce her, they had been silent for days.

"So what hospital is he in?"

"St. Francis," Sylvia said. "Harry's not his doctor, but he's keeping an eye on him."

"Good. I'm sure that gives Brenda some comfort."

"I hope so. Well, I'm going to take the Dodd kids home and put them to bed. Brenda and David are both at the hospital."

Cathy nodded thoughtfully. "Annie and I can do some babysitting, if that will help."

Annie shot her mother an unappreciative look, then shrugged and grudgingly said, "Yeah, sure."

"And maybe Mark and Rick could help keep their yard cut."

Rick leaned forward on the table. "Whatever I can do."

"I'm sure they'd appreciate that," Sylvia said. "And they'll probably take you up on it. It could be a long haul. There's no telling when a heart could become available."

Cathy sat again. "Boy. And I thought my problem with the school board was bad."

When Sylvia was gone, Cathy stared down at the letters she'd been so feverishly addressing. Somehow, they just didn't seem that important anymore.

"Mom, how do they get a heart?" Mark asked quietly.

"What do you mean, how?"

"I mean, like if they take it out of somebody else, won't they die?"

"That's kind of the point, doofus," Annie said.

Ricky's voice was kinder. "They take it out of somebody who's going to die anyway, don't they, Mom?"

Mark still looked confused. "You mean, out of somebody who's sick and isn't gonna get better?"

"No, nothing like that," Cathy said. "It's usually an accident victim. Somebody who's technically dead, but their heart is still functioning. They'll take it out and put it in somebody who needs it. They do that with all kinds of organs." Cathy had never imagined that she would have the need to explain this concept to her children.

"So somebody's gonna have to die to cure Joseph?" Mark asked.

"Looks that way."

The kids were quiet for a moment, and finally, Annie lost her belligerent look. Her voice was softer as she asked, "What if they don't get one in time?"

"They have to," Cathy said. "That's all there is to it."

Her eyes filled with tears, and she wanted more than anything to reach out and hug each of her kids, hold them until her arms got tired, rock them as she had when they were little. But she knew they wouldn't allow it. Somehow, she'd lost her privilege to do that years ago. Now she didn't know how to get it back.

She closed her eyes and let the tears flow for a moment. When she opened them, the kids had all dispersed to their separate rooms to deal with their own thoughts. And even in their stubborn rebellion and their maddening defiance, she found that she was thankful they all had functioning hearts.

Chapter Twenty-Six

The Dodd children were unusually quiet as they got ready for bed that evening.

"Mom would have called us if anything bad had happened, wouldn't she?" Leah asked.

"Of course," Sylvia said.

Daniel was watching her face, waiting for some clue to Joseph's real condition. "So how long does Joseph have to stay in the hospital?"

"No one knows, but it could be a while."

Rachel sank down on the bed and put her hand over her heart. "I think I have it, too."

"Have what, too?" Leah asked.

"Heart trouble. My heart keeps pitter-pattering."

"Everybody's heart pitter-patters," Daniel said. "It doesn't mean you have to go to the hospital."

"But if Joseph's sick, what if the rest of us get it?"

"Stop thinking about yourself," Leah exclaimed. "Joseph's the one we should think about."

Daniel was still watching Sylvia, and she felt he could read every thought as it passed across her face. "When's Dad coming home?"

Sylvia had made a valiant effort not to lie to them, but also to avoid saying too much. David and Brenda would be the ones who'd want to break the news to them. "He should be home soon," she said. "It's been a long day for both of them."

"Well, where's Mom going to sleep?"

"They have a cot in the room with Joseph."

"Did he wake up?" Rachel asked. "Is he talking?"

"Oh, sure," Sylvia said. "He's the same old Joseph, according to Dr. Harry."

She sent them all to get ready for bed, wondering whether at their ages they needed to be tucked in. She thought back to when her children were ten and twelve. Had she tucked them in? Yes—in fact, she realized, she had tucked them in, in one way or another, until the day they'd left home. At least, she had kissed them goodnight and said a prayer with them. But she didn't know how Brenda and David did things.

After a while, she found the children huddled in Rachel and Leah's room. Daniel sat on the floor, Leah and Rachel on each of the twin beds.

"You kids ready for bed?" Sylvia asked.

"We want to pray first," Leah said. "For Joseph."

"I think that's a real good idea."

Rachel and Leah got on the floor next to Daniel, and Sylvia completed the circle. "Let's hold hands," Leah suggested.

They all held hands and bowed their heads.

She was amazed at the prayers that came from those young lips, prayers that exhorted the Holy Spirit to do His work, as if they knew Him. Brenda had been doing a good job with them, she thought. They knew where to turn in times of trouble. She wondered how David could avoid being impacted by the faith of these children.

When they'd finished praying for their brother, they all wiped their eyes, and Daniel got up and headed for his own room. She tucked in the girls one by one, gave them a kiss on the forehead, then went to Daniel's room and saw him hunched on the bottom mattress of the bunk beds. She felt more awkward approaching him. He was a cross between a boy and a man—a taller version of Joseph, a smaller image of David. She tried to remember Jeff at that age. She had treated him with understanding and respect. She tried to do the same tonight.

"Good night, Daniel," she said.

"Night," he answered. "When Dad comes home, tell him I'm sleeping in Joseph's bed."

"Okay."

He looked up at her as if he wasn't quite finished. "I mean, I don't want him to come in and freak out or anything, thinking I'm not where I'm s'posed to be."

"I'm sure he'll understand."

He sat there thinking for a minute, then finally got under the covers and pulled them up to his chest. "Joseph's going to be fine. My brother's tough."

"Sure, he is. All of you are tough."

"No, but he's *really* tough," he said. "I mean his heart. It probably isn't even that bad. It's just sick. It's going to get better, isn't it?"

"He's in really good hands. Dr. Harry's taking care of him, and Dr. Robinson. They're very well trained." She knew the words didn't comfort the boy.

"You think they'll let me go see him tomorrow?"

"I don't know. There might be a problem with visitors because of germs. We'll have to see," she said.

He thought that over for a moment. "Joseph's going to have a hard time being there," he said. "Wish we could do something like make a video every day, so he can see what's going on at home. But we don't have a Camcorder."

Sylvia smiled. "I'll loan you mine. I haven't needed it since the wedding. That's a great way to keep the family together even when it's apart."

"Yeah." His voice dropped almost to a whisper. "I wish it hadn't happened to him. I wish it had happened to me, instead, 'cause I think I could take it better."

She wanted to say something about it being God's choice, but she didn't know if that particular bit of theology would comfort the child in any way.

"Thanks for coming over and taking care of us," he said.

"No problem. Good night, Daniel."

She turned off the light and headed for the kitchen. The kids, obviously well trained, had cleaned up after themselves, but still she kept herself busy, puttering around and putting things away until their father came home.

CHAPTER Twenty-Seven

Cathy stood in the doorway to the hospital room the next day, dressed in the surgical gown and mask the nurse had made her put on for her visit. Joseph was lying still with his eyes closed, apparently asleep. Brenda, dressed the same, looked as if she hadn't slept in days. "You didn't have to come by," she said, giving Cathy a hug. "I know you need to be at the clinic."

"I always close for lunch," she said quietly. She stood over Joseph's bed, looking down at him. As if he felt her gaze, he opened his eyes and looked up. "Hey," he whispered.

"Hey," she said, leaning over him. "What do you think of this mask they made me wear in here?"

He managed a smile.

"So how you doing there, Champ?"

"Okay," he said.

"He's a little groggy still from the procedure they did this morning," Brenda said. "They put the Heart Mate in."

"D'you know I'm getting a new heart?" he asked.

"That's what I hear," Cathy said, trying to sound impressed. She reached into the bag she carried and pulled out the games she'd bought for him. "Look, I brought some things to keep you busy while you're here. When you're feeling a little better."

Joseph couldn't work up much enthusiasm, but Brenda took them. "Look at all these games, Joseph."

"Thanks," he said.

"Annie and Mark and Rick want to come see you as soon as it's okay," she said. "You think you're up to that?"

He nodded.

As she looked down at the weak little boy, attached to the console with the air compressor and the monitor that ticked off his heartbeats, she wondered how she'd be able to hold off those tears threatening her eyes.

"So how's the fight with the school board?" Brenda asked, and Cathy could see that she needed to talk about something other than Joseph's heart.

"Well, it's going. Frankly, I keep wondering if all my efforts are useless. I wonder if I should even keep trying."

Brenda looked startled. "You *have* to keep trying."

"Why? Nobody's listening."

"How do you know that?"

"Well, I don't, for sure. Last night I sent out this letter to the homes in the district, and I told them about a meeting I was calling this week so we could discuss the problem and how to address it with the school board. But I have a bad feeling. I'm going to feel really stupid if nobody shows up."

"How many letters did you send out?"

"Thousands," she said. "You wouldn't believe it. If they don't come, I guess I'll just give up. Maybe it's not even worth the fight." She looked down at Joseph, whose eyes had closed again.

"Of course it's worth it," Brenda said. "Cathy, look at me."

Cathy met Brenda's serious eyes over the mask.

"I've been thinking a lot about this," Brenda said. "School's going to start in just a few weeks. Summer's going to be over, and I'm going to be here with Joseph if he hasn't gotten a heart by then. And even if he has, he'll need a lot of care. I've been thinking a lot about my other children."

Joseph's eyes opened again and settled on his mother, listening.

"I don't think I'm going be able to homeschool this year," she said. "I've been struggling with whether to put my own kids in public school. We can't afford a Christian school, and if I'm not going to be there, I don't want them to get behind and be unsupervised all day while David works. Public school may be the only answer."

"I can understand that," Cathy said. "But I know it must be hard for you. You were really committed."

"I'm *still* committed. And as soon as Joseph is better, I'll start homeschooling again. But Cathy, for people like me, who may not have a choice, please don't give up. Parents have a right to know what they're teaching our kids. They have a right to approve what's shown to them on videos, and what's put into their hands. Now, I don't know why you're the one who has this calling, but I believe that God gave it to you so you could set things right. We can't just abandon our public schools to a value system that doesn't work."

"I know," Cathy said. "I've told myself that."

"Then please don't give up. Don't quit. We need you."

Cathy breathed in a deep sigh. "Well, I guess if you can sit up here and fight this battle, I can fight that one. It's the least I can do."

"It's a lot to do. I appreciate it. And if I didn't need to be here, I'd be at that meeting."

"Okay then. I'll give it the fight of my life. For you, and for your kids. And, whether they like it or not, for my kids, too."

But the school board meeting was not the most pressing issue that evening when the families of Cedar Circle met at Sylvia's house to discuss how to raise money to help Joseph. Cathy insisted that Rick, Mark, and Annie come along with her, in case there was something they could do. Annie claimed she had a date, which Cathy promptly told her to cancel. She came grudgingly, silently threatening to make the meeting miserable for Cathy. Mark whined that he had an online appointment in a chat room with his friends. Cathy told him to cancel, too. Rick was the only one who came willingly, and he lectured his sister and brother all the way about giving their mom a hard time.

Before they went in, she threatened all of them. "Act like nice people," she said. "For Joseph, act like you care."

"Right, Mom," Annie spouted. "Like we really don't."

"Shut up, Annie," Rick said. "Just answer 'yes ma'am.'"

"Mom, I don't have to put up with this. Make him leave me alone. He's just being nice 'cause he's about to hit you up for money or something."

"Money?" Mark asked. "Will we get money if we cooperate?"

Cathy moaned. "No, you will not get money. You will do this because you care about Joseph, and for no other reason. And so help me, if you embarrass me—any of you—I'll make you sorry. Got it?"

Annie did the "Heil Hitler" sign and clicked her heels together. Cathy was proud of the remarkable restraint she showed as she rang the doorbell.

When they'd caught up on Joseph's condition, they all sat around Sylvia's dining-room table. "All right, I've got a few ideas," Sylvia said. "First of all, I've put Joseph on the prayer list at my church and Brenda's church, and I'm hoping that some of the families in those churches will pitch in and help out financially. But we're going to need a lot more than nickels and dimes."

"What can we do?" Tory asked.

"I have an idea for you, Tory," Sylvia said. "You're a writer. Use your writing skills."

"How?"

"Letters. Write letters to every church you can get an address for. Ask for donations. Harry and I are going tomorrow to set up a trust fund for Joseph at our bank. David will be the executor. All the money that comes in will go directly into that account. You can do it, Tory. I've read your work. Just tell them about Joseph—appeal to the hearts and minds of parents. Tell them about the family. The money will come."

Tory looked uncomfortable. "Sylvia, there must be something else—"

Sylvia leaned forward, brooking no debate. "Tory, honey, if you start that song and dance about how you've given up writing, I might just come across this table and throttle you."

Tory grinned. "Excuse me. I'll write the letters."

"I have an idea, too," Cathy said, glancing at her kids. "Actually, it was Rick's idea."

"Good," Sylvia said. "Let's hear it."

Rick spoke up. "See, we were thinking we could have, like, an animal fair. We could like give pony rides and stuff, and Mom could do heartworm checks on all the pets, and Annie and Mark could bathe and dip pets, and I could take pictures of pets with their owners, ten bucks a shot, 'cause I'm pretty good with a camera."

Sylvia's eyes lit up, and she grinned at Tory and Cathy.

Annie began to twirl her hair on a finger. "It was kind of my idea, too," she cut in. "I thought we could have a petting zoo."

"Yeah," Mark added. "We could go around and get some of Mom's customers' animals, and little kids could pet them. We could get baby chicks and puppies and kittens, and little sheep and some ostriches . . ."

"It wouldn't raise a lot," Cathy said. "But it would raise some. The biggest plus, though, is that it would get the community involved, alert people to what's needed, and maybe out of that we could get some big donations."

"I think it's a wonderful idea," Sylvia said. "When do you want to have it?"

"Well, we need time to get it organized," Cathy said. "I was thinking maybe the Fourth of July?"

"Sounds good. Let's plan on it. Where can we do it?"

"Well, that's a problem," Cathy said. "At first I thought maybe here, in the empty lot between Tory's and Brenda's houses.

But I don't think that'll be big enough. And we need a place more in the center of things, so people will see it and stop by. If people have to go too far out of their way, they might not come."

"We can do it at my church," Sylvia said. "We have a huge plot of land next to the church, and it's real visible."

"Are you sure they'd let us?" Cathy asked. "I mean, I'm not even a member, and already I'm using the fellowship hall for my meeting this week. Now I'm asking for the lawn?"

"The church is there to meet people's needs," Sylvia said. "You're doing that. Why would they object?"

"Well, all right. We'd promise to clean up after it's over."

"Yeah," Mark said. "Scoop up all the poop . . ."

Sylvia started to laugh. "Oh, my. I hadn't thought of that."

"It'll just fertilize the grass," Annie said.

"We can live with it," Sylvia said. "Meanwhile, I'll go around to as many big businesses in the area as I can and talk to their executives. See if some of them want to give a donation as a tax write-off."

"That's a good idea," Tory whispered.

"All right, then we each have a task to start with," she said. "We need to get busy."

"One other thing," Tory said. "Let's talk about what we can do to help them out with the rest of their needs. We could ask Brenda's church to bring food and stuff, so David won't have to cook for the kids. The rest of us could fill in on the nights when no one's doing it."

"Great. Could you organize it?"

"Sure," Tory said. "Also, I was thinking I could take the Dodd kids to church with me Sunday. That's real important to Brenda, but since none of us go to their church, I thought at least they could go with us."

"That's a good idea. I'm sure Brenda will take you up on it, especially since David won't take them."

Cathy spoke up. "Rick and Mark will be taking care of the Dodds' yard. David doesn't need that to worry about."

Mark rolled his eyes, but Rick nodded agreement.

"And Barry offered to do any home repairs they need. I don't think they need any right now, though."

"What else is there to do?" Cathy asked.

"There is one other thing." Sylvia closed the folder with her notes, then looked around the table from one person to the next. "You could become organ donors."

"Organ donors?" Mark asked. "What's that?"

Cathy touched her son's shoulder. "It's where you sign a card saying that, if you die, they can give your organs to someone like Joseph."

"Gross!" Annie said. "Why would anybody do that?"

"To save somebody's life," Sylvia said. "Why do you think that's gross, Annie?"

"Because ..." She looked from Sylvia to her mom. "They wouldn't even try to save you. If somebody needed your kidney or something ..."

"No, that's not true," Sylvia cut in firmly. "The medical team that would work on you after an accident would have nothing to do with transplants. But if you die, then they consult your family about organ donation. The transplant team isn't even contacted until the family consents."

"I still wouldn't do it," Annie said.

Sylvia sighed. "What if your mother needed a liver, Annie? If she was dying, and a transplant was the only thing that could save her? Would you see it differently then?"

Annie got quiet. "I don't know."

"I'm not trying to talk you into anything," Sylvia said. "But Joseph will die if he doesn't get a heart. Every day, nine people like Joseph die, waiting for organs."

Silence hung over the room. Finally, Tory spoke up. "Barry and I talked about it when we first got married, and decided not to sign up. We thought it would be too hard on the one left behind. But I've never known anyone who needed an organ. If it was Britty or Spencer who needed one ..." Her voice broke, and she shifted in her seat. "What do I do? Just sign the back of my driver's license?"

"That, or fill out a donor card and keep it with you all the time. But that's just a formality. It's your family that has to consent when the time comes. You have to let them know you want to be a donor."

Cathy pulled out her driver's license and flashed the back of the card. "I've already done it. See that, kids? That means that—if you're adults when I buy the farm—you sign the consent before you throw me in the tar pit."

Annie and Mark didn't find that amusing. Rick pulled out his own wallet and removed his license. "I'll do it, too, Mom."

"I'm proud of you." Cathy tried to swallow back the emotion in her voice. "Sylvia, let's offer donor cards at our animal fair, so people can sign up. Once we make people aware, they need to have a way to follow through."

Sylvia jotted that down. "Great idea. I think we're off to a good start." She looked around at Cathy and Tory, at Mark and Rick and Annie. "I sure appreciate everyone's help. It's especially nice to see how the kids are willing to help."

Cathy's three kids looked uncomfortably at each other, and Annie covered her mouth with her hand to suppress her amused grin.

"I tell you what," Sylvia said. "While we're all here, let's pray for Joseph."

"Um . . . I gotta go," Annie said. "I have, like, a date."

Cathy shot her a look.

"Me, too," Mark said. "Some people are waiting for me online."

"They can wait," Cathy said. "Bow your heads."

Huffing with resentment, the kids bowed their heads, and Sylvia began to pray. Listening to her, Cathy realized that there must be more to this prayer thing than she had thought. Some people, like Sylvia, talked to God as if He were a good friend, someone standing right in the room with them. It was an alien concept to Cathy. But now she tried to believe it as her friend and mentor appealed to God for Joseph's sake.

❧

That night, after a talk with Barry about organ donation, Tory had trouble sleeping. She got up, went to the laundry room, and turned on the computer. She hadn't touched it since the day she'd seen the book in the library that was so much like hers, and now she fought the feeling of defeat and failure that spiraled inside her as the computer booted up and the cursor began to flicker.

There was something more important than her own goals, she reminded herself. Joseph's life was at stake, and there were people who thought she had the skill to do something about it.

She thought about what to write in her appeal to the local churches, and as her fingers began to type, she found that it was liberating to not worry about publication or fame and fortune. Tory simply began to tell the story of the little boy whose heart was failing. The little boy who needed a heart transplant and couldn't afford it. The little boy whose family was willing to do whatever was necessary to get him the help he needed. And she told them how much that family needed the financial help of anyone willing.

She finished drafting the letter at three o'clock in the morning. She printed out a hundred copies for starters, and decided to address the envelopes tomorrow.

By the time she crawled back into bed, she felt the thrill of accomplishment, the peace of knowing she'd done something no one else on their street could have done. She fell into a deep sleep next to her husband, knowing that dawn would come too soon. Her brain would be weary tomorrow, and she would move slowly, but that was all right. The knowledge that those letters were on their way to people who could help would give her all the energy she needed.

Chapter Twenty-Eight

By Thursday night, Cathy had convinced herself that Sylvia's church fellowship hall would be packed with parents who'd gotten her letter and were concerned about their children's education. She had even made copies of Tory's letter about Joseph, planning to pass them out.

She got to the church thirty minutes early and tried to organize her thoughts and her notes. At quarter till, no early birds had straggled in. At five till, she looked at her watch and began to panic.

At seven, two women came to the door. "Excuse me . . . where is the meeting about the public schools being held?"

"Right here," she said, too exuberantly. "Come in."

They stepped into the room and looked nervously around. "Where is everybody?"

"I'm afraid you're the first two here."

"Really? No one else came?"

She hated to admit it. "Well, I haven't given up yet. You know people. You tell them seven and they show up at seven-fifteen. And of course, since it's a Baptist church, they figure we'll be having food and fellowship for a while before we get down to business. We have to allow for that." Instantly, she wondered if she'd offended them, and decided to amend that statement. "Of course, I'm sure other denominations eat a lot, too. Not *too* much, but . . . you know . . ."

The two women nodded skeptically and looked as if they might escape through the bathroom window. An awkward silence fell over the room as they took two seats, and Cathy pretended to be busy organizing her handouts. After a moment, she heard footsteps and looked up to see a pleasant-looking man. "Hey, I'm Cathy Flaherty," she said, her voice echoing in the near-empty room. "Are you looking for the meeting about the schools?"

"That's right," he said, hesitating at the door. "Am I in the right place?"

"This is it," she said.

He crossed the room and shook her hand. "Steve Bennett," he said. "I got your letter, and I was pretty outraged. I didn't know if I should come because I only have one child and she's just in elementary school. But I figure in a few years she'll be in those classes."

"Everybody is welcome," she said. "Even people who don't have kids. We're all paying taxes for those schools. Will her mother be coming?"

He shook his head as he took a seat in the front row. His face reddened slightly. "My wife died. I've been raising Tracy alone for the last three years."

"Oh, I'm sorry." She could have kicked herself, for she could see from the look on his face that he wasn't quite over it. "Well, I'm really glad you came. I was hoping we wouldn't just have mothers here." She glanced at the two women. "Not that there's anything wrong with mothers. I'm one, myself. I just meant . . ."

Her voice faded off as she realized what a mess she was making. She heard voices, and a half-dozen more people straggled in. She tried to greet them more intelligently. She was glad she'd brought finger sandwiches so that everyone had something to do as they waited for the meeting to start. Finally, at twenty after, she decided that everyone who was going to come was here. Counting her, there were ten people.

Ignoring the microphone she had set up, she sat on a chair facing the room and told them the story of how she'd found the condom in her son's pocket. She related her meeting with the principal and the indifference she had encountered from the superintendent. They each gave her their full attention.

"I'm not the most articulate person," she admitted. "I'm used to dealing with animals and teenagers. But my intention for tonight was to educate the parents of this community about what they're teaching our kids, and hopefully get us mobilized so that when school starts, we can all show up at the school board meeting in huge numbers." She looked around at them and gave a disappointed laugh. "Well, as many as we can get together, anyway. I'm hoping that we can go there and demand to be notified before they have this talk with our children. I think the least we could ask for is the opportunity to view the videos our children will be watching, review the material they'll be studying, and have approval rights as to what they give our children and what kinds of demonstrations they show them. Really, the line has to be drawn somewhere."

The other parents agreed, and Cathy felt validated. "For those things to happen, you'll need to tell everyone you know about this. I sent the letter to as many people as I could, but I know how it is. You get a lot of letters. If you don't know who something's from, sometimes you don't open it. I'm afraid some of the parents may have just thrown my letter away without reading it. But we need to get the word out somehow. We need dozens of parents there when we face the school board in September. We need to tell them that we won't stand for this, and that this issue isn't going to go away until something is done about it. We have to protect our schools."

She hadn't expected the applause she got from the tiny group. When it died down, she went on. "I know that the number of parents in this room tonight is not a fair measure of the number of parents in this community who care about their children. It's just that we live in a very busy culture, and a lot of parents opted to be with their children tonight, instead of coming here to talk about them. So I'm not blaming them. Heaven knows, I've missed plenty of meetings myself. So I'd appreciate it if you could talk it up, then meet me at the school board meeting on September 16, so we can make sure they understand our point."

She felt good about the meeting as it broke up and people began to go home. At the door, she handed out flyers about Joseph and his problem. Steve Bennett lingered to help her pick up the dirty paper plates and cups that had been left behind on chairs.

"Tell you what I'll do," he said. "My little girl plays soccer. I'll work something up to give to the soccer parents. And I'll do some talking, too, at the games. Give me a stack of those heart-transplant sheets, too, and I'll pass them out while I'm at it."

"Good idea," she said, getting two stacks to hand to him. "I hadn't thought of that."

He paused, looking down at the sheets. His hair was cut too short, and his skin looked weathered, as if he worked outdoors. But he had a kind face. "I really appreciate what you've done, calling our attention to this," he said. "If you hadn't, I might never have known. I've tried to be real protective of my daughter, and I can't stand the thought that these educators can do anything they want to with her when she's in their building."

"I know," she said. "Kind of scary, isn't it?"

"Let me help you get your stuff, and I'll walk you to your car."

A gentleman, she thought. A gentleman who cared about his child. Would wonders never cease? She looked at him from the corner of her eye as they walked outside. She wondered what was wrong with him. Something, no doubt. There was something wrong with all of them. They just didn't make them the way young women dreamed they did.

He helped her get her papers into the car, then shook her hand again. "It was nice meeting you, Cathy." There was nothing flirtatious or suggestive in his tone. It was a welcome relief.

"You, too, Steve. Thanks for coming. I really appreciate it." She got in the car, locked it, and watched him walk to a pickup truck that was a few years old. Not a midlife crisis sports car. Again, a welcome relief. She wondered if he dated much, then quickly chased away the thought, reminding herself that she had sworn off dating. Besides, tonight was about changing school policy, not meeting men.

She started her car, and as she drove home, she thought that things might be looking up. Maybe there was a chance, after all, that they could turn the school board around.

CHAPTER *Twenty-Nine*

Sunday morning, Tory and Barry took the Dodd kids to church with them. Brenda had been grateful for the offer, since David wanted to be at the hospital with Joseph and Brenda—and had already announced unequivocally that he did not intend to go to church under any circumstances. That wasn't like David, Tory thought. He was normally a sweet, gentle man. His distaste of church seemed unreasonable and out of character.

Brittany and Spencer were excited as they picked the older kids up and headed for Sunday school. "I want Daniel to come to Sunday school with me," Spencer said.

"He's a little old for your class, Spence," Barry said. "They don't generally let twelve-year-olds in the four-year-old class."

Daniel's smile was forced. "I have to go to my own class, Spencer."

"What about Leah and Rachel?" Brittany asked. "Can they come to my class?"

"No, we're going to send everybody to their own age-group," Tory said. "You all okay with that?"

The three Dodd children sitting on the backseat of the Caravan nodded complacently, but she could see that they were nervous about attending a new church. She remembered being the new kid once when she was a child. She'd hated it. And she couldn't even offer them the hope that they would run into school friends, since they were homeschooled. Their circle of friends was much smaller than hers had been at that age.

She took them in and walked them each to the classroom they belonged to. "This is a big church," Leah said quietly. "Our church is a lot smaller."

Tory was proud of the size of her church. "Yeah, God has really blessed us," she said. "When we first started, it was the size of your church, but we've grown over the years. There are all kinds of things to do here now. Brittany and Spencer take art classes here on Thursday mornings, and they go to Mom's Day Out, and I take aerobics three times a week and a parenting class on Sunday nights . . ."

The kids seemed to listen with polite interest. She took them each to their classrooms and watched them go in. Leah and Rachel would be fine, she thought, because they were twins and could lean on each other. But she felt sorry for Daniel. It was tough for a seventh grader to go into a roomful of kids he didn't know and try to fit in. She could see how awkward he felt, and almost considered taking him to her class with her. But she didn't know how often she and Barry would be bringing them. If it was every week, Daniel needed to get to know the kids his own age.

After Sunday school, she retrieved all five children, and they sat in a row on the pew in the sanctuary. Occasionally during the service, she glanced down the row at them. Brittany and Spencer were drawing on the program, but the three Dodd children sat silently, very still, looking miserably at the preacher. Next to her, Barry began to nod off, and she nudged him. "Wake up," she whispered. "You're setting a bad example."

After church, they took Daniel, Leah, and Rachel to the hospital to have lunch with their parents. Barry waited in the lobby with Brittany and Spencer as Tory walked Brenda's kids up. Joseph was sitting up in bed. Tory was thankful to see that the color had returned to his face, though he still seemed tired and lackluster.

Brenda threw her arms around each of her gowned and masked children as though she hadn't seen them in a week. "Leah, look at you. You're walking like a beauty queen. Have you been practicing with that book on your head?"

"Yes, ma'am."

"It's working, honey. Look how straight that backbone is. And Rachel, darlin', your hair looks just beautiful in that braid—and to think I wasn't even there to help."

"Thank you, Mama."

"Oh, Daniel, you've grown since yesterday. Look at you, you're almost as tall as I am." She tested his biceps. "Have you been pumping iron at Mark's house again?"

"Not lately."

"Good thing. If you get any bigger, I'll have to buy you a whole new wardrobe. Look at him, David. He'll be wearing your clothes soon."

With all three children beaming, Brenda finally turned to Tory. "Thanks for taking them to church, Tory. I don't know what I'd do without you."

"It was our pleasure," Tory said, staying back at the door for fear of bringing germs in, despite her own mask and gown. "How are you feeling, Joseph?" she asked.

"Good."

She doubted that was true, but it didn't surprise her that, being Brenda's son, he put the best face on things.

"He's just blossoming," Brenda said, walking to the bed and combing her fingers through Joseph's cowlicked hair. "And his disposition is unbelievable. Most kids would be whining and fussing, but he's as good as gold. I'm the lucky one, getting to spend all this time with him. So kids, how did you like Miss Tory's church?"

"It was fine," Daniel said without much enthusiasm.

"Did you make any new friends?"

"No, ma'am."

"It was kind of boring," Rachel blurted.

"Oh, I'm sure it was fine," Brenda said, shooting Tory an embarrassed look. Tory just grinned.

"Mom, can't you take us tonight?" Rachel asked. "We've been working on the musical, and I have a solo next Sunday night. I'll lose it if I don't go to practice tonight."

"And Daniel and me have speaking parts, so we—"

"Daniel and I," Brenda said, cutting into Leah's plea.

"I had one, too," Joseph interjected. "Now I have to quit. If all four of us quit, they'll have to call the whole thing off."

"We can't let everybody down," Rachel said. "Mom, please! Daddy, couldn't you just drop us off?"

"No," David said. "I need to stay here."

Tory saw the struggle on Brenda's face. She wasn't ready to leave Joseph yet.

"Look," Tory said. "If the kids want to go tonight, I'll take them. Really, I wouldn't mind."

"*Really?*" It was the most animated Tory had seen Rachel all morning.

Brenda shook her head. "Tory, you've done so much already."

"What could it hurt? I'll drop them off so they can work on the musical, and then we'll all come back for the service and we'll bring them home afterward."

"I really appreciate that, Tory."

Tory waved off the thanks. "Okay, guys, what time do you need to be there?"

"Four-thirty," Daniel said, his eyes brighter now.

"Okay, then I'll pick you up at your house at four-fifteen and run you over."

Finally, David got up. "No, that won't be necessary, Tory. I'll drop them off at the church. If you'll just go to the service and bring them home."

"Sure, that'll work out fine." She glanced at Brenda and caught her look. She knew how much Brenda wished that David would be the one to attend the service tonight.

"I'll take that time to come back and spend with Joseph," David said. "I don't get much time during the week."

Tory wondered if he would come to see the kids perform in the musical. She couldn't imagine a father as diligent as David missing something like that.

Finally, she discarded her sterile clothes and headed back down to find her family waiting patiently in the lobby. Thankful to have them all healthy and happy, she gave them each a kiss and led them back to the car.

Brenda's church was a small building with no frills. It had about fifty pews—twenty-five each in two rows—plain windows, and a simple cross at the front—so unlike their own church, which had a huge mortgage, beautiful stained glass windows, and a sanctuary that made them all proud. Tory, Barry, Brittany, and Spencer slipped in just before the service and sat near the back. Leah and Rachel found them and ran up the aisle to scoot into the pew next to them. Daniel waved from his place up front where a handful of youth were sitting.

They started the service with praise music, and the congregation clapped their hands and sang out without inhibition. Tory saw joy on the faces around her as they sang and praised God. In her church, everything was somber and reverent, and she didn't know quite how to take this new form of worship. Brittany and Spencer were on their feet singing along, instead of seated and marking up programs.

The preacher, a less-educated, less-polished man than their own pastor, began to preach. He had power and authority, and his words cut right to her heart. She saw that Barry, too, was wide awake, riveted on every word. The sermon about sharing one's faith seemed so relevant, so directly from God, so challenging and uniquely designed for her.

When the service was over, family after family introduced themselves, shook their hands, and praised them for being faithful in helping the Dodds. They left feeling uplifted and happy, instead of tired and irritable, as they often did on Sunday nights after their own church services.

They dropped the Dodd kids off at home where David waited. As they pulled into their driveway, Tory looked over at Barry and smiled. "Well, that was fun, wasn't it?"

"Yeah, it was."

"I think he wrote that sermon just for me."

"Nope. Couldn't have." Barry grinned. "He wrote it for me."

She laughed. "Seems like the Holy Spirit was really alive there. No wonder Brenda's the way she is."

"What way is that?" he asked.

"I don't know," she said. "Just real spiritual. Real in tune with God."

"It'd be hard to be a member of that church and not be."

They got out of the car and led the children in, and for a while she busied herself getting the kids bathed and put to bed.

Later, as she was preparing for bed herself, Tory paused and leaned against the bedpost. She gazed down at her husband, who was lying on the bed in a pair of gym shorts, reading a magazine. He felt her eyes on him and looked up at her. "What?"

She shrugged. "Do you ever think about changing churches?"

He shook his head. "I couldn't think about that," he said. "I'm a deacon. Deacons don't just up and leave."

"Why not?" She touched his feet. "What would be wrong with that?"

He dropped the magazine and sat up. "Tory, how can you talk like this? We've been going to that church since we were married."

"I know. It's just that I've never felt the Spirit move quite like He did tonight."

"It was nice," he agreed. "But at our church . . . we worship differently. It doesn't mean the Holy Spirit isn't there, too."

"How do we worship?" she asked Barry. "By falling asleep in church? By letting our kids color and draw and ignore what's going on? By mumbling through the hymns while we check our watches to see how much longer we have to sit there?"

"So maybe our worship methods aren't perfect," he said. "Maybe we need to work on taking worship more seriously."

"Maybe." She let it go and crawled into bed next to him. But in her heart, she wondered.

The next morning over breakfast, Spencer asked her if they could go back to that church again. "Well, don't you like our church?" Tory asked.

"No. Their church was fun."

"What was fun about it?" she asked.

He thought that over for a moment. Finally, Brittany came up with the answer. "I liked the songs."

"They're the same songs we sing."

"Yeah, but they sounded different when they sang 'em."

She smiled. "They did, didn't they? Maybe we will go back."

"Can we go Sunday morning?" he asked. "Their Sunday school rooms looked cool, and me and Britty would be in the same class, Leah said."

Tory knew that was true. Since the church was small, they divided the age-groups differently. "Maybe we'll do that just until Joseph gets better and their mom can take them again."

She knew that Barry would agree to go temporarily for the sake of the Dodds, but she decided not to bring up the subject of changing churches again. Barry was right. They were committed to their own church. For now, that was where they would stay.

Chapter *Thirty*

Sylvia had hoped that her first visit Monday morning, to her own bank, would prove fruitful. But when the bank president declined to help, claiming that bank policy prohibited them from giving to individuals, she was deflated.

Still, not one to let the word *no* stop her, she went to her bank's chief competitor and offered to move her own accounts if they would make a contribution to Joseph's fund. The bank officer told her that they would take it under advisement, but that before they could contribute, she would have to make a presentation before the board of directors, and that it could take up to six weeks for a decision to be made.

She was even less confident at her next two stops, and she supposed it showed. She couldn't get past the receptionist in the executive offices, and was told that no one had time to see her.

By the time she headed home, her feet and head ached. But it was her pride that hurt most of all. She had half expected to rake in, in one day, all the money the Dodds would need, just through sheer determination and her power of persuasion. She had not expected to arrive home empty-handed.

She fought off tears as she headed back to the bedroom. She took off her business suit and pumps and climbed into more comfortable clothes, but physical comfort didn't help her spirits any. Finally, she gave in to her tears and got down on her knees.

She prayed with all her heart, asking God to go before her and make a way—asking God to raise the money, since she wasn't able.

Finally, she headed out back to the stables to check on her horses. The teenaged boy who worked a few hours a day grooming them had already cleaned out the stables and fed the horses.

Sunstreak whinnied as she came in, and she wondered if the mare sensed and sympathized with her mood. She let her nuzzle her hand, then reached up to hug her.

"Sylvia!" She heard the voice calling from a distance and closed her eyes. She didn't want to talk. She didn't want to tell of her failures and have anyone see her tearstained face.

"Sylvia!" The voice grew closer. "Are you in there?"

She stepped out of the stables and saw Tory, her brown hair done up in a French twist and her makeup perfectly applied, despite the heat outside. She looked like a brunette Barbie doll, and Sylvia found herself envying her. Right now, in her shorts and baggy T-shirt, Sylvia felt old and useless.

"So how'd it go?" Tory asked. "I saw you come out and I couldn't wait to find out."

Sylvia looked over her shoulder between their houses and saw Brittany and Spencer, wearing helmets, riding their bikes with training wheels in the little cul-de-sac. "Well . . . let's just say it wasn't an overwhelming success."

"Didn't you get *any* donations?"

She sighed, then hated herself for it. She hadn't been a sigher before she'd married off Sarah. No wonder no one took her seriously. "I'm afraid not, Tory."

"So you'll try again tomorrow," Tory said with uncharacteristic optimism. Then she frowned and regarded Sylvia more carefully. "Sylvia, are you all right?"

"No. Not really." She headed around to her front porch so Tory could keep a closer eye on the kids. Wearily, she sat down in one of her wooden rockers. Tory sat down on the steps of the porch, looking up at her. "I should have known it wouldn't be that easy," Sylvia said. "But I was so cocky this morning. I thought I'd just prance into anyplace I tried, demand to see the president, tell him about Joseph, and voilà, he'd hand me ten grand. What arrogance."

"Don't be so hard on yourself," Tory said. "I'm the only one allowed to do that."

Sylvia gave her a weak smile. "I'm just disappointed in myself. I was starting to feel useful again. Didn't last long, did it?"

"Come on, Sylvia. It's only been one day. You'll raise money. Let's just brainstorm for a minute. Let's be creative. There must be some way to get their attention."

"Like what? I tried telling them all about Joseph; I even had pictures of him. They weren't interested."

"Well, is there some way you could find out which businessmen in town might have sick kids? Maybe Harry could get a list at the hospital or something."

Sylvia couldn't believe Tory would suggest such a thing. "That wouldn't be ethical, Tory. I would never ask him to do that."

"Why not? There must be businessmen who've had kids in Children's Hospital. If their kids are well now, they'd be able to relate to Joseph."

"Either that, or they'd resent me for asking, since no one helped them with their bills."

"Yeah, guess you're right." Tory looked around for her children, who had laid their bikes down and were crouched at a manhole on the sidewalk. Spencer was trying to open it. "Spencer, get away from that! Now!"

Spencer kept pulling at the cover. "There are fish in there, Mommy! I wanna see!"

"There are no fish in there!" Tory called. "Let go, Spencer. One . . . two . . ."

He yanked his hands away before she could reach "three," as if the manhole cover would self-destruct at the word.

Tory turned back to Sylvia. "What about heart attacks?"

"What about them?" Sylvia asked.

"Couldn't you get a list of heart attack victims? People Harry's done bypasses on? Some of them must own businesses; they might be willing to donate as a tax write-off."

Sylvia considered that for a moment. "I still couldn't get the list from Harry. That wouldn't be right."

"Okay, then walk into the lobby of a business, befriend the secretary, and ask her which executives have had heart attacks in the past. She would know. Then ask to see them. They'd be a whole lot more willing to listen than someone who's never been sick."

"Seems awfully mercenary," Sylvia said. "And dishonest, too."

"Then tell the receptionist what you're doing. Get *her* interested in Joseph. Be honest with her. She'll help you. Mark my word."

Tory glanced back at the street and saw only Brittany. Standing up, she called, "Spencer!"

"He's looking at the horses, Mommy," Brittany tattled.

Sylvia watched as Tory headed out to corral her young son. She smiled, remembering all the chases with her own children. They, too, had headed for the stables at every opportunity.

She listened as Tory shouted at Spencer, then saw the child dash back to his bike. Tory was out of breath when she rejoined her on the porch.

"Now, where were we?" Tory asked.

Sylvia grinned. "Just wondering . . . If you're so sure all this would work, why don't you try it?"

Tory stiffened. "Are you kidding? I could never do that."

Sylvia couldn't help laughing. "You know, there's a friend of ours, Ed Majors, who had a triple bypass last year. He owns a metalworks business in town. I know I could get in to see him. Maybe I could convince him . . ."

"Why didn't you start with him?" Tory asked.

"It never even crossed my mind until you mentioned the heart attack victims."

Tory arched her eyebrows. "Who's the brains of this outfit?"

"You, apparently." Sylvia laughed. "I feel better, Tory. Thank you. I think I can go out there and do it again tomorrow."

"Sure you can," Tory said. "All you needed was a plan."

The next morning, Sylvia showed up at Majors Metalworks and asked to see Ed. He came out immediately and ushered her back to his office. It took fifteen minutes, start-to-finish, for him to agree to donate five hundred dollars toward Joseph's fund. As he wrote out the check, he apologized for not giving more, but confided that his business was "in the red" and he couldn't afford more.

Sylvia expressed her gratitude with a hug, then, armed with purpose and confidence, she headed to the next business on her list. It turned out that it was time for the receptionist's coffee break, so she offered to buy her a cup of coffee in the employee cafeteria. There, she told the woman about Joseph's plight, and asked if she knew of any executives in the company who might have had heart problems themselves and would sympathize with the Dodds. The receptionist gave her the name of one of the vice presidents who'd had a mild heart attack earlier in the year. Before she sent Sylvia to his office, she gave twenty dollars herself to apply toward Joseph's fund.

The executive who'd had the heart attack wrote her a check for a hundred dollars, then walked her to the office of the president and introduced her. After hearing her pitch, the president wrote out a check for a thousand dollars.

Though the next five stops proved fruitless, Sylvia felt victorious on her way home. She had raised $1,620 in one day, and felt that if she just kept at it, they'd have what the Dodds needed for Joseph.

Harry was already home when she arrived, and she fluttered in and apologized for not having supper made.

"That's okay," he said. "We'll go out."

"Yes, let's go out," she said. "We have to celebrate."

"Celebrate what?"

"All the money I raised today for Joseph's heart transplant."

"How much did you raise?" he asked.

"One thousand six hundred twenty dollars," she said, prancing around.

"That much?"

"That's right. I know it doesn't begin to cover it, but isn't it wonderful? Yesterday I was so discouraged, but today I armed myself for battle and went at it with all I had. We're on our way. I deposited the money on the way home. The Joseph Dodd Trust Fund has something in it!"

"I *knew* you had it in you!" Laughing, he twirled her around, pulled her against him, and began to dance. "And you thought you had nothing left to contribute."

She laughed as he spun her, then launched into a jitterbug and ended with a dip that left her giggling like a teenager.

Harry grew serious at the restaurant, while they were waiting for their food. "I was thinking about a way to help little Joseph. Of sacrifices we could make to help out."

"I'm willing to give whatever we can," Sylvia said.

"Yes, but there's something we could sell, and it might help drum up some publicity to get others to contribute."

"What?"

He looked down at his iced tea and drew a line in the condensation on the glass, as if considering how this suggestion might affect Sylvia. "Before I say it, just know that if you don't want to do it, we don't have to. It's just an idea."

"Harry, what?" she asked. "You know I want to do whatever I can. Of course, with the wedding expenses and the possibility of our going to Nicaragua . . ." She halted midsentence and met Harry's eyes. It was the first time she'd brought that up since he'd first mentioned it. "I'm just saying, if we had to, somehow, we could come up with the money to help. I'm willing to do almost anything."

He looked carefully at her. "I was thinking of selling the horses."

She caught her breath. "What?"

"Just listen," he said, closing his hand over hers. "Cathy's having the animal fair at the church. That would be a good time to auction them off. It would be good advertising and draw more people to the fair. Raise public awareness."

"But Harry, I love my horses."

"I know, but hardly anyone rides them anymore. The kids aren't here—"

"They'll ride them when they come home. *I* still ride them sometimes."

"But not that often. And they're really a lot of trouble to take care of. Think how much it would mean for Joseph's heart fund. Directly and indirectly."

Tears flooded her eyes as she stared down at her silverware. She rearranged it, then set it back like it was. She wondered how he could think of giving up all the things they had loved in their lives—their home, their land, his career, and now the horses. Did he consider this the first step toward shedding all their possessions and heading for the mission field? "That's a lot to ask, Harry."

"I know." He let silence sit like a warm cat between them, and finally, he touched her chin and made her look at him. "Remember in the Bible when David wanted to buy the site of a threshing floor from Araunah, to build an altar on it and offer sacrifices to the Lord? And Araunah wanted to give it to him for free?"

"Yes, I remember," she whispered. "David said he didn't want to offer anything to the Lord that cost him nothing."

"The horses will cost us," he said. "But it won't be just an offering to Joseph. It'll be an offering to the Lord."

The struggle in her heart was almost more than she could bear, but she knew in her mind that it was the right thing to do. Finally, she brought her misty eyes back to his. "How can I say no when you put it like that?" She dabbed at the corners of her eyes. "What am I going to do around the house with no kids and no horses?"

"Maybe you'll think of something." It was his first reminder in weeks of his desire to go to Nicaragua. She chose to ignore it.

But she couldn't ignore his choice to sell the horses. She tried to find a cheerful spot in her heart from which she could make this sacrifice. "It sure will make Tory's life easier, if Spencer's not constantly trying to escape to pet the colt. She can rest a little easier if she has to turn her back on him for a minute."

He laughed softly. "That little rascal."

"Yeah," she said. "Remember when Jeff was that little? He loved those horses. We were training him for barrel races even then."

"And now he has a horse of his own in North Dakota," he said. "He'll be fine about this."

She knew he was right. It wasn't the kids who would mourn. She was the one who didn't want to let them go. "All right, Harry," she said finally. "Let's do it."

"Just tell Cathy," he said with a smile. "Then we can start preparing ourselves. It'll sure bring more people to the animal fair. Everybody wants a bargain."

She couldn't argue with that. "I just hope it makes a difference."

"It won't get him a heart any sooner," Harry said. "But it'll sure make things easier while they wait."

CHAPTER *Thirty-One*

The impromptu meeting in the middle of Cedar Circle happened by accident. Tory had walked out to check her mailbox and seen Sylvia crossing the yard, headed for Cathy's. Cathy had just driven up and was getting out of her car.

Tory waved at them both, then looked down at the mail in her hand. The envelope on top was from a church—one of those she'd sent letters to the other day. Her heart began to pound as she tore it open. She pulled out the folded note, and a check fluttered to the ground. She picked it up before the wind could blow it away and saw that it was for a hundred dollars. Quickly, she read the letter.

Dear Mrs. Sullivan,

Thank you so much for your letter regarding Joseph Dodd's heart transplant. We have shared this request with our congregation and have raised a small donation toward his medical bills. We intend to keep trying to raise more money, but wanted to make this first installment. We also pledge to pray for him and his family.

Thank you for sharing this need with us and allowing us to do our part. We have a small congregation, but because of your letter, we've reached deep into our pockets.

In Christ's name,
The Fellowship of Survey Baptist Church

Reading the check again, Tory felt the thrill of accomplishment. Survey Baptist was just a little trailer church she passed on her way down the mountain. How had they raised this much so quickly? Didn't they have a building fund? Weren't there salaries to pay? Surely there were—and yet that small fellowship had found a way to contribute.

She broke into a run across the circle.

"Cathy! Sylvia! You won't believe this!"

They both turned around, and she almost assaulted them with the letter. "Read this. Look, a check for a hundred dollars! Can you believe it?"

"You got published?" Cathy asked.

"No!" Tory said. "Better! I sent letters out three days ago about Joseph, and look! I got this response already." Sylvia took the letter, and Cathy read over her shoulder.

"Wow! It must have been some letter," Cathy said.

"That's just the tip of the iceberg," Tory said. "I must have sent letters to a hundred different churches. Do you think more money will come in?"

"Well, that hundred dollars had to have been sent out the day they got your letter," Sylvia said. "If that's any indication, I'd say yes. A *lot* more will come in." She laughed out loud and hugged Tory. "Girl, don't ever tell me that you don't know how to write."

"I just told them about Joseph," she said. "It wasn't any big masterpiece."

"Well, it got through. This is wonderful. I'll take the check and deposit it. Tory, save all the letters we get for Brenda and

David. It might be nice for Brenda to see how the Lord is providing, and I think it might be vital for David."

"I will," Tory said. She flipped through the rest of the mail, but found only bills.

"Looks like we're on our way," Cathy said. "Sylvia, tell Tory what you're going to do."

Sylvia's grin faded a degree. "Harry and I have decided to sell the horses."

Tory caught her breath. "No! You've gotta be kidding!"

"We've decided that might drum up more publicity for the animal fair that Cathy's giving, and if we auction the horses off there, we might do real well. We'll donate the proceeds to Joseph."

"But what a sacrifice! You love those horses."

"We hardly ever ride anymore. And we figure it'll give you some peace of mind about Spencer."

Tory shook her head. "He's going to be heartbroken."

"He'll get over it," Sylvia said. "Especially if he knows it's to help Joseph's heart."

"I guess you're right." She looked at Cathy. "So have we got a date for the animal fair?"

"July Fourth," Cathy said. "I talked to the folks at Sylvia's church, and they're going to let us use the grounds. And I called Brenda's church, and they're going to come over and help with food and extra booths and things. We're going to make a real big deal out of it."

"What about your church, Tory?" Sylvia asked. "Have they agreed to help any?"

Tory looked down at the bills in her hand, embarrassed. "Well, I'm sure they will. They just haven't committed yet." She sighed and looked down at the Survey Baptist letter again. It was such an encouragement. More, even, than if she had gotten published. "You know, this gives me energy. I think I'll go back in there and write some more letters. I mean, I don't have to stay in the state of Tennessee. I could write every church in the country if I wanted to. I mean, the more I can reach, the better, right?"

"Right," Sylvia said. "That's why I knew you could do it. If I'd written the letter, they would have filed it in the trash can."

"I've got work to do," Tory said with a teasing grin. "I don't have time to stand out here flapping my jaws with you. I'll see you later."

She headed back into the house, more excited than she'd been in weeks.

That night, when they were getting ready for bed, Barry sat down on the edge of the bathtub and smiled up at her as she brushed her teeth. "What are you looking at?" she asked with her mouth full of toothpaste.

"You," he said. "I'm really proud of you, you know."

She rinsed her mouth out, wiped it on a towel, and turned around to peer down at him. "Why?"

"Because your writing is so strong that it's impacting the Dodds' lives," he said.

"Well, let's not get carried away. A hundred dollars won't go *that* far."

"There'll be more," he said. "I know there will. Tory, do you realize what that means?"

"What?"

"It means you *are* called to write. You *have* got a gift. Just because some woman wrote a story you intended to write, before you could get to it, it doesn't mean you're supposed to quit."

"This isn't exactly the great American novel, Barry. It was just a few letters."

"But not just anybody could have written them. At least, not in a way that would evoke sympathy and mobilize people into action."

She smiled at herself in the mirror, wondering if that was true. Had God led her through the ups and downs of her writing "career" so that she could be the one to write the letters that would help Joseph? "Wouldn't that be something?" she asked. "If we really could raise a lot of money this way?"

"It would be miraculous," he said.

"Yeah."

They headed back into the bedroom and crawled under the covers, and she curled up next to him, absorbing his warmth. "Barry, do you think our church will come through?"

"Sure they will. I'm going to bring it up at the finance committee meeting Wednesday night."

"You are? And you think it'll be approved?"

"Well, I should hope so. The thing is, there are a lot of people in our own congregation with needs, too."

"Yeah, I know." She looked up at her husband. "Barry, remember the other night when we were at Brenda's church?"

"Yeah?"

"It was pretty wonderful, wasn't it?"

"Yeah, it was."

"It's been a long time since I've visited another church, so I didn't have anything to compare it to. But it got me thinking. Maybe there's something different that we're supposed to be doing."

"Tory, I don't want to leave our church. I'm a deacon. I don't take that lightly."

"As a deacon, do you think you can get them to help us with the animal fair? They could set up a few booths, send some volunteers over, bake some cookies, anything."

"People in our church are busy already," he said. "We have a million programs and other things we always need volunteers for."

"I know," she said. "There's a lot going on—I like that. But some things should take precedence. Hurting people should be a priority over programs."

"Our programs are *designed* to help hurting people."

"I know. I just wish they'd help Joseph, too."

He slipped his arms around her and pulled her close. "Maybe our church just needs to be appealed to differently. I'll work on them Wednesday night at the finance committee meeting. Maybe they'll let you make a personal appeal at prayer meeting."

"All right," she said. "I'm counting on you. I don't want to have to bring out the big guns."

"What big guns?"

"These typing fingers," she said, flexing them as if they were lethal weapons. "I don't think they want me to get tougher with these letters."

"You might have to," he teased. "But that's okay. Paint them a picture with words, Tory. Help them to understand who Joseph is, and why they want to help him."

"I think I can do that," Tory said.

"Oh, yeah," Barry said with a grin. "You can do it. I have faith in you."

❧

Wednesday night, Barry seemed preoccupied as he came out of the finance committee meeting. Tory met him in the church corridor. "You coming to prayer meeting?" she asked, searching his face.

He nodded.

"What's wrong, Barry?"

He shook his head and shrugged. "Oh, nothing. I'm just a little disappointed."

Her heart crashed. "They wouldn't pledge any money?"

"Not exactly." He sank onto a Chippendale chair placed fashionably next to an antique table in the hallway. "Oh, they acted real interested. Said they were glad we were helping the Dodds. But they didn't want any direct official church involvement."

"Why not?" she asked.

"They're afraid of stepping on the toes of Brenda's church."

Tory's face began to redden. "Did you tell them her church doesn't *have* toes?"

He chuckled. "I see their point, Tory. They thought it would be more powerful if her church coordinated the efforts."

"We weren't asking anyone to coordinate any efforts," she said. "We were asking for donations."

"Well, I guess that was their way of saying no. They did put him on their prayer list, though."

She sank down next to him. "At least maybe I can get some individual donations in prayer meeting."

"Well . . . actually, I guess not," Barry said. "When I asked them if you could speak at prayer meeting, they said tonight wasn't a good night. There's too much on the agenda."

"On the *prayer* agenda?" she asked. "They're putting a limit on prayer?"

"I guess there are a lot of needs." He patted her knee. "I'm disappointed, too, Tory. They think they're doing the right thing, but I don't agree."

"Barry, I'm so embarrassed. Sylvia's and Brenda's churches are coming through. What are they going to think when they hear that ours has refused? I feel like marching in there and grabbing the microphone and chewing them all out."

"We can't do that." He rubbed his face roughly. "Frankly, I can't help feeling like I'm just as guilty. I've been just as disinterested in other people's needs as they've been over the years. The only difference in this case is that we know Joseph, we care about him. They've never seen him. I just keep thinking back on all those prayer meetings I've sat through, listening to all those needs—and never uttering a single prayer for those people, just because I didn't know them. I figured somebody else would be praying for them. Even now, you don't see us in there poring over the prayer list. There are a couple dozen Joseph Dodds on that list, and we're mad because they're not making a priority out of our request."

They sat in silence for several moments. Finally, Tory looked at him. "Barry, can we just go home?"

He nodded. "Yeah. Let's go get the kids out of their classes, unless they're in the middle of something important."

They headed for Brittany's room first, and as they rounded the corner, they heard the teacher leading the class in "I'm a Little Teapot." *Well*, Tory thought, *I suppose it passes the time* . . .

She knocked on the door and got Brittany out, then headed for Spencer's room. Spencer's class was sitting on the floor watching *Mrs. Doubtfire*. She wondered if anyone had bleeped out the profanity.

"We're not through with the movie," Spencer protested as she pulled him out the door. "They didn't even sing 'Dude Looks Like a Lady' yet. That's my favorite song."

"'Dude Looks Like a Lady' is your favorite song?" Tory asked, horrified. "Where have you heard it?"

"In that movie," he said. "I've saw it four times at church."

She shot Barry an eloquent look.

"Why're we leavin' early?" Brittany asked.

Barry put his arm around Tory's shoulders and gave her a reassuring squeeze. "Mommy just wasn't feeling very well."

"Let's use this time to go visit Joseph," Tory suggested.

"Yay!" Spencer hollered. "Do we get to go in?"

"'Fraid not, Kemo Sabe," Barry said. "You're not allowed out of the lobby unless you're over twelve. We don't want to take any germs to Joseph, do we?"

"I don't got germs!" Spencer objected. "I had a bath."

Barry waited in the hospital lobby with the kids while Tory went up to Joseph's room. He was sitting up in a chair, dressed in jeans and a Mark Lowry T-shirt, trying to put together a puzzle. Brenda hugged her and welcomed her in. Though Tory had been asked to don a gown at the nurse's station, the mask was no longer required.

"Spencer and Britty are downstairs," she told Joseph. "They're terribly offended by the policy that says they can't come up."

"I could go down and see 'em," Joseph said. "Can I, Mom? Please? I have thirty minutes on the battery. They said I needed to walk!"

"Can he do that?" Tory asked. "It's allowed?"

"Sure!" Joseph spoke up before Brenda could answer.

Brenda laughed. "I guess it'll be okay, for a few minutes. But I don't want him in the lobby. I'll get permission for them to come up to the waiting room on this floor."

Tory went downstairs and got her gang, then decked them all out in gowns. Brittany bounced up and down on the elevator as they rode up, and Spencer plopped down on his little behind, because he said it felt funnier to ride up that way. Funny was a good thing to feel, Tory supposed.

She was happy to see Joseph, masked like a bandit, walking toward the waiting room to meet them, pushing a little cart in front of him to which his Heart Mate was attached. Spencer and Brittany were as impressed with all his wiring as they would have been with Robo Cop.

Barry supervised the conversation, making sure that Spencer didn't get a wild hare and decide to swing from one of Joseph's tubes. Tory and Brenda sat just outside the waiting room, away from the kids. "So how's it going?" Tory asked.

"It's going great," Brenda said. "I'm enjoying the time I'm getting to spend with him. He's not used to one-on-one attention. It's been fun. And I'm getting some fierce homeschooling in. He's too bored to fight it."

Tory shot her a disbelieving look. "No, I mean ... really. You don't have to put on that bright face with me. Your child is sitting here waiting for a heart transplant. Don't tell me it's been fun."

Brenda's smile faded. "Does it show?"

"What? The humanity? Yes, as a matter of fact, it does. You look like a mother who's scared to death. Just the way I would look."

The smile in Brenda's eyes vanished, and that worry returned. "I try, Tory. For Joseph's sake, and for David's sake ... and for my sake, I try to have faith and think about the end of all this, when Joseph is healthy and back at home. But then I imagine a different ending, and I panic ... I don't guess I hide it very well." Brenda got up and strolled to the nurse's station, where a table was set up with a coffeepot. She poured two cups. She knew how Tory liked hers; they'd visited so many times at each other's kitchen table.

Tory waited, giving her time to say everything on her heart.

"I've had a lot of time to think the last few days," Brenda said, handing Tory her cup. "A lot of time to pray. And I guess what this has taught me is that every minute is so important, with every child."

Tory's eyes were fixed on Brenda, for she wanted to take in every drop of the wisdom Brenda had to share. "But you already seem to squeeze so much life out of *every* minute."

Brenda smiled. "Well, Tory, I guess it changes you when you realize that this moment may be the only one you have with that child. It's changed the way I look at my other kids, too."

"I think I'd be hovering over them, crying and begging and bargaining with God."

"Trust me—I've done that, too," Brenda admitted. "Oh, the bargains I've made. Like God's a car dealer or something. Like if I just hit the right combination of prayer and confession and repentance and Scripture quoting and praise, He'll say, 'Finally, she's done what I've been waiting for, so now I can answer her prayers.'"

Her eyes misted as she sipped her coffee thoughtfully. "The day they admitted Joseph, I went into the chapel to pray, and Sylvia came in, bless her heart. She was a godsend. I really needed her. I was crying, upset, angry, and everything else you can imagine. And Sylvia said something to me that I've tried to remember ever since. It was that all of the blessings we have come from God. That means our children, too. We try to hold them in clenched fists, and think they're ours. But she reminded me that Joseph belongs to God, not me. I've been entrusted with him for a while." Her mouth trembled as she got the words out. "But I have to hold that blessing in an open hand, because God could take him back at any time. He has every right to. Joseph's not an object to be bargained with, and God loves him even more than I do."

Tory only looked at her, unable to comprehend that much trust in God. "I don't think I could do it, Brenda. As much as I whine and complain about my kids, that might just be the one area of my life where I can't open my hand."

"I know," Brenda agreed. "There've been times when I've read the story of Abraham and Isaac, when he was willing to offer him as a sacrifice. And I thought, how did he do it? How do you find the strength to trust God that way?" She looked at Tory with glistening eyes. "I'm afraid I might find out."

Tory's own eyes began to fill, and she wished she knew what to say. Brenda was miles above her in the areas of wisdom and spirituality. How could Tory find any words adequate to comfort her? She fought the tightening in her throat. "So how do you keep that hand open?"

"It's not easy," Brenda bit out. "Trust me."

Tory looked down at her coffee, wiping a finger along the edge of the cup. If Joseph died, what would Brenda do? Would her faith hold, or would she rail against God? "I guess we really have no *choice* but to trust God," she said, feeling the words echo with emptiness.

"Yes, we do," Brenda said. "We can choose not to, like David." She shook her head. "But the truth is, David's lack of hope gives him even fewer options than I have. If Joseph dies, David's going to feel so angry and so defeated. He'll never be able to see any good in it."

"And you really will?" Tory asked.

Brenda touched her fingertips to her mouth, as if she could stave off the tragic expression pulling at her face. "It'll be the hardest thing that ever happened to me," she whispered. "But God understands. He was there, remember? In Gethsemane, Jesus wanted to close His fist around His own life. But He didn't. He kept that hand open, and told God that if it was His will to take His life—"

"But He grieved," Tory said quietly.

"Oh, yeah," Brenda whispered. "He did that. I'll do it, too, if He takes Joseph."

Tory dabbed at the corners of her eyes. "You're stronger than I am. I think, by now, I would have broken something. Put my fist through a wall. Gone on Prozac."

"No, I don't think so." Brenda offered her a wan smile. "Look at all the money you're bringing in for Joseph. You've got a few things going for you, too."

Tory's face brightened up, and she wiped the tears away. "Yeah, we've gotten several small checks in the mail already, and it hasn't even been a week since I sent the letters out. And I'm not finished yet. I'm going to send follow-up letters to the churches who don't answer. And I've sent out thank-yous to the ones who have. I've invited them to the animal fair so they can feel even more a part of this."

"Good idea," Brenda said. "I appreciate your efforts so much. David does, too, even though he may seem ungrateful." She sipped her coffee, then blew on the steam. "He's got so much pride. Hates the idea of charity of any kind. So he's putting a 'For Sale By Owner' sign in the yard tonight."

"No!" Tory said. "Brenda, he can't. That's why we're raising the money. Selfishly, for ourselves. We don't want you to move."

"I can't talk him out of it." Brenda got up, went to the door of the waiting room, and peered in to make sure Joseph was all right. Satisfied, she turned back to Tory. "It's probably best. Even with the donations, the expenses are so high. We'll just rent an apartment for a while."

"An apartment? With four kids? And what about David's workshop?"

"He's been looking for a job," Brenda said. "Something that pays better." She couldn't meet Tory's eyes, and finally went back into the doorway. "Joseph's got to go back to the room now before his battery runs out."

Tory followed, still disturbed, as Brenda walked Joseph to his room and plugged him back into his machine. Before she left, she hugged her friend. "Brenda, God does provide."

Brenda smiled, a real, genuine, ear-to-ear smile made more profound by her wet eyes. "Sometimes He even provides a ram in the thicket. I could use a couple of them right now."

On Cedar Circle, Leah, Rachel, and Daniel sat at their front window, watching their father hammer the For Sale sign into the ground.

"I've got supper ready for you," Sylvia said, trying to distract them.

Daniel glanced back at her. "I'm not hungry."

"Me, neither," Rachel whispered.

Sylvia walked up behind them and saw that Leah was crying. She bent down to hug the girl. "Honey, don't cry."

"I like our house," Leah said. "Where are we gonna live?"

"Wherever it is, it'll be just fine." But she had no intentions of letting them move. Somehow, she would raise the money the Dodds needed before they sold the house. Then maybe she could convince David to take it off the market.

The front door opened, and he came back in. As he stood just inside, looking at the children's sad faces, Sylvia saw the raw emotion on his own. "It's gonna be okay, guys," he said. "I haven't ever let you down before, have I?"

The three children quietly shook their heads.

He glanced up at Sylvia, then went and sat down in front of the children. "Guys, I'm counting on you now. Mama's not here to keep the house clean, and people are going to be looking at it. I need for you guys to keep it clean. You already do a really good job, but without Mama it's going to take an extra effort. Just remember, we're doing it for Joseph."

"Joseph will need a place to live when he gets better," Rachel said, her mouth beginning to quiver.

"We'll have a place to live. It may be smaller, but that's okay. We can handle that."

"But what if they raise all the money we need at the animal fair?" Daniel asked. "Then can we take the sign down?"

"They're not going to raise *that* much money," David cautioned them. "It's impossible." Again, he shot Sylvia a look before she could argue. "I do appreciate what you all are doing, Sylvia. Brenda does, too. But we have to think realistically."

She nodded. "I know, David."

He turned back to the kids. "I know things are kind of topsy-turvy right now, guys. You're not getting to see Mama much, and I haven't spent much time with you, either. But things'll get better soon. We just all have to concentrate on Joseph right now. Send him good thoughts."

"Joseph doesn't need our thoughts," Daniel whispered. "He needs our prayers."

David nodded. "Prayers, then." He got up, and Sylvia realized he had aged in the last few weeks. He looked worn, weary, almost stooped with despair. "I've got to go to the hospital now," he said. He leaned over and gave each child a hug. "I love you guys."

They each returned his love, but as he left the house, they all turned back to the window and stared at the sign as if it sealed their fate.

Sylvia just hoped she could prove to them that it didn't.

CHAPTER Thirty-Two

The animal fair on the Fourth of July was scheduled to begin at noon, but by eight A.M., dozens of people had shown up to help. Cathy spent the morning setting up corrals where the children could pet the animals. By ten, the animals began to arrive in a steady stream, as if they were headed for Noah's ark.

Just before noon, a couple dozen people from Brenda's church showed up with casseroles and hot dogs and cakes of every kind to sell to raise money for little Joseph. Sylvia's church rose to the occasion as well. Someone donated ice. Someone else donated gallons of soft drinks. Others set up game booths, complete with prizes. She hadn't even asked them, but they had supplied.

The festivities spilled over onto the parking lot, because there wasn't enough room on the lawn. A contemporary Christian group from Sylvia's church turned out for entertainment.

Around noon, Steve Bennett, the man who had come to her parent awareness meeting, showed up with his little girl, a freckle-faced, pigtailed blonde named Tracy. Cathy was happier to see him than she'd expected to be, though she tried not to show it.

The little girl, Joseph's age, was a cute little thing who stuck close to her daddy. "I thought Tracy might enjoy the fair," he said. "If there's anything I can do while I'm here, just holler. I like animals, and they like me, so if you can think of a place where you need me, I'm glad to help."

"Not yet," Cathy said. "Just go have fun with Tracy. When she starts feeling comfortable enough to let you go, come back and I'll put you to work."

He grinned and winked at Tracy. "I imagine she'll see a lot of her friends here, but so far I'm her only buddy, right?" His little girl smiled shyly and nodded her head.

"Where do you get the pictures made?" she asked.

Cathy nodded toward Rick, who had set his camera on a tripod in front of some bushes, next to a sign that said, "Pet Pictures—$10." "Rick's taking them over there," she said. "Did you bring a pet with you?"

The little girl nodded again, and she looked down at her pocket, as if she had a secret there.

"Don't tell me," Cathy said, bending over. "You have a gerbil in there."

"No, ma'am." She pulled a little turtle out of her pocket and held him up, his arms and legs flapping in the air.

"What a beautiful turtle," Cathy said. "Where did you get it?"

"Down by the creek at home," she said. "I found it this morning, and Daddy said I could get my picture made with it. Then I have to put it back in the bucket so it can swim."

"Well, if you hurry, you won't have to wait in line."

Tracy grabbed her father's hand. "Come on, Daddy. Can we do it now?"

Steve laughed and followed her over to Rick.

Less than an hour later, Cathy was at the table testing animals for heartworms when Steve returned. She was trying to examine a dog who was apparently in heat, and other dogs in line were straining at their leashes, howling and barking, trying to get away from their masters so they could get to know her a little better.

"Tracy found a friend, so they're running around checking out the booths," he said. "Anything I can help with while I'm free?"

"Yes," she said with relief. "You could help keep these animals restrained. See that one over there?" She nodded toward a German shepherd twice the size of the girl who held it. "I'd prefer putting him in the kennel if you can get him in there."

"Sure," he said. "No problem."

He hurried to the dog and offered his help. "You can stay in line and we'll just keep him locked up until it's his turn," he told the owner.

"Oh, thank you!" she said, surrendering the leash. The dog bolted forward to get to the dog in heat, but Steve reined him back in and began to scratch his ears.

"What's his name?"

"Butch."

"Come on, Butch. You gotta stay away from these women. They're nothing but trouble."

Cathy laughed under her breath.

Within seconds, Steve had the dog contained in the boxlike kennel.

"Way to go," she said. "You've done that before."

"Yeah, when I was growing up, we raised black labs."

"Really? Still have them?"

"Not here. My folks raise them in Alabama."

"Then you probably wouldn't mind locking up one more?"

He dusted off his hands. "Lady, I can lock up as many as you want."

She handed him the dog she had just examined. "Would you mind helping this lady get her into the car? She's going to run her home and then come back and enjoy the fair. She doesn't have heartworms, but she's driving all the male dogs crazy."

"No problem," he said. Expertly, he lifted the dog up and carried it to the little car the lady pointed out.

Cathy couldn't help watching him walk away. He wasn't afraid of animals, or of children, or of getting dirty, and he didn't seem to have an agenda. She liked that about him. But just as quickly as that thought danced through her brain, she chased it away. He was a man, and she had given up men.

She glanced across the lawn at Leah, Rachel, and Daniel Dodd, who were working some of the booths. Sylvia and Harry mingled with families, talking up the reason for the animal fair. Already, Sylvia had collected more money just from spontaneous donations than Tory and Barry had collected at the donor-card table.

Then her eyes fell on David, who walked around behind a video camera, looking amazed at the level of activity—all of it because of his son. He hadn't had a moment free since the fair had begun. People had been approaching him all day, offering him encouragement, asking how they could help. Cathy knew he was moved; she was moved, herself.

Cathy hoped the video would be an encouragement to Joseph. But the truth was, over the past few days he had declined noticeably. When she'd gone to see him last, he hadn't been sitting up. He'd lain in bed, struggling for breath, with dark circles under his eyes. He wasn't eating well, Brenda had said, and he'd lost weight.

Cathy only hoped all of this was not in vain. It wouldn't matter how much money they raised, if they didn't find a heart soon.

"This must be one special little boy," Steve Bennett said, and she turned around. He stood behind her, his eyes scanning the crowd.

"He *is* a special little boy," she said. "But I guess when anybody that young is threatened, you just want to help."

"Tell me about it," he said. "Boy, I don't know what I'd do if anything ever happened to Tracy."

"Joseph's her age," Cathy said.

"Yeah, that's what I hear."

The band stopped playing, and Sylvia went to the microphone and called out across the crowd. "Cathy, Dr. Cathy Flaherty? Where are you?"

Cathy waved at her and Sylvia saw her. "Come up here and tell these fine folks why we're doing this, would you?"

Cathy shot Steve a grin, then headed up to the podium. Everyone quieted down as she stepped up to the microphone. "I just want to thank you folks for coming," she said. "Especially those of you who volunteered your time, people who are here because they want to help Joseph Dodd." The crowd applauded, and she waited for it to die down. "Joseph couldn't be here today, because he's in the hospital waiting for a heart transplant. And he's not doing very well, so we'd appreciate your prayers. But as you know, we need more than that. His father, David, is one of the hardest working men I know," she said, gesturing to David, who was still videotaping. "But as most of you know, insurance often doesn't cover the complete bill for an operation like this, and the Dodd family will still have to pay thirty percent of Joseph's medical bills, and that could add up to a fortune. So we really appreciate all the sacrificial giving we've seen today." She looked down at David, Daniel, Rachel, and Leah. "You want to say anything?"

Looking woefully uncomfortable, David handed the video camera to Daniel and stepped up onto the stage. He cleared his throat and adjusted the angle of the microphone. "This is a tough time for our family, but I'm really amazed at the way the community has turned out." His voice broke off, and he wiped his eyes and reached down for the video camera. Daniel handed it to him. "I'm videotaping this so Joseph can see what a lucky little boy he is." Overcome with emotion, he stopped for a moment, fiddled with the camera, then stepped up to the mike again. "One thing I do want to say." He cleared his throat. "It's real important . . . to Joseph, and a lot of others . . . that people be organ donors. We'd really appreciate it if you'd take the time to sign your donor cards. You can just do it on the back of your driver's license." He coughed, cleared his throat, then handed the microphone to Cathy.

"I second that," Cathy said. "Sign your donor cards, please. We have a table over there where you can get cards and sign up, but the most important thing is to let your family know you did. We'd all really appreciate that. Now you all just go on and have fun," she said, "and if you feel like giving any more money than you have already, just find one of us and we'll be glad to take it."

The crowd laughed softly.

By the end of the fair, they had raised five thousand dollars for Joseph's trust fund—not counting the money from the auction of the horses, which had brought in almost that much again. Cathy could hardly believe it.

When the crowd had thinned out and only the volunteers remained, she wondered if she would be able to get the grounds cleaned up before dark. But she was amazed all over again at the number of people who stayed behind to help. Steve Bennett was one of them. He and Rick disassembled the fencing and kennels she had set up, and loaded them into her truck. Tracy, his daughter, was sitting between Rachel and Leah in the bed of Steve's truck, and they were braiding her hair, one on each side of her, while she let her turtle run for its life on the hot vinyl bed liner.

Though Annie had disappeared, Mark grudgingly walked around the lawn scooping up the evidence that the animals had been there. It was all coming down quickly, and soon there would be no trace that they had been here. She looked across the lot at the church building, and realized that God was providing through His churches. All of this was about Him as much as Joseph. These churches were demonstrating what churches were supposed to be.

Suddenly, she had a fierce yearning for her children to grow up in a congregation like this, where people cared and helped and gave. She wondered if it was too late for them to be a real part of something like this.

Her eyes drifted across to Steve Bennett as he used a wrench to disassemble some of the railing. Was he one of God's provisions? If she were looking for a man—which she definitely wasn't—he was the kind of man she would look for. He wasn't the good-looking type who knocked women dead. In fact, he would be easy to overlook in a crowd. But there was something about him that was different from the other men she'd met lately, something that made her uneasy about walking away from here and not seeing him again.

For the first time since she'd become single again, she considered asking a man for a date. Then her own lack of courage won out, and she told herself she couldn't do that. If he wanted to go out with her, he knew where he could find her. She chased the thoughts out of her mind and finished her work.

When the lawn was clear and clean and Rick had driven Mark home in the truck so they could go to the fireworks at the high school football field, Steve and his daughter still lagged behind. He helped Cathy get the last few things into her car, then looked around him. Tracy was in the bed of his pickup truck, still playing with her turtle.

"Steve, I can't tell you how I appreciate your help today," she said. "I don't think I could have done it without you."

"Oh, sure you could," he said. "You had it going pretty well when I got here."

"But you helped so much with the cleanup. I would have been here until tomorrow."

"No problem," he said. "You know, this was a great idea. Look at all the money you raised, and I think it's just the beginning. I think a lot more will come in as a result of this."

"I hope so," she said. She opened her car door, but didn't get in.

He leaned his hand on the top of the door. "Well, it was good getting to know you a little better," he said. "I still plan to see you at the school board meeting in September."

"Good. That's great." They stood staring at each other for a moment, and she thought of inviting him over for dinner. Something prevented her, and she wanted to kick herself. She could just hear Annie lecturing her. *Mom, this isn't the fifties. Grow up. Women ask men out all the time.* She held her breath, wishing he would ask her instead.

He seemed to be struggling with something, and for a moment she was sure he would ask.

But then Tracy called out, "Daddy!"

He turned around. "I'm coming, sweetie." When he faced her again, Cathy knew the moment was shattered.

"Well, guess I'll see you later."

"Yeah," she said. "Thanks again."

He watched her get into the car, then closed her door and headed back across the lot to his own truck. He pulled Tracy out of the bed and tickled her on her way into the cab. Cathy watched him wait for the little girl to hook her seat belt, then pull out of the driveway.

Some tender spot she hadn't felt in a long time swelled in her heart, and she wondered if she was crazy. Men always disappointed her. She needed to stop fantasizing that this could be any different. Steve Bennett was still a man. He had a man's desires and a man's thoughts. He couldn't be that far removed from the other men she'd known.

But then she thought of Harry . . . Barry . . . David. And she wondered if it was possible that there was one more man like them, faithful and willing to do his part, without any ulterior motives or secret agenda. Maybe Steve Bennett was real.

So why had she let him get away?

She sighed and headed back home, trying to concentrate on the successes of the day, instead of the failures.

Chapter Thirty-Three

The next morning, Rick and Annie and Mark were a little less combative about getting ready to go to church. Cathy made sure they got to their classes without making detours, then headed for her own class. They had deliberately gotten there early so they wouldn't have to walk in late. She thought it would be easier on them if they were among the first ones there instead of the last.

The 8:20 singles class was just filing out, so rather than try to fight her way through the crowd, she stopped by the visitor's desk and got a name tag, then waited until the way was clear for her to get into the room for the 9:40 class.

"Cathy?"

She swung around and saw a smiling, surprised Steve Bennett, dressed in a suit and looking like a Wall Street banker.

"Steve? Do you go to church here?"

"Yeah, for the last six months. But I didn't know you did. I thought you said you were surprised the church had let you use the lawn yesterday since you weren't a member here."

She laughed. "I'm *not* a member. I've just been visiting for a few weeks."

"Really?" he asked. "I've never seen you here."

"Apparently we go to different Sunday schools and different services."

"Well, how about that?"

She felt awkward now. She hoped he didn't think this was all a clever ploy to get to see him again.

"Where are the kids?" he asked.

"They went to their classes."

"Well, good." He looked at her again, that expression of struggle on his face, just like yesterday. "Listen . . . I know you don't know me very well, but . . . how would you feel about me taking us all out to lunch today?"

"All of us? That's six people."

"I'm aware of that," he said. "Hey, I have a decent job."

She laughed. "I'm sure you do. It's just that I hate to impose like that."

"Well, if I recall, I just volunteered it."

She grinned. "We could go dutch."

"We could, but then I might be insulted, and my pride might be crushed, and—"

"Okay!" she said. "Whatever you say. We'll order the most expensive things on the menu."

"Fine with me." His smile began to fade, and his eyes grew more serious. "I hope you don't think I'm trying to hit on you the first time I see you in church."

"No, I didn't think that's what you were doing."

"Well, there are some around here who are like that."

"Yeah, I know. We've been introduced."

"I bet you have. Somebody like you? You probably get hit on all the time."

She couldn't believe she was blushing. "Actually, that's not true."

"Well, do you have a better offer, or what?"

"Not at all."

"Okay, then, I'll tell you what. I'll meet you by the elevators after the eleven o'clock service."

"Sounds great," she said.

She sat through Sunday school feeling elated that she'd run into him again and amazed that he actually went to this church. She had vowed to give up on coming with the hope of meeting a man, and now, completely unexpectedly, she'd met one. She just hoped he didn't turn out to be a frog the moment she kissed him.

After Sunday school, her kids told her one by one that they'd found friends from school with whom they intended to sit in church. It was a pleasant surprise. She found Sylvia and Harry and slipped into the pew next to them. Before the service started, Steve came to the end of her pew. "Room for two more?" he asked.

"Sure! I thought you went to the early service."

"We did," he said with a wink. "It was so good we decided to sit through it twice."

She didn't know when she had been more flattered. "Hi, Tracy. How's it goin'?" Cathy asked.

"Pretty good," the little girl said with that shy grin. "How are you?"

"Great." Cathy was impressed with the child's politeness. It spoke well of Steve's parenting skills. She only hoped her own children's manners didn't run him off.

He sat down and she introduced him once again to Sylvia and Harry. They had met the day before, but she wasn't sure they'd remember. As the service began, Cathy found she enjoyed listening to the sound of his voice as he sang the praise songs. It was as if he believed the words he sang, as though standing up and lifting his voice to God was a joy and not a chore.

Steve followed the pastor's sermon with his Bible open and a pen poised to take notes. There was something about that unpretentious, unself-conscious attitude that appealed to her. She saw Bill, the guy with the Porsche, sitting several rows away next to a size-ten blonde in a size-six dress. She kept looking into her compact mirror, and every now and then, when the mirror was turned just right, Bill stole a glimpse at himself.

Steve, in his unself-conscious plainness, was much more attractive to Cathy than the church Casanova.

As the service wound to a close, she silently prayed that having lunch with her kids would not chase him away.

Chapter Thirty-Four

Across town, as Joseph watched the video his dad had made of the animal fair, Dr. Robinson stopped by to examine him. Brenda and David watched quietly as the doctor studied his chart intensely and asked Joseph questions. The boy answered in weak monosyllables.

Finally, the doctor patted Joseph's hand and asked Brenda and David to step out into the hall.

"What is it, Doctor?" David asked when they were out of the room.

Dr. Robinson looked at the floor as if carefully considering his words. "I'm sure it's no surprise to you that Joseph's getting worse, despite our best efforts," he said. "His need for a heart is getting pretty urgent." His voice faltered again, and Brenda realized that this was taking its toll on him, as well. She wondered if treating a dying child was ever routine for him.

"Is he gonna make it?" Brenda asked him on a whisper.

It took a moment for him to answer. "I don't know," he said. "Without a miracle . . ."

He didn't have to say the words. They knew as they went back into the room that Dr. Robinson didn't think Joseph would make it. With a Herculean effort, Brenda tried not to let Joseph see her despair. Instead of focusing on what might happen, she concentrated on making him more comfortable.

Joseph was watching the animal fair with interest, but not with the joy or excitement she had hoped for. Instead, his eyes seemed sad as the footage rolled on. Finally, when it was over, she sat next to him on his bed, and leaned over him. "What's the matter, Joseph?"

He kept his eyes on the blank television screen, and Brenda met David's eyes, searching for insight into the little boy's mind. David shook his head, as if he had none.

After a while, Joseph spoke up. "They all think I'm gonna die, don't they?"

Brenda caught her breath and choked back her tears.

"Die? Of course not, sweetheart. They wouldn't have gone to all that trouble to have the fair and raise all that money if they thought you were going to die."

"But they think I'll die if we can't afford the transplant, or if we don't get a heart," he said.

With a shock, she realized that that thought, so clear to all the rest of them, hadn't yet been clear in Joseph's mind—until he saw the video. Now she wished they'd never shown it to him. "Honey, you're very sick. You know that. But they're doing everything they can for you here, and soon, you will get a heart."

"But what if it doesn't come in time?"

"It will. It has to."

He looked up at his mother, his eyes pensive. "Mama, remember when the doctor first told us about my heart, and we went to church and they prayed over me?"

David sat up straighter and met Brenda's eyes. *I told you not to allow that,* his look said. *I told you it would traumatize him.*

Her eyes misted over as she looked down at her son. "Yes, I remember," she said softly.

"That was nice," he said. "It felt like the prayers would work."

"Prayers always work, sweetheart."

"I know," he said. "But, sometimes . . ."

Her throat was so full that she couldn't answer him, and tears brimmed in her eyes. Concerned, Joseph reached up and touched her face. "Don't cry, Mama. I know I'm going to heaven."

She wanted to scream out that he wasn't going anywhere, not yet. Not now. But she couldn't make the words come out.

Squeezing his mother's hand, he turned his head to his father. "Daddy?"

"Yeah, son?"

"How do they get a heart?"

David got up and came to his side. "What do you mean, how do they get it?"

"I mean, where does it come from?"

"They get it from another person."

"What person is mine coming from?" he asked.

"We don't know yet."

Joseph thought that over for a moment. "What happens to them?" he asked finally. "I mean, after I get their heart?"

David breathed a deep sigh and leaned wearily over the rail. He began to stroke his little boy's red hair with callused fingertips. Brenda struggled to choke her tears back. "Well, son, what usually happens is that somebody is in an accident. And they die. Except their organs still work, so the doctors can take them out and give them to people like you, who need them."

A troubled expression fell like a shadow over Joseph's face. "Somebody has to die so I can live?"

David's mouth twitched at the corners as he nodded. Brenda slid her hand along her husband's shoulder, hoping to comfort him.

"Kinda like Jesus, huh, Mama?"

Brenda tried to smile. "Yeah. Kinda like."

The thought didn't seem to give Joseph much pleasure. Still frowning, he looked at the television screen again, thinking that over. "Is it going to be a kid? The person that has to die, I mean."

"We don't know," Brenda whispered.

"We can't know that, buddy," David said. "They'll give you whatever heart is available when you're at the top of the list, as long as it's a match for you. It might even be an adult's heart. It depends more on the size of the heart than the age of it. But it'll be random."

"It's not *that* random," Brenda corrected. She bent over her son, making him look into her face. "Honey, God is in control. He already knows whose heart He's going to give you. And when that person is in an accident, or whatever happens, God's going to take his or her spirit out before anybody ever takes the heart."

"So they won't feel it?" Joseph asked.

"Not at all."

"But what about their parents? Won't they be sad?"

She smeared the tears across her cheek. "Sure, they will," she whispered. "But it's up to God when that person goes home."

Silence fell between them as Joseph stared into her glistening eyes, processing his thoughts. "It's up to God when I go home, too, isn't it?"

She paused, almost unable to answer. "Yes, honey. It is."

Several moments went by as he gazed at his thoughts. "I feel bad taking somebody else's heart."

She struggled to steady her voice. "But that might be how God answers our prayers," Brenda said. "To take someone's death, and turn it into life. It's just like God, isn't it?"

Joseph didn't answer.

Later, Joseph fell asleep, and David stepped out into the hallway. Brenda followed, and found him leaning against the wall. Her eyes were swollen from crying, and she felt as if she hadn't slept in years.

"I wish you wouldn't tell him those things," David said, staring at the opposite wall.

"What things?"

"Things about your spirit leaving your body and God being in control."

"I was telling him the truth, David."

He moved his gaze to her. "I don't see that as the truth, Brenda, and I have a hard time with those concepts being put into the head of a little boy who might die."

"What would you rather he believed?" she asked, growing angry. "Would you rather have him believe that it's all random and hopeless? That his life or death means nothing? Would you rather tell him he's insignificant, that life will go on with or without him?"

"You know I wouldn't," David said.

"Then what is wrong with my telling him the truth? That God is in control, that He's taking care of him, and that *if* and *when* he gets a heart, it'll be because God chose it for him."

"And what if his body rejects it?" David flung back. "Will you tell him then that God made a mistake?"

She wanted to scream that she couldn't take much more of his disbelief. But she had no choice. "David, I don't know what's going to happen. God may take Joseph out of our hands, and we may go home and have three children to tuck in at night instead of four." She began to sob but didn't let it stop her. "But if He does, David, it won't be because of any *mistake*."

Slowly, he pulled her into a hug and held her tightly against him. "I'm sorry," he whispered. "I didn't mean to hurt you."

She tried to pull herself together, but her face was still twisted in pain. "When you talk about God as if He doesn't exist, I take it real personally, David."

"Why? We have different philosophies, that's all."

"It's not a philosophy," she whispered. "He's real. He's part of me. I love Him. And He gave up His life for you and for me. Just like somebody is going to have to give up his life to save Joseph. The difference is that they won't volunteer. It won't be a choice they make. But when Jesus came down here to die for our sins, it *was* a choice He made, David. He didn't have to do it, but He did. And when you talk about Him the way you do, it hurts me, because I'm part of Him!"

David held her face against his chest and let her weep. "I'm sorry. I guess I haven't been very sensitive to that."

"Joseph knows Him, too," she cried. "You promised, David. When I became a Christian, you told me I could raise our children that way. You said it wouldn't hurt anything. Don't pull it out from under Joseph now when it's all he has left. It's a lot, David. It's a lot. It's more than most people have."

"Shhh," he whispered. "I'm sorry. You tell him what you need to get through this. I wish I could believe it."

"I wish you could, too," she cried. She spoke the words as a prayer.

CHAPTER Thirty-Five

Cathy's lunch with Steve was fraught with tension. Her children hadn't embarrassed her yet, but she fully expected their disrespect to manifest itself at any moment.

They were halfway through the meal when Annie fulfilled that expectation. "Mom, can Rick run me home? Allen's coming to get me, and we're going out to the lake."

Cathy didn't look up as she cut her steak. "No, Annie. I'll get you home after we eat."

"But I'm finished."

"Well, I'm not," Rick said. "Besides, I'm not running you anywhere."

"Mom, make him," she whined. "Allen will be there soon. It's rude to make him wait."

"It's rude to whine at the table," Rick shot back. "So shut up, will you?"

Cathy shot Steve an apologetic look. He seemed a little embarrassed. Keeping her voice calm, Cathy leaned toward her children. "Could we refrain from the whining *and* the bickering?" she asked.

"I'm not whining," Annie said through gritted teeth. "I'm just telling you that I need to go. You don't need me on your date."

Mortified, Cathy glanced at Steve again. He was busy cutting Tracy's meat and acting as if he hadn't heard. But judging from the sudden hush, Cathy realized that even the people at the next table had heard. "Annie, unless you change your tone and lower your voice, you won't be going anywhere today. Now close your mouth and wait until we're finished."

"Fine." Annie threw her napkin on the table and slid her chair back. "I'll just call him and tell him to pick me up here!"

Cathy stared at her as her face turned scarlet. "You can call him, all right, and tell him that you won't be leaving the house today because you couldn't control your mouth." She picked up her purse and dug for some coins. "In fact, I'll pay for the call."

"Mom! You can't do that!"

"Watch me," Cathy said.

Furiously, Annie stormed from the table.

Cathy wanted to cry. "Steve, I'm so sorry."

"No problem," he said, but she could see on his face that it was a big problem.

It grew bigger when Annie didn't come back to the table. By the time they'd finished the meal and returned to the car, she realized that Annie had left.

"Ten bucks says Allen picked her up," Rick wagered.

Cathy tried to keep her rage contained as Steve paid the bill.

As the kids got into the cars, Steve lingered behind. "You all right?" he asked.

She thought of lying, but realized he'd see right through her. "No, actually. I'm not. I've got to get a grip on her. I'm just so sorry she ruined our lunch."

"She didn't ruin it," he said. "It was still nice."

"Be honest," she said. "It was the most expensive fiasco you've ever experienced."

"Not true," he maintained. He glanced into his truck at Tracy. "Well, I'd better get Tracy home. I'll talk to you later, okay?"

She knew better than that. "Yeah. See you later."

When they had pulled out of the parking lot, Cathy looked over at Rick. "Well, that was a nightmare."

"Not my fault," Rick said. "Annie was the brat. In fact, if you don't ground her up one side and down the other, there's just no justice."

Cathy drove in silence until they got home. She hurried into the house. Annie wasn't home. Her church clothes were puddled on the floor of her room where she'd stepped out of them, so Cathy knew she hadn't been kidnapped at the restaurant.

"She went to the lake, Mom," Mark said. "She does whatever she wants to."

"Rick? Mark?" Both boys looked at her.

"Yeah?"

"Leave the parenting to me, thank you. I'll be in my room. Let me know if your sister comes home."

Then she marched to her room and slammed the door behind her. Throwing herself on the bed, she wondered where she'd gone wrong.

CHAPTER *Thirty-Six*

School started the last week of August, and Brenda came home from the hospital early that first morning to get the kids ready. They were nervous and full of questions about what was going to happen. She had already done what she could to make the transition to public school easier on them, arranging for Leah and Rachel to be put in the same classroom and for Daniel to be placed in several of Mark Flaherty's classes. Knowing that none of the three would be totally alone gave her some peace of mind.

She tried to sound excited as she packed their lunches. "Won't this be great? Instead of listening to me all day, you'll get to hear other teachers. And all those new friends you'll make . . ."

The kids were quiet. "What if people make fun of us because we've never been to school before?" Rachel asked.

"They won't. And if they do, when they see how smart you are, they'll stop."

"Mom, can't we wait until Joseph comes home and you can homeschool again? We'll work hard to catch up."

"I promise, when things have settled down, we'll start back. But just in case this takes longer than I think, I want you learning. It'll be a good experience. Trust me."

As she drove her kids to their respective schools and made sure they got through the paperwork of registration, she hoped she hadn't asked them to trust her in vain.

With every day that passed, Brenda tried to assure herself that they were one day closer to getting a heart for Joseph. But it was a thin, fragile slice of hope, for Joseph was declining daily. He spent much of the time sleeping, and twice his blood pressure slipped so low that she thought they were going to lose him.

The only color left in his complexion was the sickly gray of his freckles. He didn't get up anymore, even to go to the bathroom, so they had inserted a catheter. Monitoring his urination made them aware that his kidneys were beginning to lose their function, too.

The doctors moved Joseph into cardiac intensive care but allowed Brenda to stay with him, since she was able to take some of the burden off the nurses, who had other patients to watch. At night, David would sit with Joseph while Brenda visited with her other children in the waiting room. Taking their cue from their mother, they tried to paint a happy face on their stories about school, but Brenda could see that this crisis had taken its toll.

The fact that they were close to selling the house didn't help her spirits, either. One couple had looked at it three times and had assured David that they would be back in touch soon. In all, he had shown the house at least a dozen times. The pressure that put on the kids to keep it spotless was almost cruel, but she knew there was no way around it.

In her despair, she turned to God for comfort, but found herself praying incessantly for the heart that would save her son. God seemed to be saying "no," and she couldn't understand it.

One Monday morning, Dr. Robinson came into Joseph's area and asked her to get in touch with David because he needed to meet with both of them. As she called her husband, her heart deflated.

When Harry and Sylvia came to sit with them during their meeting with Dr. Robinson, Brenda knew that this was going to be the prepare-yourselves speech. She leaned on David as they went in, and trembled as they sat down. Sylvia sat on the other side of her, holding her hand.

"Brenda, David," Dr. Robinson began in a soft, gentle, apologetic tone. "I know it doesn't surprise you to know that Joseph is declining. You saw his blood pressure this morning. You know about his kidney function. We've done as much as we can, and we're going to keep doing it. If his kidneys don't rebound by tomorrow, we're going to put him on dialysis. Even as we speak, we're adjusting his medications. We're doing everything we can to keep him alive."

"But?" David prompted, waiting for what seemed inevitable.

"But . . ." The doctor glanced at Harry, who looked very tired, as if he, too, had been losing sleep over Joseph. "But we may not succeed. We're hoping to get a heart in time. Joseph's at the top of the list. We could get a match at any time. But if we don't . . . I'm afraid there may not be much more we can do for him."

Brenda wilted against David.

"But that Heart Mate was a bridge," David insisted. "It was supposed to keep him alive . . . until . . ."

"It has its limitations," Dr. Robinson said. "Most of the time, we have good luck with it. But in Joseph's case—"

"The dialysis," Brenda cut in. "Won't it help? Won't it get the poisons out of his body and make his heart work better?"

"It will filter out some of the toxins," Harry said. "And it might make him feel better, for a time."

"Then we can keep doing it," she said. "Just as much as we need to." She looked at David, who still looked stunned. "I don't care about the cost. We're selling the house. We can sell our furniture, our cars . . . anything. If the dialysis can make him feel better, and keep him alive . . ."

"It's his heart," Dr. Robinson cut in gently. "That's the main problem. His heart may not make it."

Brenda doubled over, covering her face with both hands as she wept into them. Sylvia embraced her and began to weep with her. David sat as still as a statue, staring at the air.

"I'm sorry," Dr. Robinson said. "I don't want you to give up hope. But I've found that it makes it easier when the parents know what to expect. When they have time to prepare themselves."

"I can't prepare myself for this," David whispered in a thick, broken voice. "I'll never be prepared."

"We're still praying for a heart," Sylvia told them. "It's not over yet. God still hears. His timing is perfect."

Brenda didn't voice the questions swirling in her mind: Why was God waiting when Joseph was so sick? Why was someone so young and bright and innocent so close to death? She tried to remember the last time she'd had a prayer answered, but it seemed so long ago. All of her prayers lately had been about Joseph—or David. None of those prayers had been answered, and now her heart demanded to know why. How long would it take for God to save Joseph?

"How long?" David asked, still wooden. "If he doesn't get a heart, how long has he got?"

Brenda looked up, trying to read the exhaustion and dread on the doctor's face. "A few days at the most," he said.

"*A few days?*" She collapsed into Sylvia's arms again, then pulled away and turned to her husband. "Oh, David." He opened his arms to her and held her as she cried, but he was so rigid, so quiet, that she feared what might be going through his mind.

It had to be even worse than what was going through hers. Anger, confusion, despair—what were they going to do with all these feelings?

When they got back to Joseph's room in ICU, there was no change. David wanted to stay with him, so Brenda went out to the waiting room, where Sylvia was waiting.

"How is he?" Sylvia asked.

"Terrible," she said. "Asleep."

"No. I meant David."

Brenda shook her head and sat down next to her friend. "David is ... stone cold and silent. I can see the anger brewing inside. I think that, for the first time, David *wants* to believe in God—so he can lash out at Him." She met Sylvia's eyes. "I understand that feeling, Sylvia. I've been doing a little lashing on my own. Why won't God answer this prayer? Why won't He heal my baby?"

"He will, Brenda. One way or another, He will." She breathed a deep sigh. "I've asked Him the same questions myself over the last few weeks," she said. "When I've been out trying to raise money for Joseph. I've asked, 'Why won't You send the money they need? Why does it all have to be so hard? Why can't just part of this turn out right, to encourage them?'"

"I appreciate all you've done," Brenda said, wiping her eyes. "I know that your efforts, and Cathy's and Tory's, are going to make such a difference. I'm sorry it's been so hard for you."

"Thank you, but that's not what I was getting at," Sylvia said. "Brenda, when I've prayed those things, the Lord has reminded me that things *are* working out. Let's not forget the answered prayers, the blessings ..."

Brenda closed her eyes and tried to think of what those blessings were. "Blessings. Let's see ..."

"How about Dr. Robinson? Hasn't he been a good doctor?"

"Yes. And Harry. He's been a huge blessing. And so have you. I don't know what I would have done without you."

"What else?"

"The time with Joseph. Every minute. When he's been awake, we've talked and played games ... I've never *had* time alone with Joseph. He's always had three siblings competing for his time. It's been good."

"Anything else?"

Brenda thought for a moment, then a sad smile stole across her face. "You know what this reminds me of? A few months ago, the day of Joseph's birthday party, when he collapsed for the first time, we sat in the doctor's office and played a game.

He had to pretend he had a million dollars and spend every cent. The things he came up with were so sweet."

Sylvia's eyes lit up. "Then pretend you can have a million blessings—anything you want. What would they be? Just think of the snapshots of those blessings."

"A heart for Joseph," she said without thinking. "One that works." She paused. "Snapshots. Joseph on his bicycle. Joseph hugging the dog. A family portrait when the kids are grown—all four of them, not just three." Her gaze lowered, and she tried to think of more. "But if he dies, those snapshots will be so different."

"What will they be?" Sylvia asked, taking her hands and making her look at her. "Not the loss, the sorrow—what's the blessing?"

Brenda paused, forcing her mind by sheer power of will to see her situation from a different angle. "Reunion," she said finally. "In heaven. When I get there, and Joseph comes running, with Jesus right behind him. And the love he's brought to our lives, that you can't put in a snapshot, but it's there, in our family. It won't ever die. That will be one of the blessings."

"And the friends who've been praying for you and loving you," Sylvia said. "Hasn't that meant something?"

"Yes," Brenda said. "It has. I just . . . I want them to see that God does still answer prayer."

"Don't you think He does?"

She wasn't sure. "It's just like I've told you before. I want this to be answered a certain way. But I know God may have another plan. And I don't want Joseph to suffer. I want to put him into God's hands. I just don't know how." She broke down, and Sylvia hugged her again. "Pray for me, Sylvia. Pray that I'll be able to lay Joseph in God's arms, and trust Him to do the perfect thing. Even if it hurts me. Even if it hurts all of us. Right now, I feel like if I lose my focus, Joseph will die. If I close my eyes and sleep, he'll slip away. If I go downstairs to eat, he won't be there when I get back." She got to her feet. "Even now, it makes me crazy sitting out here, knowing that he could breathe his last breath.

I feel like his living depends on something I can do. But in my heart, I know better. Pray that I'll trust God about Joseph, Sylvia. Pray that I'll have enough faith to let go."

"I have been all along, sweetheart," Sylvia said. "And I think that prayer is being answered as we speak."

CHAPTER Thirty-Seven

The urgency surrounding Joseph's heart transplant became more apparent to Cathy each time she visited him that week. It was clear that he was running out of time.

On Thursday, Cathy came home from the hospital more depressed than she'd been all week. Annie was sulking in front of the television, unable to leave the house or talk on the phone since the stunt she'd pulled at the restaurant. Cathy had threatened to keep her from getting her driver's permit if she was disobedient during her punishment, and that had worked. Annie hadn't made any more surprise disappearances.

The phone rang as Cathy searched the refrigerator for something quick to cook for dinner. Annie leaped for it. "Hello?" she almost shouted. Cathy gathered from her scowl that it wasn't for her. Rolling her eyes, Annie shoved the phone toward her mother.

Cathy froze for a moment. "Is it Brenda?"

"No," Annie said. "Some guy." She looked up as Cathy took the phone. "Why? Is Joseph worse?"

"He's real bad," Cathy said. She thought of getting Annie to take a message, but the thought crossed her mind that it might be Steve. She hadn't heard from him since their lunch Sunday, and didn't really expect to. Still, she didn't want to take the chance of missing his call. "Hello?" she said.

"Cathy? This is Steve."

Her spirits instantly inflated again. "Hi."

"Hi. Listen, it sounds kind of busy there . . ."

She reached for the remote control and turned down the television, then took the cordless phone into the dining room. "No, no. Not at all."

"Well, I won't keep you, right here at supper time. I just wanted to see if you'd like to have dinner tomorrow night."

She was so stunned that she almost couldn't answer. "I can't believe you'd ask me again after being around my kids."

He laughed. "I'm not inviting them."

"Still . . . I thought I'd heard the last of you."

His laughter faded, and there was a moment of silence. "I meant to call before now. I just . . . didn't."

She didn't tell him that she'd noticed, or that she'd had at least two depressing, miserable nights hoping he would. It had taken all week for her to get philosophical about it. "It's okay. I've been busy, anyway. I didn't know if you had or not."

"Sometimes . . ." His voice faded off. She frowned, wondering what he was going to say. "Sometimes dating seems too complicated," he went on. "I start to worry about Tracy's reaction, and I think about all the potential problems . . ."

She swallowed, but tried to keep her voice light. "Hey, it's not like we're walking down the aisle together. Just two friends having dinner. Without their kids."

He laughed again. "So—Tracy will be spending the night at her grandmother's tomorrow night."

"My kids'll be at their dad's."

"Then tomorrow sounds good."

But by the next evening, Cathy's spirits were lower than they'd been all week. She was looking forward to her dinner with Steve, but she had talked with Sylvia on the phone that afternoon about Joseph's plight, and the news wasn't good.

Steve arrived exactly on time, and she tried not to look too eager as she let him in. "Hi," she said.

"Hi."

There was a chemistry between them, an electric spark that she hadn't felt in years. She liked being around him. His very presence made her feel better. "I'm almost ready," she said. "Just let me get my sweater."

"Sure," he told her. "No hurry."

She ran to get her cardigan, then hurried back to the front room. He took it out of her hands and helped her put it on. "So how's Joseph?" he asked.

"Not well," she said. "I'm starting to think he may not make it until he gets a heart."

Steve's expression mirrored her own concern. "No kidding."

"Yeah, it's getting pretty bad. I don't know how Brenda does it. She reads to him, sings to him, talks and tries to play with him. But he just lies there, too weak to do anything."

"What's your friend next door saying? The doctor?"

"They don't give him much time," she said.

His expression collapsed, and he sank onto her couch. "Wow. I didn't expect that. Guess I thought that, with all the success at the fair and all the money we raised, he'd *have* to get better. Stupid thinking, I guess."

"I had the same idea. It just seemed like everything was working out." She got her purse and looked down at him. "So where are you taking me?"

He thought for a moment. "Well, I was thinking of some place where we could get some good seafood, but ..." He hesitated.

"But what?"

He got back to his feet and met her eyes. "Cathy, I don't know how you'd feel about this, but I had this idea this afternoon ..."

"What?"

"Well, I was thinking we could go to Kinko's and print up some flyers about Joseph. Get about a thousand run off, and then go to the coliseum where they're having that big gospel thing tonight, and we could go around and put the flyers on the car windows asking for prayers and donations. I mean, if they don't send any money, we need the prayers even more."

She gazed at him for a moment, moved to tears. "You're right."

"Does that sound like a good idea, or would you rather go eat steak?"

She laughed. "How can I say no? Steve, it sounds like a wonderful idea."

"The restaurant will still be open when we finish," he said. "We'll miss the movie, but I don't care about that if you don't."

She could hardly speak. As they walked out to his car, she prayed silently that God wouldn't let her fall head over heels for this man unless it was part of the plan.

Chapter Thirty-Eight

The home video of the Dodd kids singing a song for Joseph played across the hospital television screen. Brenda watched Joseph staring at the screen with dull eyes. The videos weren't cheering him anymore, and she wondered if he had the energy to smile. The song ended, and the video camera began recording the supper table conversation. They had set the tripod in Joseph's place, so it would seem as if he was there, listening to the idle chitchat and the family bantering.

On the video, David looked tired, bedraggled. She knew he'd been taking in more work than he could handle and working around the clock to get it all done. He was a proud man who didn't want to depend on donations to pay for his son's medical bills, if there was any possibility of his paying them off himself. Often, his days were interrupted by real estate prospects wanting to view their house. At night, he spent as much time as he could at the hospital with Brenda and Joseph, while Sylvia sat with the kids. She saw the despair on his face as he ate, and she wished there was something she could do about it. But she was as helpless to make things better for David as she was to help Joseph.

"You want me to turn the video off, honey?" she asked her son.

For a moment, Joseph didn't answer, then finally, in a voice just above a whisper, he said, "No, I like it."

She turned on the bed so that she was facing him, and gazed down into his pale little face. "What's wrong, honey? You seem kind of sad today."

He looked up at her and tears filled his eyes. "Mama, if I die, how long before you'll come to heaven?"

A cold hand gripped her heart. In all the books she'd read on parenting and homeschooling, she'd never seen advice on answering *this* question. "You're not going to die."

"But if I do. How long?"

She swallowed down the lump in her throat. "I can't say for sure," she whispered. "But I bet it'll just be a blink of an eye. Time passes differently in heaven, you know."

He nodded pensively and looked back at the television screen. "You think Daddy'll ever get there?"

She turned her head back to the screen so Joseph wouldn't see her tears. The video showed David piddling in the kitchen, chattering with the kids, talking to Joseph every now and then as if he was at the table with them. "Honey, I pray every day for your daddy," she said. "Something's going to get through to him one of these days. I know it is."

His silence pulled her gaze back to him. A tear rolled down his face, but he didn't seem to have the energy to wipe it away. She did it for him. "What if I never see him again?" Joseph whispered.

She looked down at him, waging a war within herself to keep from falling apart. "It could still happen, Joseph," Brenda said in a shaky voice. "You might still get a heart." It was the only answer she was capable of giving him. That stubborn faith was the only thing keeping her functioning—keeping her in this room day by day, hour by hour, minute by minute, talking to

Joseph, trying to keep him from despairing—trying to keep *herself* from despairing.

Joseph shook his head feebly. "What if I don't, Mama?"

She didn't know if her voice would make it through an answer. "We're still praying, Joseph," she said. "God's still in control. He knows about your heart. He hasn't forgotten."

"Then why hasn't He given me one?"

"It's not time yet," she said.

He stared up at her, thinking, and she wanted to tell him to stop it, that it wouldn't do any good, that he needed to spend his time thinking little boy thoughts, pretending he was a wounded cowboy, an injured soldier, a football player who'd just scored a winning touchdown. He needed to pretend he was going to get better and get up out of this bed and go home. But he wasn't having little boy thoughts. His thoughts were those of an old man who'd lived his life to its end, and now faced the death that his loved ones weren't prepared for.

"Mama?" he whispered, finally meeting her eyes.

"Yes, sweetie. What is it?"

"I want to go home. I want to sleep in my own bed."

She stroked his forehead and tried valiantly to hold back the tears. "Of course you will, when you get that new heart and the doctor releases you. We'll have a big party. The whole neighborhood."

He stared at the ceiling for a long while as his thoughts reeled by. Finally, mercifully, his eyes closed. He fell into a light sleep. Relieved that she wouldn't have to answer his questions anymore—not for a while, anyway—she tucked his blanket around him, then went to the end of the bed to make sure his feet were warm. His toes were swollen, further testimony that his heart wasn't adequately pumping his blood. She got a pair of socks and slipped them on him, then tucked the sheets and blanket around them. She stood at the window, staring out into the night. Crossing her arms across her stomach in a self-embrace, she let the tears flow harder and faster than they'd flowed yet.

After a while, she turned back to the bed and regarded her little boy with his gray face and his bluish lips, held hostage by a heart in rebellion. Soon, that heart would go on strike altogether. It might be a quiet, merciful ending. Or there could be pain that grew worse hour by hour, long past the point either mother or son should be able to endure. Only God knew.

She heard footsteps in the corridor outside, then David appeared in the doorway. It was after visiting hours, and she hadn't expected him.

He saw her crying and quietly came to her and pulled her into his arms. She clung to him with all her might. "Did you leave the kids alone?"

"No," he whispered. "Sylvia came over to spend the night so I could come back. It was good that she did." He seemed to hesitate, then added, "I felt like I should be here tonight." His voice caught on the last words, and still holding her, he looked at his sleeping son. "Any change?" he asked.

Brenda shook her head. "He's talked a lot about dying."

David closed his eyes. His throat bobbed as he swallowed.

"We talked about heaven," she said quietly, her eyes fixed on Joseph's face. "He's worried that he'll get there but never see you."

He looked down at his little boy, then back up at his wife, and shook his head drearily. "I'll tell you something, Brenda. I find it real hard to believe in a God who would let a little boy like this get sick and die at nine years old."

The angry, whispered words cut through her heart. "David, you didn't believe even when things were fine. If none of this had ever happened, it wouldn't have made any difference to you—not spiritually."

"Well, we'll never know that, will we?" Wearily, he went to Joseph's bed, leaned over, and pressed a kiss on the boy's forehead. Then he dropped his head to the sheet next to Joseph's head, and his shoulders began to shake as the sobs tore silently out of him. Brenda put her hands on his shoulders and pulled him up. He turned around and held her, his body quaking with despair.

"You know, if I could cut out my own heart, I'd give it to him."

"I know," she whispered. "I feel the same way."

"None of this should be happening. Life stinks."

She couldn't answer. They sat down together on the vinyl couch, wiping tears from their faces as they watched their little boy sleep, checking every rise and fall of his shoulders, every weak, irregular bleep of his heart on the monitor. It was nearing midnight, and except for the occasional footsteps outside the door, there hadn't been a sound. It was as quiet as death, and she wondered if Joseph would just slip away from wherever he was right now—just stop breathing quietly, without a fight, and never open his eyes again.

Hours passed, and without meaning to, she and David dozed off, their heads resting against the back of the small vinyl couch. When Brenda awoke, it was one A.M. She felt instantly guilty for falling asleep when her son was dying, and she got up and went to Joseph's bed.

Behind her, she heard David stirring. "Is he all right?" he asked softly.

Joseph hadn't moved since falling asleep last night. Studying the monitor, she was discouraged by how weak his heartbeat was. Would those little peaks flatten out altogether before morning came?

"Brenda?" David asked, getting up and joining her beside the bed.

"He's . . . I don't know." She checked the pulse in his neck. It was so weak she almost couldn't find it. "He hasn't moved. He's just lying there, on his back. He never sleeps on his back."

They turned him on his side, and began massaging his back and legs, trying to get his blood circulating. His heart rhythm changed as they did, which brought two nurses in to check on him. They seemed somber and concerned, which made Brenda worry more. The activity around him didn't waken him.

They sat back on the couch, watching their son as if he would pass from life as soon as they took their eyes off him. When the monitor began to show a weaker beep, they both stood up.

Brenda went to Joseph's bed and shook him, watching the monitor as she did. His heartbeat didn't change. "Joseph, no!" she cried.

Suddenly the line on the monitor flattened, and an alarm sounded. Nurses bolted in and pushed her aside. Doctors rushed in behind the nurses. They all began working on her son, shouting instructions to each other and calling for equipment. Someone ushered them out into the hall, and she buried her face in David's chest as she waited for them to pronounce her son dead.

CHAPTER *Thirty-Nine*

Daniel Dodd couldn't sleep that night. Sylvia heard him walking down the stairs, and she rolled out of Brenda and David's bed, pulled on her robe, and followed him down. "Daniel? Is something wrong?" she asked.

He headed into the kitchen and turned on the light. His eyes were sleepy and his hair ruffled, but he didn't look like the twelve-year-old child he was. He had changed in these past few months, just as Leah and Rachel had. He was older. Sylvia could only guess at the thoughts that went through his mind. "I couldn't sleep," he said.

"Are you worried about Joseph?"

He didn't answer. For a moment, he just looked down at the floor. "I was thinking about his shoes," he said finally. "He couldn't get them on his feet when he left for the hospital because his feet were swollen. I thought maybe he could wear mine. But they're so sweaty and dirty, I thought I'd wash them. We could take them to him tomorrow. He likes my shoes."

"Then what will you wear to school?" Sylvia asked.

He shrugged. "My flip-flops, I guess. Doesn't matter."

She remembered when her children were twelve. Shoes had mattered a lot. Sarah had gone through a stage where she'd wanted black sneakers that she'd neon-painted herself. Jeff had insisted on a certain brand of high-tops that he swore enabled him to make the junior high basketball team.

Neither of them had suffered through sleepless nights over a sibling whose shoes didn't fit.

"Do you know how to wash them, Miss Sylvia?" Daniel asked. "I know how to wash jeans and underwear and stuff, but not sneakers."

"Sure," she said, taking them out of his hands and heading into the small laundry room. She dropped them into the washer, poured the soap in, and started the cycle. When she turned back around, Daniel was still staring at the floor.

"What are you thinking, Daniel?"

Again, he shrugged. "Just that I wish I could miss school tomorrow and go to the hospital. There are things I need to tell Joseph when he wakes up."

Sylvia pulled the chair out from the table and sat down. "What things?"

"Things like ... what a cool little kid he is. I never told him that. I just called him dumb and stuff."

She watched him standing there in a baggy T-shirt and gym shorts, his feet bare. "I'm sure he knows you didn't mean it."

"I'd still like to tell him." He was struggling with the emotions pulling at his mouth.

She knew he would never allow her to do what came most naturally—pull him into her arms and hold him. She felt helpless, inadequate. "How about some warm milk?" she asked finally.

He nodded.

She warmed it up in a saucepan, then poured two glasses, praying it would help him sleep. When he'd finished, she set her elbows on the table and gazed at him. "Feel pretty helpless, don't you?"

He stared down at the empty glass and nodded.

"Me, too," she said. "I've been praying and praying. It's like my mind won't let me rest. It keeps saying that we have to keep praying."

"We do," Daniel said. "Joseph needs us to."

"That's what I was doing when I heard you on the stairs."

He gave her a half-smile. "That's what I was doing before I came down." He got up and put his glass in the sink, then slid his chair back under the table. "Thanks for the milk. Guess I'll go try to sleep."

"Okay." She watched as he padded to the kitchen doorway. "Daniel?"

He stopped and turned back around.

"Lots of others are praying, too, you know. Joseph's pretty well surrounded with prayer."

"I know," he whispered. Then he headed back into the darkness upstairs, where she knew he would pray some more.

CHAPTER *Forty*

Brenda was exhausted and emotionally drained as the last of the doctors filed out of the room. Joseph had been revived. He was alive, but she knew it was just a matter of time before his heart failed for the last time. He looked as if his soul had already left his body—or as if it would flee again at any moment.

It was the longest night Brenda and David had ever shared together, yet the moments seemed so short. When morning came, she realized that Joseph hadn't stirred since he'd been revived. She went to his side and found his hand under the covers. It was cold as ice. His fingers were blue. She remembered when his hands were hot and his palms were sweaty, when his cheeks would get red after running from Daniel or chasing the dog.

Hours passed. Nurses moved Joseph, gave him injections, changed his IV, checked his monitors. He never woke up. David didn't leave the hospital. He left ICU only to get them food, which neither of them could eat. Neither of them had showered, and Joseph's breakfast tray went untouched. When the lunch tray came, they took the breakfast tray, then at supper, replaced the lunch. Still, Joseph did not wake up.

When he had been asleep for twenty-four hours, Brenda bent over his bed. "Where is he?" she asked David. "Why won't he wake up?"

David, draped across the rail on the other side of the bed, looked ragged and exhausted. She was exhausted, too, but could not take the chance of resting again.

She thought of her son's questions yesterday about death and heaven, and suddenly the thought of his dying here was unbearable. Old people died in hospitals, suffering people that saints were praying home. Not children. Children needed to be in their own homes, with things that gave them comfort.

"The last thing he said to me yesterday ..." she whispered to David. "He told me he wanted to go home. Sleep in his own bed."

David closed his eyes, and tears plopped onto Joseph's sheet.

"David, Joseph's going to die, isn't he?"

He nodded, unable to speak. She covered her mouth and bent down to press her forehead against her son's. "What if we took him home?" she asked.

There was a moment of silence, and finally she looked up and saw the tragic look on David's face.

"What do you mean?" he asked painfully.

"I mean ... if he's going to die ... let's take him home, David. Let's let him die in his own bed. Not in a cold hospital room with tubes and alarms. Not here."

Again, silence. "But the children," David whispered finally. "It would be too hard on them."

She covered her face with both hands, wishing she knew what to do. "I'm thinking of them, too. They need to say goodbye to him. He's their brother."

He stared down at the boy, his face twisted as the thoughts turned in his mind. "But Brenda, as long as he's here, there's still a chance he'll survive until—"

"David, I *don't* want my son to die here."

"What difference does it make where he dies?" he whispered harshly, the corners of his mouth trembling with the words. "Here or there—what difference does it make?"

"He wanted to go home. He wanted to be in his own bed."

"But there's still a chance . . ." His voice trailed off as despair flooded up in him, rendering him unable to finish.

"We could take the machines with us," she said. "We could take him home in an ambulance. Get a private nurse. We would keep giving him what he needs. But he would be home, in his own room, with his own family. Harry would be right across the street. If they *do* find a heart, we can have him back here in just a few minutes. And if they don't—he'd be at home, David. His own home."

David stared at her for a long moment, turning the idea over in his mind. She could see the turmoil the suggestion created in him.

"What if his heart stops again?" David whispered at last. "Who would revive him?"

The words came so hard that she almost choked them out. "How many times do we want the heroics, David, if there's not a heart? Joseph may be suffering. Maybe there's a time . . . to let go."

The rims around David's eyes reddened, and he sucked in a sob and covered his face with a callused hand. He wept for a moment, as hard and as deep as she. But finally, he raised his head and met her eyes. "Okay," he whispered. "Maybe I can catch Dr. Robinson before he leaves the building. And I'll call Harry."

David left the room, and Brenda looked down at her son, wanting so much to hold him, to cradle him in her arms, to let him feel the love she had for him. So she climbed onto the bed next to him, careful not to pull any of the tubes coming out of him. Carefully, she slid her arm under his head, and held him as she wept against his face.

Joseph never moved.

After a few minutes, David came back in. "They're still waiting for Dr. Robinson to answer his page," he said softly. "I called Harry, and he tried to talk us out of it. But when I explained, he said he understood. He said he'd help all he could."

Brenda squeezed her eyes shut. "We're taking you home, Joseph. Can you hear me? You're going home."

But Joseph didn't respond.

He just lay there, limp and gray.

Chapter Forty-One

Harry couldn't sleep after David's phone call, and with Sylvia at the Dodds' house, he saw no reason to stay in bed. He spent some time praying for Joseph, and for Brenda and David, then decided to go to the hospital and see if they needed help getting Joseph ready to go home.

He tapped on the glass at the side entrance and waited for the security guard to let him in. As the door opened, he heard the sound of a woman wailing.

"What's that?" he asked the guard.

"Big accident on the interstate," he said. "Some lady's losin' it over in ER."

Concerned, Harry detoured through the emergency room. Ambulance lights flashed just outside the glass doors, but the patient had already been brought inside. A woman wept loudly, uncontrollably, in her husband's arms. Her legs gave way, and he bent with her until she was on the floor, balling up as if that could assuage her grief. The man wept, too, but more quietly, in a way that was perhaps even more tragically helpless. Clearly, someone they loved had died. No matter how many times Harry had seen it, he'd never gotten used to it.

Outside the emergency room, two paramedics turned and moved slowly down the hallway, a look of defeat on their faces.

Other patients—a man with a broken arm, a woman with a cut on her foot, a teenaged boy with asthma—all quietly watched the family's anguish. Harry, too, stood watching, wishing there was something he could do. He thought of approaching the family, but he saw that someone was already there, urging them into a conference room. He wasn't needed.

Whispering a prayer for them, he started through the swinging doors that would take him to the elevators. As he pushed through, he ran into Dr. Robinson, rushing out.

"Chris! What's the rush?" Harry asked.

The man looked shaken, distracted, and his eyes sought out the weeping parents. "I'm glad you're here, Harry," he said quietly. "I may need you."

"For what?" Harry asked.

"To talk to these parents," he said. "They just lost their eight-year-old son. But, Harry—there was no injury to his heart."

Half an hour later, Harry left the room with Dr. Robinson, feeling drained of every ounce of energy. The parents were distraught to the point of needing sedation, but they had refused any.

At first, they had rejected the idea of giving up their son's heart. They hadn't yet accepted his death, and the idea of donating his organs was more than they could bear. So Harry had begun to tell them about Joseph—lying upstairs, hours, maybe moments, from death himself. He told them about Brenda and David's intentions to take Joseph home to die.

Finally, they had realized that their son's heart could spare another family the pain they were suffering. It could keep another child alive.

Reluctantly, miserably, they had agreed to sign the papers.

Drained, Harry followed Dr. Robinson to the elevators. "What now?"

"I'll contact the transplant team. We have to make sure it's a match for Joseph. If it's not, we transport it to a recipient who does match. If it's a good heart for Joseph, we'll operate within a few hours. Right now, we have to tell the Dodds."

The elevator doors opened, and they both stepped on.

"What if it doesn't match?" Harry asked. "Is there any way to keep from getting their hopes up?"

"No," Dr. Robinson said. "We have to start prepping Joseph. You might start sending up some of those prayers you're so popular for. Joseph is going to need them."

CHAPTER *Forty-Two*

Brenda and David heard a flurry of activity outside Joseph's room. She looked into the hall and saw Dr. Robinson and Harry at the nurse's station. Dread constricted her throat. She was sure they had come to help them get Joseph ready for his last trip home. Then she saw that the nurses seemed to be celebrating, hugging each other and smiling. She looked back at David.

"What is it?" he asked, stepping to the doorway behind her.

"I don't know."

Harry and Dr. Robinson started toward them. Both of them seemed breathless, though they seemed less celebratory than the nurses.

"What's going on?" David asked as they reached them.

"Brenda, David, I may have good news," Dr. Robinson said. "We may have a heart. We're running some tests now, and the transplant team will determine soon whether it'll work for Joseph. If so, we'll do the surgery in the next few hours."

Brenda stepped back, trying to process what Dr. Robinson had just said. She couldn't speak. Hope flooded her—she had almost forgotten what it felt like. Stunned, she turned to David.

"Doctor, how long will it take for the heart to get here?" David asked.

Dr. Robinson hesitated a moment. "It's already here. The transplant team is on their way."

Brenda saw the beginnings of the first smile she'd seen on David's face in days. "There's hope, David," she whispered. "There's hope."

But both of them knew it could be false hope, so they settled in for a long, anxious wait as the nurses began to prep their son.

Within two hours, Dr. Robinson was back in their room. This time he was smiling. "It's a go," he said, and they sprang to their feet and threw their arms around each other. "We'll start the surgery soon."

"We've got a heart! We've got a heart!" Brenda squealed, nearly dancing.

A nurse who was painting Joseph with iodine laughed. "I'll bet you have some phone calls to make," she said.

"Yes!" Brenda said. "We've got to get everybody praying."

CHAPTER *Forty-Three*

The telephone rang, waking Cathy, and she squinted at the clock. Which one of her children's friends would be rude enough to call this late, she asked herself, and picked up the phone to tell them it wouldn't be tolerated. "Hello?" she snapped.

"Cathy, this is Brenda."

She sat up straight in bed. "Brenda. What is it?"

"We've got a heart. They're taking Joseph to surgery now."

"Yes!" Cathy shouted triumphantly. "I'll be there in fifteen minutes!"

"You don't have to come. That's all right."

"Are you kidding? I'll be there." She hung up and began throwing her clothes on as fast as she could.

Annie appeared at the door, still wearing her jeans and T-shirt. She hadn't yet gone to bed. "Who was that, Mom?"

"Brenda. They've got a heart. Joseph's going into surgery."

"I wanna come!" Annie cried.

Rick stepped into the hall in a pair of shorts and a T-shirt. "What's all the noise?"

"Joseph's got a heart," Annie said. "Mom, wait, I have to get my shoes."

"Hey, I'm goin', too," Rick shouted.

"But there's nothing to do but wait. Anyway, somebody has to stay with Mark."

Mark stepped groggily into his doorway. "What's all the yelling about?"

She pulled on her shoes and headed to the stairwell. "Joseph is getting his new heart," she shouted. "I'm headed for the hospital. You three just stay here."

"Please, Mom!" Mark protested. "I wanna come with you."

She stopped and turned back on the stairwell. Annie had found her shoes and was leaning over the banister with a pleading look on her face. "Mom, we're in this, too. We helped. We want to be there."

"Please, Mom," Rick begged.

She sighed. "Everybody has five minutes to get dressed and into the car, or I'm leaving without you." She went back into her room and brushed her hair and teeth, and hoped that her gang would bring more encouragement than noise to the hospital.

Tory wasn't conscious enough to make sense out of the ringing telephone. Finally, Barry answered it. "Hello?"

She felt him sit up quickly in bed, then shake her shoulder. "Wake up, babe, it's Brenda."

Tory grabbed the phone and tried to shake the cobwebs out of her brain. She gave Barry a dreadful look. He returned it. Was Brenda calling to tell them Joseph had died?

Already feeling sick, she brought the phone to her ear. "Brenda?"

"Tory, we've got a heart," Brenda said.

Relief washed over her. "You're kidding! That's great! I'm coming to the hospital to wait with you."

"All right," Brenda said. "You might be able to catch Cathy and come with her."

Tory hung up and threw open her closet door. "Barry, they've got a heart! I'm going to the hospital. Will you stay with the kids?"

"Sure," he said. He was on his feet, too, wide awake now.

"If it goes all night, I'll try to get back in time for you to go to work."

"Don't worry about it," he said. "I'll go in late."

She pulled out the clothes she would wear, then swung around. "Oh, Barry, pray hard!"

"You got it." He slid his arms around her. "You be careful, okay? Don't drive like a maniac."

"I'm not driving if I can catch Cathy," she said. "Barry, will you call her while I get dressed and ask if I can have a ride?"

He picked up the phone.

"Oh, Barry, this could all be over soon."

As Barry punched Cathy's number, he looked up and said, "Maybe our prayers are finally being answered."

At the Dodds' house, Brenda's phone call to tell Sylvia about the heart had awakened Daniel. By the time Sylvia hung up, Daniel was standing in the doorway, listening.

"What is it, Miss Sylvia?" Daniel asked.

When she saw the fear on his face, she got up and put her hands on his shoulders. "Daniel, they've found a heart for your brother. They'll be taking him into surgery soon."

Daniel stared at her, then swung around and ran back up the hall. "Leah, Rachel, wake up! Joseph's got a heart!"

Sylvia thought of trying to stop him, but it was too late. The girls sprang from their beds, dancing with joy. "Joseph's got a heart! Can we go there, Miss Sylvia? Please!"

Sylvia decided there were things more important than keeping hospital rules. "Get dressed," she said. "I'll take you."

They whooped and hollered as they pulled on their clothes. Within minutes, they were in the car, headed for the hospital.

Chapter Forty-Four

Cathy, with Tory and her kids, made it to the hospital in record time. They parked near the emergency room because the lights in the parking lot were stronger there, and they felt safer cutting through the building than walking through the parking lot. They headed to CICU first to see if the Dodds were waiting there. A few reporters with television cameras were standing in the hallway, and Tory wondered if they considered Joseph's transplant newsworthy. But how would they have known about it?

"I'll go see if Brenda and David are in there," Tory said, and left Cathy and the kids in the corridor. She pushed through the press into the CICU waiting room. She didn't see the Dodds—only a scattering of strangers, most of them asleep in chairs. In the corner, a woman was crying, and her husband was holding her as a doctor in scrubs spoke softly to them. Against her chest, she clutched a pair of small, dirty tennis shoes.

Tory turned to leave, but before she reached the door, she heard the woman's voice. "Please . . . can you put these on his feet? I don't want his feet to get cold."

Tory turned back to the couple and saw the doctor take the shoes as the woman crumpled painfully against her husband. Tory met the woman's eyes, saw the shattering despair, the tragedy. *There must have been a death in that family*, she thought. Compassion surged through her . . . but then she remembered Joseph. A passing nurse pointed out the surgical intensive care waiting room, and Tory rushed back out, grabbed Cathy and the kids, and headed for it.

The waiting room filled up fast. By the time they had all arrived, the surgery had begun. Tory looked around at the tired, jubilant faces, so thankful that they had this chance to save Joseph. At first, the conversation was hyperactive and ecstatic, but as the hours ticked by, Brenda and David got noticeably quieter. Brenda couldn't seem to sit still. She kept crossing the room, back and forth, back and forth, going down the hall to the Coke machine and back, and constantly checking the telephone in the waiting room for a dial tone, since the doctor had promised to call the moment surgery was over.

Once, when Brenda left the room, she didn't come back for a while, and Tory decided to look for her. When she didn't find her roaming the halls or in the bathroom, she checked the chapel. Brenda was sitting on the pew at the front of the small room. Tory started to turn back and leave her alone to pray, but when Brenda turned around and saw her at the door, she said, "Come on in, Tory. It's okay."

"Go ahead," Tory said. "I don't want to interrupt."

"No, really," Brenda said. "Come on in."

Tory walked the short aisle, feeling as if she were entering holy ground. Though Brenda's eyes were red and wet, her face glowed with a beauty Tory knew no amount of makeup could achieve. It came from deep inside, nurtured and cultivated by the trials Brenda had endured. Tory sat down next to her. "It's taking a long time, isn't it?" she asked.

Brenda nodded and got to her feet. She paced in front of the altar, then stopped and stared at the stained glass. "But we knew it would. You don't swap hearts out just like that. I don't want them to rush."

Tory thought of how impossible heart transplant surgery seemed, and how miraculous that doctors had ever found a way to make it work. The thought of her own children lying on that table under oxygen masks and anesthesia, their chests open and exposed, and their very life sitting in a container waiting to be put into their bodies—the thought made her eyes well up with tears. She tried to fight it, for Brenda's sake.

Brenda turned around and settled her misty eyes on Tory. "I was just thinking," she whispered, "about the parable of the talents."

Tory looked at her, wondering how that particular parable could possibly apply to what was happening here. Had she been worrying about the money?

"I was thinking how those talents could just as well be our children," Brenda said. "God gave them to us, and we have the option of either hiding them in the ground or investing them."

Tory tried to make the analogy, but came up short. "What do you mean hide them in the ground?"

Brenda shrugged. "Oh, I don't know. Ignore them, maybe. Stay too busy to spend time with them. There are an awful lot of stray kids running around with no one to take care of them. Oh, I don't mean that they're homeless or orphaned. Their parents are meeting their physical and material needs, but that's about it. They're not loving them, teaching them, training them up in the way they should go."

Tory kept her eyes on Brenda, trying to follow where she was leading.

"In fact," Brenda went on in a shaky voice, "they're wishing they didn't even have them, because they cramp their style and interfere with their goals."

Tory felt slapped down, as if Brenda had just nailed her. But she could see in Brenda's face that she hadn't directed that at

Tory. She wasn't pointing a finger; she was just painting a picture. Maybe she didn't realize how close to home she had hit.

"So many people just keep looking to the future," Brenda went on. "They think, 'Someday my kids'll grow up and I'll be happy.' And others look back and think, 'If only my kids were home again, I'd be happy.' And some think, 'If I could just do this or be that, I'd be happy.' But it's funny how they're never very happy. Even Christians," she said, as if that surprised her. She looked down at Tory. "But you know what?"

Tory wiped her face and shook her head. "No, what?"

"I've been happy. God's given me these four children, and I've invested them. They're my life's work. I know you want to be a writer, Tory," she said, sitting back down and taking Tory's hand. "You'd love to win a Pulitzer prize and have your books on the shelves of bookstores. But you know what? To me, that's not as exciting as what you and I get to do every day. Think of it," she whispered. "We've got these little human beings in our hands, and it's our job to raise them up in the way God wants them, so that when He comes back for them, we can say we invested them wisely."

Tory stared at the altar, trying to let the words sink in. She had never thought of her children as being much of a blessing. They had come easily, just when she'd planned them, and most days, she found them to be an obstacle between her and her ambitions. That exasperation was an occupational hazard, she had told herself. All mothers felt this way. Worn out, overworked, spinning their wheels. As much as she loved them, she often resented them.

She looked up at Brenda, and saw that her eyes were brimming with tears. "God may take Joseph back today," Brenda went on. "But if He does, I'll know that I gave Joseph all I had. I invested him wisely." Her voice broke, and her lips trembled as she got the words out. "If he grows to be an adult, I've prepared him to be a godly man. And if he doesn't, I think God will be happy with what I did for him, anyway."

Silence fell like snowflakes between them.

After a while, Tory whispered, "Imagine that. Guilt-free parenting, knowing you could look God in the eye, because you did your best." It was a concept hard for her to grasp.

Finally, Brenda wiped her tears with both hands and got to her feet. "We'd better get back. The doctor might call."

Tory couldn't manage to move just yet. "I'll be there in a minute," she said. "I just want to pray a little myself."

Brenda nodded and gave her a tight, lingering hug. Then she left Tory alone.

Tory looked up at the stained glass dove, then down at the altar, letting the words her friend had just spoken seep into her heart. She began to weep harder. "Lord, forgive me," she whispered. "Forgive me for seeing my children as an inconvenience. For not investing them wisely. For not giving them everything I have." She went to the altar and knelt, her face in her hands. "Lord, little Joseph has been invested wisely, and if he's allowed to grow up, there's no telling what he can do for Your kingdom." A sob rose in her throat, and she wiped the tears away. "Oh, Lord. Please let him live. And thank You, thank You, for my children."

She felt the peace of the Holy Spirit fall over her. Bone tired and still reeling with the wisdom Brenda had planted in her mind, she headed back to the waiting room.

CHAPTER *Forty-Five*

By daybreak, the tension had grown unbearable. Brenda paced back and forth, back and forth in the surgical intensive care waiting room, waiting for word. David stood in the doorway, watching for the doctor.

Cathy sat with her head back against the wall, unable to move because Annie had fallen asleep on her shoulder. It was the closest her daughter had been to her in months, so she didn't dare wake her up. Daniel and his sisters, who had been elated at first, had now grown quiet as they saw the stress mounting on their parents' faces. Mark and Rick, who'd chattered a lot earlier in the morning, had now grown quiet, too.

Sylvia and Tory sat next to each other, conversing quietly about what kind of geraniums Tory should plant on the east side of her house, and whether the Bryans should tear down the stables since the horses had been sold. But they kept their eyes on the door, waiting for someone—anyone—to bring them word.

Mark and Rick finally offered to go to the cafeteria and get everyone a breakfast roll, but before they'd reached the elevator, the doors opened. Harry, dressed in scrubs, got off. They knew he'd been assisting in the surgery, so they stopped cold. "Is it over?" Mark asked.

Harry put his arms around their shoulders. "Yeah. It's over." He led them back into the waiting room, and everyone froze.

Harry looked first at Brenda, then at David. The exhaustion on his own face matched the fear and anxiety on theirs. Neither of the Dodds could ask the question they were all waiting to have answered, and Harry seemed too drained to speak. Finally, with obvious effort, he took a deep breath and looked around.

"Joseph came through just fine," he said, and a whoop went up as Brenda and David threw themselves at each other. The Dodd kids got to their feet, cheering and embracing. Sylvia threw her arms around Harry, and he laughed as tears came to his eyes.

"Can we see him?" Brenda asked over the noise.

"He's still in recovery. It was a perfect heart, Brenda. Strong and healthy." His voice broke, and he cleared his throat. "You can see him when they get him into surgical ICU. Meanwhile, the transplant team needs to see you both downstairs. There are a lot of things they need to go over with you."

❧

Tory was exhausted by the time she got home. Her children were still sleeping, but Barry was sitting at the kitchen table, drinking a cup of coffee and watching the news on television. He got up when she came in, and gave her a kiss.

"Is he all right?" he asked.

"The surgery was successful. Joseph has a new heart."

"And?" Barry asked. "What happens now?"

"Well, it's kind of touch and go. He's going to be in SICU for a while. They're watching him real closely. But they're saying they'll have him out of bed walking around by tomorrow, and he may be able to come home in a week or so if all goes well. The drugs suppress his immune system, so they figure he's safer at home than in a hospital full of germs. We just have to see what happens."

"You must be tired," he said. "Let me get you some breakfast."

"No, that's okay. I'm not hungry."

As she watched the news absently, a snapshot of a little boy with a buzz cut and huge brown eyes flashed on the television screen, and she glanced up as the anchor read, "Eight-year-old Tony Anderson was killed instantly when the oncoming car crossed the median and barreled into his family's Ford." The little boy's face was replaced by scenes of the wreck that had killed him—and then by footage of the grieving parents in the hospital waiting room. Tory slowly got to her feet. The camera zoomed in on a little pair of dirty tennis shoes, clutched against the heart of the grieving mother. It was the same couple Tory had seen in the waiting room before the surgery, when she'd been looking for the Dodds.

". . . pronounced dead at one thirty-five at St. Francis Hospital," the report went on.

That woman, whose eyes she had met, the woman who had been clutching her child's shoes and wailing with such horrible grief, had lost her child last night, not an hour before Tory had gotten to the hospital. Her eyes filled with tears.

Barry noticed it. "Honey, what's wrong? Are you okay? What is it?"

"The news," she said. "That little boy."

"Did you know that family?"

"No, but last night . . ." She caught her breath. "I saw them in the waiting room. They were devastated. And there were cameras in the hall. I must have seen them right after the cameras filmed them." She looked up at Barry, her eyes intense. "Do you think that could have been the heart that Joseph got?"

He looked thoughtful. "Did they say where his heart had come from?"

"No," she said. "But Brenda was surprised at how fast they had gotten it. It was already at the hospital when they told Brenda and David. That wouldn't have happened, would it, unless the child had died there?"

"Probably not," he whispered.

He held her, letting her cry against his shoulder. "Why is this upsetting you so?" he asked.

"Because I looked that mother in the eye," she said, "and I saw her pain. Then I went up to the room where everybody was celebrating that Joseph had gotten a heart. But it was *that* little boy's heart."

"Maybe," Barry said. "But if it weren't for that heart, Joseph's parents would have been the ones grieving."

"I know," she whispered. "I know. It just hit me so hard. When you see dying children, and you come home to your own, you wonder why they were spared." She pulled out of his arms and tried to catch her breath. "The kids aren't up yet?"

"No," he whispered. "They're in Britty's bed. Spencer claimed to be scared for her, so he got into bed with her."

Tory managed to smile. When something frightened their son, he always claimed he was scared for his sister. "I'll go see if they're awake."

She pulled out of his arms and headed for Brittany's room. The two children lay tangled in the covers, Spencer in his Superman pajamas, Brittany in a Tennessee Oilers T-shirt.

She started toward them—and promptly tripped on Spencer's shoes, lying in the middle of the floor. Steadying herself, she bent down and picked them up—and was immediately reminded of those shoes the bereaved mother had clutched last night, and the despair in her voice as she'd asked the doctor to put them on her son so his feet wouldn't get cold.

How irrational. How perfectly understandable.

The woman had lost her son.

Tory closed her eyes and clutched Spencer's shoes against her chest. New tears came to her eyes. Feeling Barry's hands on her shoulders, she turned around and looked intently up at her husband. "I'm going to change, Barry. You'll see. I'm not going to whine anymore. Why did I ever think that my only goal and purpose in life is to write, when I have these wonderful children?"

He just held her tightly.

"Mommy?" It was Spencer's voice, and he yawned and stretched, then got up and reached for her. She sat on the bed and pulled him into her lap. Brittany woke up then, too, and sleepily said, "Hey, Mommy."

"Hey, darlin'. Guess what? Joseph got a new heart last night."

"Does he like it?" Spencer asked.

Tory grinned. "I'm sure he does."

"Will he come home now?" Brittany asked.

"I think so. In a few days. If everything goes well." She patted Spencer's bare little leg, then ruffled Brittany's hair. "So what do you guys want to do today?"

"Aren't you tired?" Barry asked. "Don't you need to sleep?"

"I've still got a little energy left," she said. "I want to invest it in my family."

CHAPTER *Forty-Six*

Sunday morning, Barry and Tory decided to take Brenda's children to their own church again. Brenda and David wanted to stay at the hospital with Joseph, who was doing well but wasn't out of the woods. Because of the animal fair and the amount of time Tory had spent at the hospital with Brenda, she felt as if she knew a lot of the members of Brenda's church already. They welcomed her and Barry as if they were family, and the children couldn't wait to get to their Sunday school classes to tell of the miracle Joseph had received.

Instead of Sunday school that morning, the adults of the church met in the sanctuary for what they called a "power session." Barry and Tory weren't sure what they were getting into, but when they learned that it was an intense hour of prayer for Joseph's recovery, they were all for it.

They all met around the steps at the front of the small podium and prayed from the bottoms of their hearts, one at a time as they felt led. By the end of the hour, both Barry and Tory felt as if they had been touched personally by the Holy Spirit. Their hearts felt cleansed; their minds were clear and alert. When it was time for the service, and they had Spencer and Brittany and the Dodd children back with them, they sat close to the front. Barry stayed awake the whole time—in fact, Tory saw him smiling and nodding during the sermon. And at the end, when they were singing the final praise songs before closing the service, Barry surprised her with the exuberance in his voice and the tears she saw in his eyes.

When they had dropped the Dodd kids off at the hospital and were on their way home, Tory glanced at her husband. "So what do you think about that worship experience?"

He smiled. "I think I need to quit worrying about being a deacon. It's time to change churches."

The kids erupted with excitement in the backseat. Tory only smiled. "Are you sure, Barry? They depend on you a lot at our church."

"They can depend on others," he said.

"Maybe we're supposed to stay and light a fire under everybody."

Barry considered that for a moment. "I think we're the ones who needed a fire lit under us. We're not in any position to activate anyone right now. Let's go to Brenda's church for a while longer, and then decide whether we should go back to our church and get something going. But personally, I need some discipling." He paused a moment. "You know what the pastor quoted today from Second Peter, about growing in respect to your salvation? I don't think I've done that. As far as I know, I've never borne any fruit."

"Me, either," Tory agreed. "And then I see Brenda, and I think, Lord, if I can't be like You, let me be like her."

When the children were down for their naps, Barry came into the kitchen where Tory was reading the paper. He picked up his car keys.

"Where you going?" she asked.

He shrugged and looked down at the floor. "I thought I'd go up to the hospital and see David."

"Really?" They had never been close friends. The relationship between families had primarily been between Brenda and her. "Okay. I'm sure he'd appreciate that."

He nodded. "I'll be back in time to take us all back to church."

"Okay, you can bring the Dodd kids back with you."

"Good idea," he said.

As he headed to the door, Tory sat back in her chair, thinking. She wasn't sure whether Barry had ever shared his faith with anyone before, other than cursory conversations with the children—but she had no doubt that's what Barry was intending to discuss with David. That sermon must have given him a sense of urgency. She was thankful. She only hoped that David would listen—so that Barry would be encouraged to share his faith even more.

Then, maybe, she'd start doing it herself.

Chapter Forty-Seven

At the hospital, Brenda was surprised when Barry arrived alone. He bantered with the kids for a while, welcome entertainment when they were all confined to the SICU waiting room—they were only allowed to visit Joseph for a few minutes every couple of hours. When Barry asked David if he'd like to go down to the cafeteria for a cup of coffee, and David agreed, Brenda was more confused than ever. She watched, perplexed, as they left the room. Then she turned back to the children, who were playing a game of Monopoly.

"Mama, I think the Sullivans really liked our church this morning," Daniel said.

"Really?"

"Yes, ma'am. Mr. Barry even had tears in his eyes."

"How about that?" Brenda said, amazed. She looked at the doorway again, wondering if that had anything to do with Barry's visit. Just in case, she breathed a silent prayer for him.

Downstairs in the cafeteria, Barry and David sat at the table across from each other, eating a piece of pie. "So how are you holding up?" Barry asked.

"Fine," David said. "I'm not going to lie to you. It hasn't been easy."

"I went to Brenda's church this morning," Barry told him, as nonchalantly as he could manage. "They had a power session for Joseph during the Sunday school hour."

"Power session? What's that?"

"It's when they all get together and pray intensely for someone. I'd never heard of it before, but it was a really good idea. And then I come here and I see how well Joseph's doing, and I'm just amazed. I really think prayer has had a lot to do with it."

David smiled and nodded his head politely, as if he didn't want to argue with Barry. "Doctors had a little something to do with it."

"Of course," Barry said. "But I believe that Joseph is doing so well because so much prayer went into it. Not that those of us who are praying should take any credit—I just mean that God answered."

"Yeah, that's what Brenda tells me. But you know me. I have trouble with that." He crossed his arms on the table and looked up at Barry. "We were about to take Joseph home that night. We didn't want him to die in the hospital. And then—there was a heart."

"And you don't think God was working all that out?"

David smiled and shook his head. "I can't believe that. I think things just have a way of working out sometimes. And other times they don't."

"So you put more faith in accidents and coincidence than you do in God?"

"Not really," David said. "I don't have faith in accidents or coincidence either. They just happen. I guess I don't have faith in much of anything, except for my wife and my kids."

Barry didn't know how to respond. He knew that Brenda had shared the gospel with David many times, and that nothing he said today was going to change David's heart. Only the Holy Spirit could do that. Silently, he prayed for words that weren't confrontational, but that would shoot through the faithlessness straight into David's heart.

"You know, Brenda said something just before we got the heart," David said. "We thought we were going to lose Joseph. I told her I couldn't believe in a God who would take our child from us. And she pointed out that, even when our children were all healthy, I didn't believe." He glanced up at Barry. "She was right. You know, if there was any way I could force myself to believe, for Brenda's sake, I'd do it. I've thought of faking it, going to church with her, sitting beside her, singing those songs loud and clear like I was one of them. But church and I have a long history together, and it's not a very pretty one. I've done enough faking in my life. For now, I'd rather be honest about my disbelief. I'm not willing to fool my wife just for the sake of peace in the family."

"I don't know about your history," Barry said. "But maybe if you went to Brenda's church once, you'd find out it's not like you remember."

David looked down at his plate, frowning deeply, as if something Barry said had triggered a flood of memories. "I don't think that would happen. I have trouble with the way they do things there. Even those power sessions or whatever you call them. I mean, they seem like name-it-and-claim-it mumbo jumbo to me."

"It wasn't anything like that," Barry said. "We prayed that God's will, whatever it might be, would be done."

"Yeah, well, I really resented the elders praying over Joseph. But then the way they've supported us through this, bringing meals to the house, donating money, coming to the hospital . . ." He cleared his throat. "It wasn't that way for us—my mother and me—when I was a kid." David leaned back and stretched, and Barry knew that he'd said all he was going to say about his past.

"But that whole business about God's will—that's another area where I have trouble. There's something a little superstitious about trusting completely in God's will, no matter what happens. Whether you lose your father, your husband, your home, your friends . . ."

Barry suspected that David hadn't meant to say those last few words, but he decided it might be the opening he'd prayed for. "Are you talking about your mother?"

David looked down at his hands, folded in front of him. "It was like a mental illness with her. No matter what my father did, no matter how cruel the church was to us, even when we were out on the street, she kept saying it was God's will. But it was just her excuse not to do anything for herself, not to try to make it better . . ."

"Sounds like a real burden to have to carry around," Barry said quietly.

"What do you mean?"

"You have a lot to forgive. An awful lot, I'd say. That kind of stuff can weigh you down, control your life, until you cut it loose."

"I'm over it," David said, shrugging it off. "I'm just telling you, church and I don't go together. But I live a good life, even without believing what you believe. Brenda keeps talking about abundant life. I feel like our lives are pretty abundant. Sure, I could want more financially, that kind of thing, but other than Joseph's illness, things have gone pretty well."

"But when you have trouble, like this business with Joseph, there's an awful lot that's out of your control."

David took a skeptical breath and looked off across the room. "So you think I should believe that God's in control?"

"Sure. Because He is, whether you believe it or not."

David shook his head and finished his pie, then abruptly changed the subject to football and fishing. Finally, they made their way back up to the SICU waiting room. Brenda looked up.

"I'll take the kids with me now if you want me to," Barry said. "We'll get them back to church. Tory and I are planning to go back tonight. We're thinking about moving our membership."

Brenda caught her breath. "That's wonderful! We'll be going to church together."

"Yeah," he said. He glanced at David. "You tell Joseph to keep getting better, okay? Tell him they're really missing him back at that church."

"I will," Brenda said.

Then with a wave, he headed out of the room, praying silently that the Holy Spirit would finish what he'd started.

Chapter Forty-Eight

The night of the school board meeting, Cathy dressed in her most conservative dress and prayed that people would come. For the past couple of weeks, she had used those skills she'd learned raising money for Joseph's bills. She'd gone from parking lot to parking lot, putting out flyers about the Monday night school board meeting. She'd made countless phone calls. She'd gone to baseball and soccer parks, left flyers on windshields, and chatted with parents she met there. She didn't think she could have worked any harder if she'd been running for congress. All of this was hard for her. She wasn't a confrontational person; she wasn't used to rocking the boat or making people angry. But that, she suspected, was exactly what was going to happen tonight when she got up to speak to the people making decisions about her children.

She had seen Steve only once or twice since their date and had decided that he was no more reliable or interested in commitment than any other single man she'd met. Yes, he was apparently attracted to her—but he seemed torn between that attraction and his allegiance to the wife he'd lost. And he was lukewarm, at best, about Cathy's kids.

Still, when he did call, she found her heart racing and hoped he would suggest another date. She refused to show it, and even prided herself in pretending she was so busy she hardly had a moment to talk.

She expected him to be at the school board meeting, and he didn't disappoint her. In fact, he was still sitting in his car in the parking lot when she arrived, as if he was waiting for her. She got out of the car and looked around at the other cars already filling the parking lot.

"Looks like a big turnout," he said.

"You think it's for us?" she asked.

"I don't know. Let's go in and find out."

Inside, she studied the crowd that had filled the room. There was standing room only. The school board members were scurrying around, trying to find places for everyone to sit. It was an open meeting, but it was clear that the board wasn't used to a crowd this size.

She made the rounds, shaking hands with some of the people who were still standing, and learned that they had, indeed, come to find out about sex education in the schools. Her heart leaped as she realized that her work had not been in vain. The school board would have to listen to her now!

When they had found enough chairs to seat everyone, the meeting came to order. She waited as the board covered various housekeeping items. Finally, the school board president called on her to speak. She went to the microphone at the center of the table in front, facing the school board with the audience behind her.

"As most of you know, I'm here about something that happened in the junior high and high school at the end of last year, something I've been told happens every year," she said. "I found a condom in my son's pocket. You can imagine how upset I was. I naturally assumed that he had bought it. But when I confronted him, he explained that he'd gotten it at school, and that they'd had a video about safe sex and how to use condoms. I was told that this was not the first time. I was very disturbed." There was applause behind her, as if other parents in the room were equally disturbed, and she paused and looked over her shoulder, gaining strength as she went.

"As you can see, I'm not the only concerned parent here," she said when the applause had died. "And I wanted to appeal to you as the people with the power to stop this madness. Our children don't need the school system to teach them about sex—*especially* about condom use. They have parents to do that."

Again, there was applause.

"I think with teen pregnancy at an all-time high," she said, "what we need to teach our students is abstinence, not supposedly safe sex."

"Dr. Flaherty," one of the board members said, taking the floor, "I understand your concern, but the kids are going to do this anyway. We have to teach them how to keep from getting deadly diseases. I, personally, don't want to have to bury my son because of AIDS."

"I wholeheartedly agree—not your son, or mine, or any of the other students in our district," Cathy said. "But the best way to prevent that is to teach them to control themselves."

Again, there was jubilant applause behind her, but she held up her hand to quiet them. Her eyes blazed with passion as she went on.

"A few months ago, someone told me that the best we can hope for is to raise our children to adulthood without pregnancy or disease." The memory of her ex-husband's statement reddened her face. "But for the last few weeks, I've been watching another parent fighting for the life of her child—a child that did have a disease. But that child had such character, even when we thought he might die. Character that his mother instilled in him, not from teaching him a list of do's and don'ts, and not from giving him tools that enable him to make bad choices. She taught him character by giving him a value system that never changes."

Her voice broke, and she blinked back the tears in her eyes. "If—no, when—that little boy grows up, he probably won't ask her what's wrong with sex before marriage as long as nobody gets hurt. He'll already know that everybody involved is hurt by premarital sex, because he'll know where his values come from." She cleared her throat, and tried to steady her voice.

"I haven't always known that myself, so my children *have* asked those questions. I'm ashamed to say that sometimes I haven't had answers. But watching my friend has shown me that we *can* teach our children better. We *can* expect more of them. We *can* demand more from ourselves. If we want to do the best for our children, we can give them a firm base of values that come from someplace specific, someplace like the Bible, instead of passing out condoms or showing titillating videos. We can show them how a moral life works, instead of giving them the means to *ruin* their lives."

Again, applause erupted, until Superintendent Jacobs began to speak. "You think they'll stop having sex just because we tell them to?" he asked. "We have to arm them, Dr. Flaherty."

Cathy leaned in to the microphone again. "It's interesting that you would use a metaphor involving weapons, what with all these recent school shootings." The room got so quiet she could have heard a pin drop. The school board members sat straighter in their chairs. "You don't give a violent kid a gun and think it'll deter him from shooting it, and you don't give a hormonal teenager a condom and think that's going to somehow keep him from having sex."

Again, there was raucous applause behind her, and she felt her face reddening and perspiration tingling on the edge of her lip. "As you can see, I'm not the only one here who feels this way." She looked from school board member to school board member and realized that some of them were smiling and nodding their heads, as if to encourage her. This confused her. Were some of them on *her* side? Deciding not to dwell on it, she pulled out a magazine article she had brought. "If you'll turn over the sheet I just passed out," she said, "you'll see an article that came out in a major parenting magazine recently, describing an abstinence program that has worked in many cities, bringing down the teen pregnancy and AIDS contraction rate drastically."

"I've read all about this program," Jacobs said. "But I don't think it would work well in this community."

"Why wouldn't you try it?" she demanded. "Don't you think our children are worth that?"

"I wouldn't try it because it's a waste of time."

"A waste of time? You'd rather encourage them to go to bed with each other than to teach them how *not* to act like animals?"

The crowd roared behind her, and the superintendent slammed the gavel and took control of the microphone. "Thank you, Dr. Flaherty. I think you've made your point. Does anyone else have anything to say?"

At least fifty parents stood up and raised their hands, and the members began to look at their watches as if they might be there all night. Finally, the superintendent leaned back hard in his chair. "All right, please line up at the microphone. You have three minutes each. We won't have time to hear all of you out, but we'll hear some of you before we take a vote."

Cathy left the microphone and sank down in the seat Steve had reserved for her. She felt as if a hundred pounds had floated off of her shoulders. He was grinning from ear to ear. One by one, other parents added to what she had said, conveying comments their children had made after viewing the video, and tearfully sharing incidents of teen pregnancy and abortions—in some cases, as a result of the sexual activity that began the day they'd been given condoms.

After forty-five minutes of testimony, the superintendent suggested that they take a vote. When all was done, the school board had voted six to two to allow parents to view any sexual material before it was shown to their children, and to do away with the current sex education program. To Dr. Jacobs' chagrin, the school board president assigned someone to look into the abstinence program Cathy had suggested, and set a date to vote on its use locally. When the gavel struck to adjourn the meeting, the parents all cheered.

After the meeting, Cathy was treated as a celebrity. They patted her on the back and thanked her for what she had done. Steve stood back, letting her bask in the adulation. When the room had mostly emptied except for the school board members, one of them came and set her arm around Cathy's shoulders. "Way to go," the woman whispered.

Cathy gaped at her. "You were on my side all along?"

"You got *that* right," the woman said. "I'm a parent, too. I have kids at the middle school and high school."

"Then why haven't you objected to what's going on?"

"Didn't know about it," she said. "Here I am sitting on the school board, and none of my kids ever told me what's going on. Until it came up on this agenda, I didn't have a clue. I've only been on the board a year; they implemented this program before that."

"I'm glad I came, then," Cathy said.

"Good thing you did," she said. "You know, the people on this school board are good people. They're trying to do what's best for the kids. But sometimes we need the help of parents like you to call our attention to problems and help us get things across to those of our members who don't agree. It's not easy, this education thing."

"No, I don't suppose it is."

She squeezed Cathy's shoulders, then let her go and started out the door. She stopped at the door and turned back. "Woman, you pack a wallop when you want to. Next time you've got a beef with the school board, how about giving me a call first so I can brace myself?"

Cathy laughed and followed her out.

Steve was talking to a few stragglers in the parking lot, and when she got into her car, he came to the window and leaned in. "I'm pretty proud of you, lady," he said.

She laughed. "I'm kind of proud of myself. So . . . you want to go have a milkshake and celebrate?"

He smiled apologetically. "Wish I could, but Tracy's home with a baby-sitter and I promised I'd be the one to tuck her in."

"Can't argue with that," she said. "I like a man who's a good dad."

His smile faded. "I like a woman who's a good mom."

She hadn't heard those words in a long time. There was no one to praise her mothering skills and tell her she was doing a good job. More often, she had a million reasons for self-condemnation. It almost brought tears to her eyes. "Do you really think so?" she asked, feeling a little foolish.

"I know so," he said. "How many moms would have fought this hard for their kids?"

"Well, my children wouldn't agree. They're embarrassed to death. They said their friends are calling me 'the condom lady.'"

He laughed softly. "They'll appreciate it one day."

"Yeah, maybe." She cranked her car. "Well, looks like we're the last ones here." Their eyes met, locked for a long moment. Finally, he leaned in and pressed a kiss on her cheek. Her heart jolted.

"I'll call you tonight, after I get Tracy to bed," he whispered. "And then we can relive your moment in the spotlight."

"I'll look forward to that."

As she drove home, she thanked God for helping her to pull the whole thing off, for getting the school board to vote for her instead of against her—and, most of all, for letting her still have a chance with Steve.

Chapter Forty-Nine

Sylvia sat at the patio table covered with papers, and looked out at the empty corral. She had expected to be sad about the loss of the horses, as she had been after Sarah's wedding, when the house had felt so empty. But she realized now that it was a blessing and not a curse.

Harry came out drinking a glass of iced tea and sat next to her. "So whatcha doing with all these papers?" he asked.

"Counting up all the money we've raised," she said. "It looks like we've covered all of the bills they've received so far. Of course, most of the bills haven't come in yet. But I still have some pledges coming in. You know, I think we might just cover it all, if we work really hard. I think God is helping us keep the Dodds on our street. Since the couple who wanted to buy their house didn't qualify for the mortgage, we have a little more time. If we can raise enough money, I'm sure David will take the sign down."

"So how much of these donations came from your visits to corporate America?" he asked.

She smiled. "About half."

He leaned on the table. "Excuse me, but aren't you the woman who had nothing left to contribute?"

She threw her head back and laughed. "Okay, so I may still have a little life left in me."

He picked up the letter from the Nicaraguan couple who had asked for advice and help. "You know, I feel bad. All this time we've been so busy with Joseph, I haven't had time to look into much of anything for Maria and Carlos."

"It's not too late," she said. "Besides, I've done a little thinking."

He set the letter down and looked up at her. "Yeah?"

"Yeah." She fixed her eyes on him for a moment. "Harry, what would you think about our offering our house to Carlos and Maria while he's in seminary? We could also pay his way, and line up a job for him and a school for their son while they're here."

He frowned. "You wouldn't mind having them live with us?"

She held his gaze for a moment. "We're not going to be here, Harry."

He sat up straighter, and his eyes widened. "What do you mean?"

She reached out and clutched his hand. "We're going to Nicaragua."

His eyes misted over. He studied her face for a moment as if waiting for her to scream out, "Gotcha!" But she didn't. "Are you sure?" Harry asked.

"I've been praying a lot about this," she said, "asking God to change my heart. A few months ago, when all this came up, I didn't think I had much to contribute. But now I can see that I do still have talents God can use. I *can* work with the children, and I can teach the mothers. I want to go. You have so much you can take to those people, and I think I have some things I can take, too. I may not be able to cure their diseases, but I can help to cure their hearts."

"You're absolutely sure?"

"Absolutely," she said. "And if Carlos and Maria stay in our house, I'll have the peace of knowing that we'll have it to come back to. Or, after they finish seminary, we can sell it if we want."

Harry leaned back hard in his chair and let out a laugh that seemed to shake the trees. "I can't believe I'm hearing this!"

"Believe it," she said. "I asked God to change my heart if He wanted us to do this. I didn't *want* Him to, and I didn't expect Him to. But He did. Now I'm getting excited."

Harry got up and hugged his wife with all his might.

Chapter *Fifty*

That night after supper, Tory, Sylvia, and Cathy went to the hospital to sit with Brenda and Joseph. He had been moved to his own room and was doing well, so while he slept, they went into the small waiting room across the hall and talked softly about the best moments of the last few months.

"When they told us they'd found a heart," Brenda whispered. "That was a good one."

"Me, too, when you called to tell me," Tory agreed.

"When my kids wanted to help raise money," Cathy said.

Sylvia began to laugh. "When Ed Majors gave me that first check."

Brenda grinned. "Rolling my own yard with my kids for Joseph's party."

"The animal fair," Tory added, "when Spencer finally got to ride Sylvia's horse before she sold it."

Brenda smiled. "When they prayed over Joseph at church."

"When I met Steve Bennett," Cathy added. They all looked at her and smiled knowingly.

"When we discovered Brenda's church," Tory whispered.

"When *I* discovered Sylvia's church," Cathy echoed.

"When Harry came in and told us the surgery was a success."

"When your kids made all those videos," Sylvia said.

"When Joseph opened his eyes after the surgery."

"When you told me what you did about investing our children wisely."

"When I told Harry I wanted to go to the mission field."

They all got quiet for a long time, their thoughts centered on blessings instead of trials, on joys instead of heartaches. It was so much different than the night they'd gotten together months ago, after Joseph's first collapse—when they'd thought they had so much to complain about.

"Some of the best moments," Tory whispered finally, "have been sitting right here with you tonight, and knowing that we're all different people than we were when we started out."

"Yes," Sylvia whispered. "These are definitely some of the best moments."

Barry was asleep on the floor with the children—in front of the television—when Tory got home that night. She stood quietly over them, filled with an overwhelming love for her family. She knelt there beside them and wept for the blessing of them.

An idea came to her, and quietly she went into the laundry room, turned on her computer, and began to write her feelings down. She wrote about the little cul-de-sac of Cedar Circle, about the child who needed a heart, and how the neighbors had banded together to raise the money. She wrote about the things she'd learned about loving her own children, about the blessings she was too busy to see, about the joy she was too rushed to experience. She wrote about God changing her heart, and

Sylvia's and Cathy's, and she wrote about the courageous love of Brenda, who trusted God enough to open her hand for Him to take Joseph away from her. She talked about the lessons of investing her children wisely, and how God had taught her, through Brenda, that her children, not her writing, were her life's greatest work.

When she finished, it was five A.M., and she realized that she'd written an entire article. She would send it to her favorite magazine and see if they wanted it. If they didn't, that was okay too. After all, it wasn't the words, but rather the meaning behind them, that was most important: the changes in her heart, and the changes that would occur in her family as a result.

Quietly, she slipped outside. The sky was just surrendering its darkness to the beginnings of day. She walked down the driveway to the mailbox, slipped the envelope in, and put the flag up. Then she turned and saw the sun's rays just coming up over the mountains. She watched, breathlessly, as the sky grew brighter, brighter, until the sun burst like a fireball above the mountain peaks.

For a moment, she stood and took it all in, like an epiphany in her heart as this new morning in her life dawned. Joy and incredible gratitude washed over her like the sun's light, and suddenly she couldn't wait to see what the day would bring.

She could have stood like that for hours, just watching the miracle of God's new day, but instead, she went back into the den, where her family still slept on the floor. Instead of waking them and taking them all to bed, she lay down with them, curled up between her two children, her hand on Barry's arm. There was no place she needed to be, nothing calling her away. This was her work and her greatest joy.

This was where she belonged.

THE END

Enjoy This Excerpt from Book Two

Showers in Season

As crises went, Tory Sullivan usually put nausea at the bottom of the scale. When it was her children who were sick, she dealt with it just fine. She washed their faces and rinsed out their mouths, and lay them down on the bed with towels in case another wave assaulted them. Then she would matter-of-factly clean up the mess while she thought about the lantana plants that needed watering, or how badly she needed to paint the living room.

But she didn't handle it as well when she was the patient. Queasiness seemed like an insult to her, as if her body were taking away her control and running rampant like a rebellious child. She wouldn't have it. If she stopped thinking about it, it would go away.

Tory stopped rocking and tried to concentrate on the leaves whispering in the breeze. Her friend Brenda Dodd kept moving in the matching chair on her porch, but the sound and motion made Tory close her eyes. She didn't have time to be sick, she thought. She simply didn't have room for it on her schedule.

The sound of Brenda's voice, as sweet as it usually sounded, droned on as she read the words of the article that Tory had written. Tory would have thought it was the terror of having her words read aloud that had turned her stomach, but the truth was that she was exceptionally proud of them. She had deliberately brought the article here so that Cathy and Brenda could be amazed. Cathy Flaherty, in her light blue veterinarian's lab coat, responded with dutiful admiration as she chomped on the Fritos she was having for lunch.

Tory wondered if the smell of Fritos made others want to gag.

"Cool, you got a zipper on your front!"

Tory looked down at her four-year-old son, Spencer, who sat with Joseph on the steps. Joseph, Brenda's nine-year-old, had his shirt pulled up and was showing four-year-old Spencer the scars healing on his chest. The fact that he'd gotten a heart transplant just a few weeks ago fascinated Spencer.

"It's not a zipper, Spence," Joseph said. "It's where the doctor cut—"

"No, Joseph!" Tory cut in. "Don't . . . please don't . . ." But she couldn't get the words out. It took too much concentration not to let her body have its way.

Brenda shot Tory a puzzled look and leaned down to her startled son. "Your surgery may be a little too graphic for Spencer," she explained softly.

"Just give him the broad picture," Cathy suggested with a wink.

"No." Tory didn't want them to think she was angry at Joseph for going too far. Spencer had seen much worse on television. Just the other day, she had caught him watching a facelift on cable. "It's me." She touched her stomach and tried to turn back the wave of nausea.

Brenda and Cathy gaped at her as if waiting for the rest of a sentence. After a few seconds, Spencer lost interest in Joseph's chest and began turning cartwheels in the grass. "Look, Mommy!"

Tory couldn't look.

"Tory, are you okay?" Cathy asked. "You look as white as a couch potato."

Brenda laughed. "A couch potato?"

"Well, yeah. They never get any sun. Tory?"

Tory couldn't manage a smile. She opened her eyes and got slowly to her feet. "I don't feel so good."

Brenda looked up at her, alarmed. "Tory, you really don't look good. What's wrong?"

"Just a little . . . sick." She stood there for a second, then bolted for Brenda's front door. "Bathroom . . ."

Brenda launched out of her chair and threw open her front door, and Tory dashed into the house and made a beeline for the bathroom.

When she came out several minutes later, Cathy, Brenda, Joseph, and Spencer were all lined up in the hall, looking at her as if she'd just performed an amazing stunt.

"Tory, did you eat breakfast this morning?" Brenda asked her.

"Of course," she said, still feeling wobbly. "Wheaties. Breakfast of Champions, huh, Spence?"

"Maybe the milk was bad," Spencer suggested. "Bad milk makes me hurl."

"The milk was not bad," she said. "I've been feeling a little sick off and on for a while, but it hasn't gotten me like that before. Maybe it's a bug. Guess I'd better get out of here so Joseph doesn't get it." She realized how serious it could be for Joseph to contract a virus. Because of the high-dose steroids he was taking to keep from rejecting his heart, his immune system couldn't protect him at all. "Oh, Brenda, I'm so sorry."

"It's fine," Brenda said, though Tory knew she must be concerned. "Just passing you in the hall isn't going to make him sick. The kids are bringing home backpacks full of germs every day."

"Do you have any Lysol? I really should sanitize the toilet so Joseph won't be hurt by the germs."

"Don't worry about it. I'll do it. You go on home."

"No, I think she should do it," Cathy said with that amused look on her face. "Just pull that puppy up and go boil it for a couple of hours. David must have a vat you could use."

Joseph looked horrified, and Spencer looked fascinated. "They boil toilets?" Joseph asked.

"No." Brenda playfully shoved Cathy. "She's kidding, guys. Tory, you don't have to sanitize my toilet. Just go take care of yourself."

Tory was too distracted to laugh. She knew that Brenda was too kind to tell her that the more time she spent here apologizing, the more germs she would spread. So she took Spencer's hand and started out the door.

"Want me to walk with you?" Cathy asked, hurrying out beside her. Thankfully, she had gotten rid of the Fritos while Tory was in the bathroom.

"That's okay. I'll be fine. I have to go pick up Brittany."

"I could do that for you before I go back to the clinic."

Tory considered that, then decided that it wouldn't be necessary. "No, I think I'm over it now. Really. Boy, I hate being sick."

"Unlike the rest of us who enjoy it?" Cathy asked with a smirk. Her blonde ponytail bobbed as she walked along beside them. She wore a white T-shirt under her lab coat, jeans, and Nike tennis shoes. Tory envied Cathy for being so unselfconscious. "Spencer's probably right," Cathy said. "You probably ate something that made you sick. What'd you guys have for supper last night, Spencer?"

"Pork chops," Spencer said with a sour look. "They tasted like Daddy's shoes."

Cathy laughed and looked at Tory. "Mmm. Sounds good. He's tasted his daddy's shoes, has he?"

Tory couldn't help grinning now. "The pork chops were dry. Barry said they tasted like shoe leather. They did not make me sick. No one else in my family is nauseous."

"That's 'cause we all spit them out when you weren't looking," Spencer announced.

Cathy's mouth came open in delight. "You see there?"

"Okay, so I'm sick from the pork chops," Tory conceded. But that didn't explain the queasiness that had assaulted her for several days.

Giving up, Cathy told Spencer to take care of his mom, then bopped back across the cul-de-sac. "Call me if you need anything," she said over her shoulder. "I'll be home around four."

"I will."

As they reached their house, Spencer looked up at her with big, serious eyes. "Want me to get you a barf bag?"

She couldn't imagine where in the house they might have such a thing. "I'm okay, honey. Let's just get in the car and go get Britty."

The wave of nausea passed over her again as she drove to Brittany's school at noon to pick her up. Beside her, Spencer was chattering nonstop about the action figure he wanted for Christmas, even though it was only October.

The nausea ambushed her again as she got into the line of traffic picking up kids at the school. Quickly, she pulled out of the line and parked the car.

Spencer looked up at her, puzzled. She saw in the rearview mirror that Brittany was standing on the curb staring at her with a troubled expression, not knowing whether she should launch out in front of the stream of cars to her mother, or wait patiently as her teacher had told her. To her children, obedience was always a cause for careful consideration. It was one of the few things they thought about before doing it. "Come on, Spence. I need to run in and use the bathroom."

"Are you gonna barf again?"

The crude question made her situation even more urgent. Without answering, she got out and waited for Spencer, then grabbed his hand and crossed the busy lane of traffic.

"Mommy, what are you doing?" Brittany asked as she approached.

She kissed Brittany's forehead, then put Spencer's hand in hers. "Both of you just stand here for a minute. Mommy has to use the bathroom." She darted into the school just as she heard Spencer explaining, "She's been puking all over the place."

Wondering where he'd gotten these expressions, Tory made it to the bathroom, into the stall, and stood with her back to the door, thinking, perhaps, that the feeling would pass. She took a deep breath and tried to concentrate on something other than her stomach.

She really did not have time for this.

She had promised herself she would write this afternoon while the children were napping. She wanted to tweak her article one more time before sending it off, and she had that deadline looming over her. Nausea was an unexpected factor in this equation.

As if in answer to her mental declaration that she didn't have time, her body proceeded to show her that it could make time for whatever illness had gripped her.

She couldn't remember feeling this way since the last time she was pregnant.

She rose up slowly, trembling, as the thought seemed to settle on her consciousness like a visitor who liked the view.

No, she couldn't be pregnant. Not when she had just gotten one child in school and the other in a Mother's Day Out program three mornings a week. Not when she was finally writing and selling her work. Not when she had gotten her priorities straight and listed them so tightly that there was little room for adjustment.

The wave came over her again, and she leaned over the toilet.

She *couldn't* be pregnant!

As if in answer, that stranger settling on her consciousness seemed to say, *Of course you can.*

She went to the sink and cupped water in her hand, drank some, and splashed the rest on her face. Her makeup wasn't waterproof, so she set about trying to blot it and repair it, but it was no use. At least her hair still looked decent. The teachers at the school had never seen Tory when she looked less than her best. Beauty and control were both near the top of her priority list, and today she seemed to be losing her grip on both.

The worst part of the nausea was gone, though she still felt the queasiness lurking somewhere in the back of her mind. She forced herself to head back to her kids.

Spencer had engaged the poor, bedraggled teacher in conversation, and was telling her about his mother getting sick all over his friend's bathroom. She supposed that, in Spencer's mind, that wasn't a patent lie, for he'd probably misinterpreted the Lysol exchange. But she found it hard to look the teacher in the eye as she took her kids' hands.

"Are you all right, Tory?" the teacher asked.

"I don't know what's wrong with me," she said on a laugh. "Just not feeling my best."

"I've thought you were getting too skinny lately," the teacher said. "You've always been thin, but you're even thinner than usual. My friend started losing weight like that and found out she had stomach cancer."

Tory tried to plaster a pleasant look on her face, and fought the urge to thank the woman for her cheery optimism. "I watch my weight, that's all." She took each child by the hand. "I probably just have a stomach virus. Either that, or I'm pregnant."

She couldn't believe she had said the words out loud, and as the teacher's pointy eyebrows shot up, Tory began to laugh, as if that was the funniest thing she'd ever said. The woman joined in with as much mirth as Sarah and Abraham must have had upon hearing of Sarah's pregnancy.

Fortunately, her kids were fighting at the time, because Spencer was certain that Brittany had gotten their mother's good hand, and he wanted to trade. Brittany never did anything Spencer asked without a fight, even when she knew that one hand was as good as the other. Neither of them heard the explosive word that had rolled off her tongue like a prophecy.

She got them both to the car, belted them in, and sat with the car idling as she tried to decide if she needed to run back in for one last round with the toilet. As she did, she tried to count back to her last period. Was it late?

She had it written down, she thought. On the calendar in the kitchen, she always used little dots to indicate her cycle. She could count up the weeks.

But as she drove, she began to feel that loss of control again. Her well-planned life was tipping a little on its axis. She and Barry had planned for both Brittany and Spencer. They hadn't planned for a surprise. Tory didn't like surprises, and she didn't like disruptions to her schedule. She had her days planned down to the moment. Brittany could tie her shoes, and Spencer could make his own peanut butter sandwich. She didn't have the heart to start over with an infant.

The nausea seemed to subside as she blew the air conditioning into her face, despite the fact that Brittany and Spencer complained about being cold. Usually, she deferred to them, but today she had no choice. By the time they pulled into their driveway, she was feeling better.

She got out of the car and helped her children out, then went straight for that calendar.

She counted the weeks—one, two, three, four, five . . .

She shook her head. That couldn't be right. She would have realized it.

. . . six, seven, eight, nine . . .

She stood there for a long moment, gaping at the calendar weeks, while Brittany and Spencer began to fight over whether to watch reruns of *Full House* or *Saved by the Bell.*

How could this be? How could she have missed an entire period without realizing it?

The answer came to her suddenly. *Joseph.*

Her first missed period had been during the worst part of Joseph's illness, before they had found a heart. He had been dying, and Tory had hung on with Brenda. She and Sylvia and Cathy, her other neighbors, had been steeped in grief and worry, not to mention the stress of trying to raise money to pay the medical bills. As Joseph slipped away, Tory's period must have slipped her mind.

Now she had missed another one.

She stood there with her mouth open, counting the weeks over and over, wondering if she had just forgotten to mark the calendar. But she knew it wasn't an oversight. All the signs pointed to pregnancy.

But it couldn't be! She and Barry hadn't planned to have more kids. She was thirty-five years old, and their family was complete. Could she really be pregnant?

"Everybody back in the car!" she yelled, desperately trying to take back the reins of her life. "We have to go to the drugstore."

"Can I get a Darth Vader?" Spencer asked, seizing on his mother's obvious distraction.

"Yes."

"I want M&M's," Brittany shouted.

"Okay."

As she grabbed her purse and headed back out to the car, she checked off her list in her mind. Action figure, M&M's . . .

And the fastest pregnancy test she could find.

Seaside

Terri Blackstock

Seaside is a novella of the heart—poignant, gentle, true, offering an eloquent reminder that life is too precious a gift to be unwrapped in haste.

Sarah Rivers has it all: successful husband, healthy kids, beautiful home, meaningful church work.

Corinne, Sarah's sister, struggles to get by. From Web site development to jewelry sales, none of the pies she has her thumb stuck in contains a plum worth pulling.

No wonder Corinne envies Sarah. What she doesn't know is how jealous Sarah is of her. And what neither of them realizes is how their frantic drive for achievement is speeding them headlong past the things that matter most in life.

So when their mother, Maggie, purchases plane tickets for them to join her in a vacation on the Gulf of Mexico, they almost decline the offer. But circumstances force the issue, and the sisters soon find themselves first thrown together, then ultimately *drawn* together, in one memorable week in a cabin called "Seaside."

As Maggie, a professional photographer, sets out to capture on film the faces and moods of her daughters, more than film develops. A picture emerges of possibilities that come only by slowing down and savoring the simple treasures of the moment. It takes a mother's love and honesty to teach her two daughters a wiser, uncluttered way of life—one that can bring peace to their hearts and healing to their relationship. And though the lesson comes on wings of grief, the sadness is tempered with faith, restoration, and a joy that comes from the hand of God.

Hardcover: 0-310-23318-6

The Act of Marriage after 40

Making Love for Life

Tim and Beverly LaHaye with Mike Yorkey

In this upbeat, medically informed sequel to their 2.5 million-selling book, *The Act of Marriage*, Tim and Beverly LaHaye candidly share their expertise on such topics as:

- Enhancing sexual intimacy with your spouse
- Adjusting to sexual changes resulting from growing older
- Openly facing menopause and ED (erectile dysfunction)

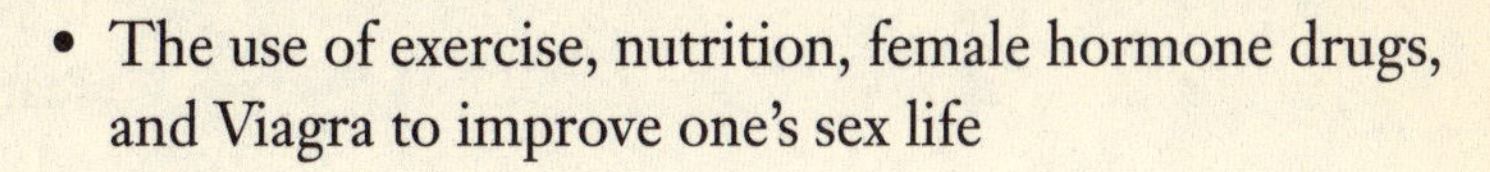

- The use of exercise, nutrition, female hormone drugs, and Viagra to improve one's sex life

. . . and much more.

The LaHayes have helped thousands of couples build stronger, happier, more intimate marriages. Discover that intimacy with your spouse after age 40 can be just as good, if not better, than ever before.

Hardcover 0-310-23114-0

Pick up your copy today at your favorite bookstore!

ZONDERVAN™

We want to hear from you. Please send your comments about this book to us in care of the address below. Thank you.

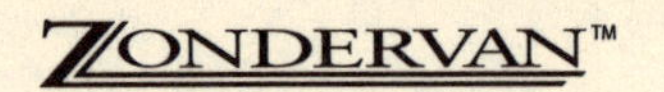

GRAND RAPIDS, MICHIGAN 49530

www.zondervan.com